RELIABLE IN DANANG

An Asian Thriller

by
Valerie Goldsilk

First published by Thaumasios Publishing Ltd. in 2020

Other books by the same author

Negative Buoyancy
The Oldest Sins
Sins of Our Sisters
Sins of Our Elders
The Reliable Man
Reliable in Jakarta
Reliable in Hong Kong
Classified As Crime
Dragon Breath
Perfect Killer
Fatal Action
Random Outcome
White Bishop

About the Author

Valerie Goldsilk is English and has lived in Hong Kong for over thirty years. She is now retired but used to run her own business, travelling frequently around Asia working with factories. Her better half is a former Hong Kong police inspector.

This story takes place in the mid 1990s

James Bond, with two double bourbons inside him, sat in the final departure lounge of Miami Airport and thought about life and death. It was part of his profession to kill people. He had never liked doing it and when he had to kill he did it as well as he knew how and forgot about it. As a secret agent who held the rare double-O prefix – the licence to kill in the Secret Service – it was his duty to be as cool about death as a surgeon. If it happened, it happened. Regret was unprofessional - worse, it was death-watch beetle in the soul.

Ian Fleming

Many individuals have, like uncut diamonds, shining qualities beneath a rough exterior.

Juvenal

There are many sham diamonds in this life which pass for real, and vice versa.

William Makepeace Thackeray

To Dago Gonzalez and Rory – now the whole world will know how you got those crocodile tattoos.

To James Phuong - Danang sure has changed since our time there.

To Tommy Doncaster - RIP.

To Jack Herr – thanks for taking one for the home team.

To Wing - thank you for letting us borrow your factory.

To Milford - you know who you are.

To Paul Miles – thank you for all the Madeira.

To the Plantmeister - this time next year we'll be in Hollywood.

To Jonny Hall - 'Alpha Reader' Extraordinaire, amazing how useful an English degree from Balliol can be.

1

I'd just landed in London, where I had gone to kill a man who was responsible for the death of a close friend.

That was done now, and it was time to relax and enjoy the pleasures of the Old World for a little while. I wasn't a great fan of London. I'd left England to seek my fame and fortune in the Far East when I was still in my twenties and rarely came back to the dank, dirty metropolis.

A few days here would be more than enough for me but in the company of Julian McAlistair, mysterious man of letters married to a Thai heiress, they promised to be a sybaritic few days.

He'd woken me up in my hotel room at four in the afternoon with the comforting news that everything had been taken care of and that the police were professing bafflement all across the media. The girl I'd shot was doing fine in hospital and would have full use of all her limbs in good time. It was nice to hear that she would only be a temporary casualty of my war of vengeance.

I'd dragged myself into the shower, spruced myself up and met McAlistair in the lobby of the Hilton where we were both staying. He suggested we did some shopping like proper little tourists and we took a cab to

Knightsbridge where we were now wandering the halls of Harrods.

"So there is a rumour that Princess Diana is going out with a mysterious Muslim man," McAlistair said as we walked into the outdoor clothes section, "and some people are saying it's the son of the owner of Harrods."

"That's just tabloid nonsense," I said.

"Apparently he's given her a massive diamond ring, even bigger than the 12-carat oval blue Ceylon sapphire engagement ring that Prince Charles gave her," McAlistair said as he fingered a heavily waxed Barbour jacket on a rack.

We were on the third floor and a po-faced salesman in a well-cut suit hovered out of earshot but within nodding distance from us.

McAlistair said to the man: "Do you have this one in blue?"

I said: "How can you remember such ridiculous trivia. Who cares about the size of a woman's engagement ring?"

"I need it in a size 52," McAlistair said to the salesman who had brought him two choices of the waxed, water-proof jacket. "What do you think, Kevin?" McAlistair had bent forward to read the man's name-tag. "Is Princess Diana dating a mysterious Muslim man?"

"I really can't say, sir."

"Go on, tell us what the Harrods rumour mill is saying."

"I haven't heard anything of the sort," the salesman said, looking marginally embarrassed at these two mad men standing in his haberdashery section. He touched the quiff on his head with a self-conscious movement of his hand.

"Would you disapprove of her marrying again?" McAlistair said to Kevin, the salesman.

"It's really none of my business, sir," the man said.

"I think the green colour looks much better. More classical," I said to take the pressure off the young man. "Blue just isn't right. It's a hunting jacket, McAlistair. You've got to be able to hide in the gorse bushes with it."

"The Queen might disapprove. It's not the done thing," McAlistair said. "They might have to hire someone to assassinate her."

"Professionals don't like killing women, children or royalty," I pointed out. I didn't like the way this conversation was going.

"Who cares anyway," McAlistair said and tried on the next jacket that Kevin the salesman had brought. "Bit too short this one. Are there longer ones? This greasy wax really gets on your hands."

"You could try the Northumbria model, sir."

"Let's try that one. We've got to get some riding whips, Bill. I've got a new maid from Buriram who needs a bit of discipline in her life."

Kevin stared at him in horror and McAlistair turned and gave me a quick wink. He was pulling the man's leg but that didn't mean McAlistair wasn't capable of inflicting vicious pain. He had once been a police inspector in Hong Kong and he was renowned for his imaginative interrogation techniques. Eventually his reputation had preceded him and he'd been advised that there would be no long term career in the Force if he didn't change his ways. He'd resigned and married his Cathay Pacific stewardess girlfriend whose father was one of the richest men in Thailand.

"I'm sorry about my friend," I said, stifling a jet-lagged yawn. "He's recently had a vasectomy and he hasn't been the same since."

Mezzo was still as popular as when I'd last been in town and the models and their dates had not changed either – tall, skinny birds accompanied by short, paunchy geezers. It was a fun place for sightseeing. McAlistair was in one of his ironic moods and the fact that it was just the two of us meant he didn't have to put on any act. He viciously critiqued all that he saw around him and we laughed ourselves stupid at the expense of self-conscious Soho.

We were the wild colonials, out on the town but not part of it any more. Our roots were in Asia and to us London was as alien as Paris and New York and, through our tourist eyes, equally entertaining, the way one might go to the zoo for a fun afternoon.

McAlistair lit one of his stumpy Bolivars and with his left hand emptied the second bottle of St. Julien. I was staring across the room at a coffee-coloured vision that could have been Naomi Campbell's bustier sister. Her companion was a small Asian man who pawed her continuously as if she were a pretty piece of jade he'd picked up in the night market. The escort exhibited an icy patience that reminded me of a Shanghai karaoke singer I'd once dated for an evening.

"Veal was great," McAlistair said. I thought I'd detected a slight chubbiness in his cheeks that had not been there the last time we met in Thailand. Obviously he wasn't hitting the gym as hard as usual in between enjoying the fruits of his labours in London. He still looked impressively fit. Both of us had chosen to wear dinner jackets and black bow ties. Mine was frayed-at-the-edges Savile Row, but his was pristine new Armani. Although we didn't feel uncomfortable in the up-market crowd we did stand out amongst the pinstripe suit brigade and the nouveaux wearing open collars displaying heavy gold pendants.

"Can't get into any of the night-clubs in jeans and trainers," McAlistair had commented earlier at the hotel.

"We'd better dress properly then," had been my reply.

I reminded him of the time when I'd got into trouble with the Chief Superintendent while I was still a young Inspector. I'd been turning up for work in jeans and a T-shirt and the boss had blasted me for dressing casually. The next morning he stopped by my office as I was coming off duty from the night shift. He was furious to find me wearing a dinner jacket, convinced I was trying to make fun of him. He ripped me another arsehole, gave me four weeks of 'C' shift and would hear nothing of my explanation that I'd been to a formal dinner party at the Mandarin Hotel shortly before reporting for work.

McAlistair tossed his Platinum Amex card at the waitress and settled up. We then strolled out into the cool evening air in search of the elusive cabbie.

An hour later we had managed to skilfully glide into a hot new club called 'Incandescence' tucked down the back of a cobbled alley somewhere in Mayfair.

"Hey, are you the writer guy, man?" the selector with the clipboard and electronic earpiece asked McAlistair as he gave his name. McAlistair smiled modestly. This didn't happen too often. His books were rather niche but beefy, bodybuilding bouncers were probably part of his target audience. Sex and violence featured heavily in McAlistair's oeuvre. "I've read all of your books. Is that real shit? All those Triads and stuff?"

McAlistair assured him it was mostly true. "Why not check it out for yourself. Come to Asia."

"Ah, I'm not too sure, man. I've got to think of my career."

We didn't ask him to expound on this as he led us inside but assumed he meant something else besides manning the red sash at the front door of an edgy West End nightclub.

The place was just filling up so we managed to find a spot at the bar and staked it out. Within a minute a pretty teenager came bounding up to McAlistair and held out a felt-tip pen. "My boyfriend says you're famous and you should give me your autograph," she giggled.

"Where would you like it? On your left or right breast?"

She took it quite well but ended up with his name scrawled on her bare thigh instead.

The music was some form of high speed techno. There seemed no noticeable transition between songs but people moved to and from the dance floor periodically. Once on the dance floor they would close their eyes in rhythmic contemplation while shaking the upper parts of their bodies to the pounding of the speakers.

"It's not quite Marine Disco in Pattaya," McAlistair commented after watching the action for ten minutes.

"It's not quite Tanamur, Club of Clubs in Jakarta," I replied.

"It's London, capital of Europe."

"Don't tell any Frenchman that."

"Ah, it's okay. Look there's the gorgeous black bird with the little choggie. He does love stroking her arse, doesn't he?"

"Should I go and rescue her?" McAlistair said. He wasn't really into African girls but I knew he liked the idea of messing with the Chinaman. He had always had a nasty streak in him.

By now I'd noticed something far more interesting at the other end of the room: she had jet black hair that fell to her shoulders and marvellously expressive almond brown eyes. Her lips were that classic Chanel cherry red and there was a slight cleavage in her little black dress which emphasised an apparently perfect pair of breasts. I doubted she was Chinese, although on first glance that's how her features appeared.

"What do you think?" I said to my friend, prodding his arm and nodding in the right direction. He focused, pursed his lips, creased his brow. "Marvellous. Singaporean, I'd say."

"Why?"

"Great hour glass figure. Probably some Malay blood. Look at the lips. Way too voluptuous for a Cantonese."

"I'm not sure. It's not quite a Chinese face."

"Who is the wanker with her?"

"Mike Tyson's taller brother?"

"She's not comfortable talking to him."

We watched for a while, entranced by her grace and the crassness of the guy trying to chat her up. Suddenly the man looked up and saw both of us staring at him. We were both ex-coppers and the habit of holding someone's eye dies hard. Tyson-fellow didn't like what he saw – two guys staring him down. He turned in our direction and, after hesitating for an instant, moved towards us. I hadn't noticed it before but now it became obvious that he was being trailed by two other heavy-weights in fancy clothes and glittering chains.

"Have you got a problem?" Tyson-fellow said, squaring off against us. I thought I'd leave the talking to McAlistair. He needed some action and I'd had all of mine for the month. I shook my head mutely.

"Maybe you didn't hear me proper, lads. Have you got a fucking problem?"

"We don't have a problem, mate," McAlistair said quietly and I noticed he shifted his body sideways while apparently looking down into his empty glass. "But you obviously do. You have an attitude problem, sport."

Tyson-fellow was speechless for an instant. He was a head taller than both us. But McAlistair hadn't finished: "Now run along with your hard-men and don't bother us any more, or the young lady for that matter."

"You've got some fucking cheek," Tyson-fellow managed to say. He was still off balance from the unaccustomed challenge to his dark presence. "Do you know who I fucking am?"

"Does it matter?" McAlistair carried on baiting him.

"You're obviously from out of town," Tyson-fellow concluded and he looked left and right for assurance from his associates who were putting a lot of effort into appearing tough and intimidating.

"I'm from Bristol," said McAlistair economically. The big black man studied us for a long ten seconds wanting to build the tension while he weighed up the odds. "Anyone know you in Bristol?" he demanded, fishing for more information that might tell him if McAlistair was just mad or so well connected he could risk picking fights with strangers.

"Some people know me."

"What's it you do in Bristol?"

"Is it any of your business?"

Tyson-fellow shrugged, keeping the mean, mad look on his face. McAlistair added, "I write children's books, if you must know. And you?"

When the punch came it had been telegraphed a long time. Tyson-fellow's features might be identical to the world champion boxer but his fighting skills left much to be desired. McAlistair didn't even break into a sweat. He rolled sideways from the round-house blow, ducked under the black man's armpit, turned and delivered a savage elbow just over his opponent's heart. As Tyson-fellow gasped in pain and fought to get a breath of air McAlistair turned again and while sliding a leg behind the other's produced a small black truncheon from nowhere and delivered a smart crack against the man's jaw. Before Tyson-fellow even hit the ground, unconscious and with a broken face, the truncheon had vanished again into its secret pocket.

I hadn't moved during the entire sequence but I'd held the other two guys with my eyes. Given the swiftness of McAlistair's response neither was ready to respond. When they saw their mate bleeding on the floor they chose quickly to stay cool. However they shuffled angrily and a third guy pushed forward and began attending to the victim.

"Nice move that, McAlistair. I thought you were looking out of shape," I said in a low voice, reaching back for my vodka. A small crowd had gathered and bouncers were shoving their way through the bodies in our direction.

"What's going on here?" a manager asked angrily.

"Guy tripped and knocked his head against the bar," I explained.

"They fucking coshed him," one of Tyson-fellow's mates accused.

McAlistair held up his empty hands and shrugged innocently.

"Look at the guy. He tripped. Nobody's been picking any fights here," I said and caught the eye of the Asian girl who was staring at me with a neutral expression that could have hidden any thoughts imaginable. Perhaps she actually was the girlfriend and they were just in the middle of a tiff.

The bouncer from the door had arrived and he was whispering urgently in the manager's ear.

"Has someone called an ambulance?"

"Okay, everyone, there's nothing to see here. Just a little accident," one of the other bouncers was saying.

Tyson-fellow was groaning and his friends were still staring daggers but not daring to take it any further.

"I'm going to have to ask you gentlemen to leave," the manager spoke to us.

"For what?" McAlistair said.

"I think you know exactly why, but let's not make a big deal out of it."

"McAlistair. The man's right. This is a dangerous place. Time to move on."

There was a hint of relief on the manager's face. "Come back tomorrow perhaps," he said.

"We might," I replied giving the Asian girl a wink as I turned and moved towards the door. It wouldn't take long for Tyson-fellow's buddies to follow us out so we watched our backs as we worked our way through the busy throng at the front of the club. The bouncer at the door told us to take care, a look of respect stretched across his face. I patted him on the arm. McAlistair's book sales in London might be going up next week.

We walked down the road, waiting to be followed but nobody came. McAlistair knew another place close by that wasn't as trendy but proved to be equally busy. It was a revue bar and we ensconced ourselves in a gloomy corner with a bottle of Dom and watched tall, Eastern European students remove their undergarments to the sound of eighties music. It wasn't chic but it was sordidly entertaining.

It was after three in the morning when McAlistair dragged me to the after-hours club just off Oxford Street. Youths of all ages were lounging around on the pavement and there was a general atmosphere of decadence as we descended the stairs into a smoky, perfumed cellar. This looked like the final stop. As if every discotheque in town had poured its dregs into one wide funnel and now all the human flotsam milled around pushing up against a cracked vintage bar.

"You bring me to the finest establishments," I slurred and McAlistair just thumped me on the back gleefully and ordered a bottle of their best wine which turned out to be a vinegary Beaujolais from the year before.

Every nationality was represented, including what looked like a group of Romans in togas and a band of transvestites (or probably blokes in drag left standing from a Tarts and Vicars party).

"London isn't as boring as you think, old boy," McAlistair assured me and I assured him that I never said it was. An American next to us tried to join in our conversation and we told him to shove it, although admittedly there wasn't much conversation left in either of us. I decided it was time for the gents and swayed in the direction of what looked like the right corridor. Both toilets were occupied and a line of mostly females told me that it would be a while before I could relieve myself. They had commandeered the men's room and would not be giving it up.

"You can piss on the street," a 200-pound person in a skirt told me delicately. I checked her out cautiously but she wasn't one of the men in drag, so I took her advice. Upstairs the air was bracing and a welcoming alleyway beckoned. I had to make my way further down the dark passage, as a few drunks were in the process of chucking up their onion bahjis and a couple, oblivious to the Indian food, were getting it on against a dumpster. The man's striped boxer shorts were around his ankles as he gripped the girl's bare leg under his arm.

The sweet sound of tinkling was a relief to my deafened ears. Once done I zipped up and made my way delicately past the other occupants of the alley. I stopped on the main road and took in the scene. The night was still in full swing and standing by the entrance, having a conversation with a tall blonde was the Asian girl from 'Incandescence'. I sobered up slightly thinking that Tyson-fellow's friends might be with her but a quick glance around proved that wasn't the case.

At that moment she looked over and recognition came to her eyes. She was between me and the club's door so I approached.

"Hi, still hanging on in there?" I said, pausing.

She nodded cautiously. "Where's your friend?" she asked.

"Downstairs."

"I saw what he did to the guy who was chatting me up. He's vicious." Her accent was a cross between Wimbledon and the Mekong Delta. It was an odd sound but it gave me pleasure.

"I'm Bill. What's your name?"

"Brigit. This is Stella." We shook hands. Stella gave me a cool glare as she'd obviously heard the full story of McAlistair's cosh attack and despite still wearing my DJ and not having lost my bow-tie I didn't seem like the kind of man one should be talking to on the street, shortly before dawn.

"Going downstairs?" I asked. They hesitated for a moment but decided it wasn't time to call it quits yet and so followed me into Dante's Inferno below.

"I know you." McAlistair said pleasantly when I turned up with the girls.

"They don't want to know you," I pointed out. "You are a nasty, short and brutal creature."

"But I'm an artist. And five foot eleven."

"You are a thug," I told him and this time Brigit's friend, Stella gave me an approving nod. "This is my beastly friend McAlistair who has no redeeming features except the enormous size of his bank account."

"Bank account?" Stella sneered.

"It's a euphemism."

"For what?" She seemed to fall for it.

"His manly dangly bit."

The girls snorted with derision. Brigit said pleasantly, "You're sick and he's vile."

"But not so bad you'll refuse a night cap with us?"

"It's too late for that," the Asian girl said.

"Is that a yes?"

"Okay, two white wines."

It turned out that Stella was in PR and Brigit worked in an exclusive Knightsbridge boutique. To keep things simple we told them that McAlistair was a struggling author and I was a financial consultant. We explained that we were old colonials in town for some rest and recuperation.

Brigit asked why McAlistair had been so violent and where he'd learnt to do such things.

"We were in the police together in Hong Kong. You learn to hit first before some big coloured fellow lands a punch on you that knocks all of your teeth out."

"He seemed like a nice guy."

"I don't think you really believe that," I said.

She considered for a while as she sipped the sour chardonnay which the bar had served. "No, probably not. And neither are you two. Nice fellows that is."

"We had already established that at the beginning of the conversation." I looked across her and noticed a gleam of interest in Stella's eye as she was listening to McAlistair trying to be lucid. At times – when shit-faced - he could still be quite hilarious.

"Anyone for dinner at my suite? They make excellent Eggs Benedict at the Hilton. No funny business. Purely above the belt entertainment," the brutal writer suggested half an hour later as the Club began noticeably slowing down.

"I don't do this all the time you know," the girl said. She was lying on her side, covered mostly by the sheet as if, after what we'd done a few hours earlier, she still had a reason to be coy about the shape of her fine figure.

"What I like to hear is that I have an irresistible charm which makes women behave in extraordinary ways," I said dreamily, one eye open to watch the movement of her face.

"You behaved in an extraordinary way. My English boyfriend never did that before."

"Lazy git."

"I realise that now." She pursed her lips and gave me a long, serious stare. "But you do believe me that I just don't do this sort of thing... normally."

"I do." Slowly I stroked her cheek with the back of my hand.

"Now you're making fun of me."

"Shh," I told her and began kissing her lips, the ones below her dainty nose this time.

Her full name was Brigit Nguyen and her family had brought her to England when she was eight years old. Her parents had since died and she only had her brother left who had recently graduated from Oxford taking a First in chemistry.

"You live in Asia. So you know how to behave around an Asian girl," she explained once we'd finished this round of smooching. My Rolex said it was shortly after two in the afternoon. But it was Sunday and neither of us apparently had anywhere else to go.

"So why did you leave the police, Bill?"

"If I had a dollar every time I've had to answer that question."

"Did they kick you out?"

I chuckled. "In a manner of speaking. They made it plain that things were going to be different once 1997 came so my hopes for a career in law enforcement were dashed." I winked so she could tell that I wasn't being entirely serious. "It started to get boring and we were all drinking way too much and working way too little and it suddenly became obvious that the time had come for new challenges."

"So you've kicked the drinking habit I noticed."

"Touché."

She frowned and brushed some of her raven hair away from her ochre cheek.

"Where did you get this?" I said grasping hold of her hand. I'd noticed it earlier but was too busy with other matters. On the back of her left wrist was a small tattoo. "What is it?"

"It's a crocodile," she said, watching me curiously.

"And it means?"

"Nothing really. It means: I'm wild and wicked, I've got a tattoo."

"But girls are supposed to have roses on their ankles. Or something sweet like that."

"How boring. I've got a crocodile."

"You're a man-eater."

She smiled. "Right first time. It's embarrassing but it was something amusing. A bunch of girls did it at school. A long time ago."

"Show us your teeth."

"Shut up. How about some cold coffee."

The phone rang and McAlistair explained he was indisposed for the rest of the afternoon and perhaps we could reconvene for dinner. I ordered room service and got back to kissing Brigit.

It was a pleasant way to pass the rest of the morning and an even better way to spend the afternoon. My jet-lag had me drifting off to sleep periodically only to be woken again by the Asian vixen between my sheets. Room service came two more times. Not quite as often as I did.

"When do you go back to Asia?" the girl said at some point while munching on a muffin covered with a generous dollop of cream and some fine cherry jam. A sliver of the red confiture had got stuck on her cheek and it looked as if she had cut herself shaving until I wiped it away with my tongue.

"In a week or so. I've got some business to attend to in Holland. Depends on how long that takes."

"Do you go to Vietnam on business sometimes?" she asked. Her eyes, for a moment, held a look of anxiousness.

"Sometimes. In fact I was thinking of going after I get back from Amsterdam."

"What is it you do again? You're not really a financial consultant, nor is McAlistair really quite what he pretends," she said perceptively.

"I consult on security matters but projects are a bit thin on the ground at the moment. So I've been running some errands for friends."

She considered this for a few seconds then said, "Would you have time to run an errand for this new friend?"

I shrugged. "If it's something I can do. You want me to deliver something to someone in Vietnam?"

"Not exactly." She paused and frowned, trying to explain things carefully. "You see, my brother Stephen went back to Saigon a few months ago. Four weeks ago he stopped sending me e-mails and I haven't been able to get through on his mobile. I'm worried he may have had a motorbike accident or something."

"Sounds a bit odd. Probably he got involved with a local girl, lost his mobile phone and is so busy working he's forgotten to keep you updated."

"He's my only brother and we've always been close."

"Why did he go back to Vietnam?"

Brigit shifted around on the bed. She'd been sitting cross-legged, wearing one of my T-shirts which drowned her in a most charming manner. I had a brief glimpse of dark hair between her thighs as she got herself more comfortable against one of the pillows.

She slapped me playfully when she noticed me peaking.

"He wanted to explore our roots. It's fashionable now that Vietnam is more open and modern. Lots of people have been going back. They call us Viet Kieu, when we go back and get jobs and help the country move forward."

"Did he have a job lined up or something?"

"No, he just went on spec. But he had a few names and met up with people and then he got a job in some company importing stuff."

"Is that what he wanted? He studied chemistry. There are lots of oil companies down there. That sounds more like the kind of job he should have been angling for."

She raised her shoulders up and down in a Gallic gesture. "I can show you all his e-mails. I've got them on my computer."

I cleared up the food and pushed the tray outside the hotel door. It sounded like a simple project. I didn't have anything else on and had time on my hands. It would take my mind off what had been done yesterday and what had gone before. We didn't talk about it much more after I'd agreed to help her. She showed her appreciation by giving me a massage that would have done a temple-trained Bangkok masseuse proud. By eight I was alone but we'd agreed to meet for lunch the next day and she'd bring along what I needed to know.

McAlistair finally surfaced and we went around the corner to a pub that did snacks. After a few pints of their local bitter I felt energised again. I'd lost a lot of fluid in the course of the day. McAlistair grinned lasciviously but did not elaborate on why he was wearing a turtle neck sweater.

2

We had lunch in a little Italian restaurant around the corner from the British Museum. Brigit looked prim and secretarial in a black Fendi dress. Not that I recognised the brand but when I told her what a fine outfit it was she explained its provenance.

"London is an odd place to live," she said, "most people just make enough money to pay for their tiny flat and the occasional cab fare but everyone dresses up to the nines. Except the tourists, of course."

I looked down at my new Calvin Klein jeans and my open collared Thomas Pink shirt and decided she wasn't really referring to me.

"The cannelloni is brilliant here," she said tapping the menu and we agreed to share. I asked for a bottle of Bardolino to be opened but Brigit wasn't going to join me. "I'll fall asleep at work. And … by the way. I'm aching all over." She gave me a stern look as if it had all been my fault and wasn't at least half her own doing.

We talked about this and that, getting to know each other better but mostly it was superficial stuff about her life in the big city, being an Asian in a Western culture and how lonely it could be sometimes when both one's parents were dead. I avoided giving too many details about my life. I was practised at telling half-truths and fleshed out only the trivial details. She wanted to know why I had never married and what my previous girl-friends had been like. I selected a few stories that were innocuous enough and we ended up having a civilised lunch.

She gave me a brown manila envelope and a long, lingering farewell kiss when we parted.

"It's all there, Bill. E-mails, passport details, a good photo of Stephen. Keep calling me. I'll miss you." She hesitated for a second then said, "I hope it wasn't just a one night stand and you'll be back in London again soon." Her eyes seemed to glisten slightly.

"I'll be back soon and just to see you," I replied and meant it, then giving her a quick warm hug sat back down again to finish the bottle, while she hurried off to her workplace.

An hour later I'd checked out of the hotel, given McAlistair a bear-hug and hopped into a taxi for Heathrow.

There was no point in hanging around. Any more days in London and it would turn sour on me. Nor did I want to stay and let Brigit become too sweet on me. I'd let matters cool for a few weeks and then hopefully find her brother and come back the conquering hero.

The newspapers had calmed down a lot about the murder of the man at the airport. A new scandal involving Premier league footballers was dominating the front pages. McAlistair would keep an eye on the affair and keep me posted in case the police came up with any real connections. I doubted it. Somewhere someone would have said: it's just as well. The man was an embarrassment. Let sleeping corpses lie. And somewhere in Singapore an irascible, liver-spotted military man would be signing off on his file with a satisfied grunt and more than likely opening a fresh one. I hoped that whatever it was, it did not involve me. The last time he'd cajoled me into that business with the Filipino colonel had been hairy enough for me. Hairy had been the defining word of that contract.

The flight to Schiphol Airport was mercifully brief and painlessly smooth. The Italian red and a few vodkas from the lounge were still with me by the time I boarded so I nodded off after take-off. From the airport I took a train into the centre of town and found a hotel within walking distance of the railway station. It was a clean Dutch three star and despite the tourist season they had rooms available.

My reason for coming to Amsterdam was purely commercial. I had an idea that I wanted to turn some of my hard-earned cash into diamonds and while pursuing that idea thought I might try and buy and sell some diamonds for profit. There was always some canny Asian who'd be willing to buy under the table for his jewellery shop. I knew a wealthy Filipina girl who ran her family business in Manila and she had expressed interest when I sounded her out. She would take the diamonds up to her factory in the provinces where cheap labour would fit them into rings and necklaces for the moneyed elite.

The man I'd arranged to meet in Amsterdam came originally from Golders Green but he didn't like the competition so moved to Holland where he had developed a slick niche operation. How much of it was above board remained unclear and didn't interest me.

By the time I got to the Irish pub – you can be sure you'll find one in every city of the world – it was eight fifteen. I ordered a pint of Kilkenny and sat myself down in a dark, mahogany corner waiting for the arrival of Jeremiah Rosenstein. A couple of Dutch youngsters were talking in loud voices and some British tourists were discussing the merits of the red-light district, an area that holds a perverse fascination for uptight, sex-starved Anglo-Saxons. Amsterdam had always been the favoured stag week-end destination for the young men who could afford the trip.

Jeremiah arrived, a bit late as was his habit. He slouched in, glancing around shiftily until he spotted me.

We shook hands and he hung up his frayed raincoat, then blew his large nose into a heavily soiled handkerchief.

"Ballantine's and soda, my boy," he said. Once he was installed with his tipple we exchanged pleasantries.

"Business has been slow. DeBeers is playing all sorts of games as usual and the big volume buyers just aren't there," he moaned as always.

"Still driving the Bentley then, Jeremiah."

"I drive a Renault," he corrected me with irritation. "An old one."

"Get back to London much?" I asked.

"For what? Expensive, everything is so damned expensive there."

"See the family?"

"That woman can rot in hell," he snapped. He meant his ex-wife rather than his mother. I got another round of drinks. In twenty years of knowing Jeremiah I'd never seen his hand come out of his pocket with anything else in it but his grubby handkerchief. But he was a nice man otherwise, if you forgave him his idiosyncrasies.

"What do you want then?" he finally demanded.

I pushed a little list across the wooden table towards him. He studied it for a full two minutes, nodding, pursing his lips, expelling air through his teeth. Mostly I wanted one or two carat white stones, nothing fancy, just the regular fare for engagement rings and easy to transport.

"How much of this is for you?" he wanted to know.

"About half."

"Where will you keep them?"

"Safe Deposit Boxes."

"Don't bury them in the garden." It was his idea of a joke so I grinned politely. "It will take me a few days. I'll have to make some calls."

"You don't have it in stock? It's not a big amount."

"I don't have any stock. I'm a trader. The only stock I keep is what belongs to me and that's in a bank in Liechtenstein."

"It's where I keep most of my money," I commented. "Pretty little place, Vaduz." I knew he had an account with the Liechtensteinische Landesbank because that's where I transferred the money when I'd previously bought diamonds from him.

"Yes, the Swiss are not like they used to be and the European Community is making everything more complicated. I heard the Russians were talking about enacting new bank privacy laws that would attract foreign investors but you never know with them. The government will probably borrow any money you place in their country." He muttered on for a while along this tack and then finished up his Scotch.

"Where're you selling this stuff then?" he wanted to know.

"Philippines. I might try Vietnam. I've got to go there and see some people."

"Vietnam?" Jeremiah's face lit up, which was something I had rarely seen with the grumpy old Semite. "Where in Vietnam?"

"Saigon, Hanoi. Nowhere specific yet."

"I've got a small package I need sending to Vietnam," he said, fidgeting with excitement, sensing an opportunity, "but those bastards at Brinks are too expensive. There's a feller who usually helps me out but I can't contact him. Probably lying on his back getting lobster-red in Thailand."

I smiled. "So?"

"Will you deliver it for me?"

He would not have respected me if I did not ask him to pay me for the job so we haggled for a while and he agreed to give me cash to cover a First Class air ticket out of Amsterdam. He grumbled a lot about that one and wanted to palm me off with a bigger discount on the diamonds I was going to buy from him but that meant nothing to me.

"It's me or Brinks."

"They're professional jewellery transporters and you're asking for more than them."

"I'm professional in my own way. And you always pay more for personalised service."

Of course he wasn't paying more or he'd never have agreed to the deal.

"I'll give you the package when you come around to pick up the other stuff. It's just a few uncut stones but they could turn out very nicely."

"Not bulky is it?"

He made a square with his fingers and thumbs. Transporting large quantities of diamonds in your cabin luggage was not strictly speaking legal. Customs expected you to declare valuables. I had no intention of doing that in any of the countries I would be visiting. Customs officials had sticky fingers and small salaries.

Jeremiah looked into the base of his whisky glass. There was nothing left. Even the ice had disappeared. He said, "Have to go now. Call me tomorrow afternoon. See how much of your order I can scrape together by then."

"Take care, Jeremiah." I patted him on his back and helped him on with his tawdry mac, after which I went to the gents to wash my hands. I never liked the look of his grubby handkerchief.

When in Rome ... but this was Amsterdam so I thought I'd go to a hash café and amuse myself there and then wander along the canals gazing at half-clad sirens displaying their wares in the shop windows of Gomorrah.

The Dutch are very pragmatic people. They have always been tough traders, daring merchant adventurers, harsh colonialists and expert linguists. They know when to pick their fights and when to run. The Anglo-Saxon paranoia about the evils of gratuitous fornication and the use of recreational drugs did not make sense to the politicians and social workers of the Netherlands and so both activities are of course legal, although carefully monitored.

With the criminal element removed from drugs and prostitution there was a lot less trouble for the police and the general public. Whatever country you were in, if you wanted to get stoned and laid you could always find a place to do it. Laws or not. 'Why not roll with the punches and concentrate on the real problems?' was the approach of the phlegmatic Dutch burghers.

I made my way to the 'Grasshopper' which had been around since before I was a student and they sold me a baggy of green leaves which were assured to make my evening a relaxed one. Two pints of Kilkenny had already set me on the right path. I watched the hippy attendant, who spoke perfect idiomatic American-English, as he stuffed the water pipe and explained how it all worked. Not too complex: the water bubbled up and cooled the smoke. It was much mellower to draw down into your lungs than a stick of Philip Morris's best Virginian.

I read the International Herald Tribune for a while and puffed through half of my baggy. At the back of my mind I let my concerns bubble away like the water in the pipe. What principally concerned me was the thought of why two people had, within two days, asked me to do them favours in Vietnam.

Some say there are no coincidences in life and there is only fate and pre-ordination. I wasn't given to this type of contemplation. I didn't like coincidences because too often I'd found they were man-made and not induced by the fortuitous movement of the stars. And when they were man-made a heap of cow dung usually came flying in my direction.

But those were negative thoughts and it was such a nice relaxing evening in a chilled out continental capital city, surrounded by splendid looking folks who were all gazing at each other in contentment and brotherly love. After three quarters of an hour I decided I'd had enough, wrapped up my tranquility inducing herbs and strode out into the mild night air. A great hunger pounced on me and it took all the self-control I had to rush into the nearest Chinese restaurant instead of snatching the hot dogs from a passing vendor's wheel barrow.

A can of Tsing Tao beer and a big heap of chicken and cashew nuts and steamed rice calmed me down. I looked at the waist-coated Asian waiters scurrying around the tables and wondered how much of their business came simply from proximity to a busy 'brown café'. They'd know from my pin-prick pupils that here was a customer who was capable of ripping the raw chickens off the meat-hooks by which they hung at the window.

"Mai dan, m'goi," I said in Cantonese and the waiter looked impressed. He would recognise it but most likely his dialect was Hokkien. Many Chinese emigrated to Indonesia from the mainland in the early half of the twentieth century but their lot had not been a happy one in the sixties and seventies due to racial discrimination by the indigenous Javanese, so many had opted, and succeeded in their next migration to head for Europe. Holland, as Indonesia's former colonial master had welcomed a big chunk of Indonesian Chinese over the last twenty years.

I took the change and left a handsome tip. The food had been fine but it was probably still a hash-induced magnanimousness. Walking around the cobbled roads my head cleared quickly and I began to concentrate on the pleasures of the night. Each building had shop windows just above ground level and reclining or posing in most of these were mostly attractive women dressed in scanty lingerie. There were buxom blondes, and svelte brunettes, there were charcoal women from the dark continents, there were brown Brazilians, and petite Asians which my practised eye told me were all Thai. They all beckoned with eyes or hand movements or simply with the sensual enticement of their poses. The night had turned more chilly but inside awaited warmth and fifteen minutes' worth of ardour for the punter who surrendered to the temptations of the flesh.

I wandered in ever decreasing circles for the best part of two hours. It was the most pleasant type of exercise. Whenever a particularly gorgeous girl caught my eye suddenly there appeared another one a few windows down. I felt like a rat on the spinning gig forever moving, paw in front of paw without being able to stop.

But then I did pause when I noticed what could have been a familiar face. I'd passed by this darker alley before. On the left side there were four stocky Africans with thighs that would have credited a baby elephant and breasts that could have suckled half the Zulu nation. On the opposite side there were five more windows. Before, they'd all been covered up implying that a visitor was inside or the girl wasn't working.

Now two of them had the curtains drawn back and a petite Thai girl in leather boots was beckoning me.

I moved closer to the window because her face was partially in shadow but there was something distinctive in her pose.

She yanked open the street door and gave a squeal of pleasure. Next I knew she was flinging her arms around my neck and her legs around my waist. A minute later I was installed in the little room and the curtains were drawn hiding us from the ogling outside world.

"What you do here, Bill?" the girl was saying.

I laughed. "I should ask you that question but the answer is obvious both ways."

"I'm working," El said. The last time I'd seen her was in the Lucifer disco in Patpong where she'd been chilling out with a bunch of her girlfriends.

"How did you get to Amsterdam?" I asked.

"Have some man they know about how to get girls the visa and then we have to pay and work for 6 months."

"And you're okay?"

"Sure, it's good here. But too many men come and not want to pay big money. Lots and lots of small money." She grinned like a pixie and rubbed her crotch to imply that it got painful after a long night. In Bangkok if a woman went with a man for sex it was usually one man only and for the entire night. It was a different game in Amsterdam.

"They not have shower here you know. That no good. Only the wash basin." She pointed around the small room. A curtain separated us from the corridor and beyond that another girl would be working.

"Looks reasonably clean," I said.

She shrugged and said, "My sister also come. We have maybe ten girls together."

I had to think about that one. I didn't recall her having a sister on the game. Perhaps it was a half sister or a friend or …

"Your sister?" I said.

"Sure, my sister."

The curtains parted at this moment and another Thai girl stepped into the room and they exchanged quick sentences. The new girl gave me a wai, the traditional Thai greeting that consisted of a slight bow, with the palms pressed together in a prayer-like fashion, as we were introduced. I took a moment to size her up and then I confirmed my suspicions. This wasn't El's sister. This was her brother and he was looking as feminine and gorgeous as any drunken Dutchman's Asian fantasy. Politeness demanded I did not mention that I knew this was a 'ladyboy' and should treat Him like a Her. With the perfect silicone breasts and the long, smooth legs it was easy to ignore the anomaly. She'd had some silicone injected into her chin and a bit on her nose but otherwise not much more than was needed except for the regular hormone tablets which were nothing more than female birth control pills.

We went into the little pantry to drink some coke. The girls lit up Marlboros and I explained vaguely what business had brought me to Holland. El's brother/ sister had a high-pitched twittering voice that occasionally slipped a key and it was amusing to hear. I had a bottle of Heineken from their little fridge. Standing on a side table somewhat incongruously were various sex aids including a whip and a giant dildo that must have been painful for anyone at the receiving end of its bulbous plastic knob.

I was just lighting El's second cigarette when the curtain that led into the back of the house was pulled aside and a man stood staring down at us. At first I thought it was the pimp and he was going to yell at the girls to get back to work. Then I thought for a micro-second that it was the waiter from the Chinese restaurant where I'd just eaten.

Then, whoever he was, was coming at me with a meat cleaver and I thought I was back in Hong Kong all over again. The girls screeched in terror and I ducked in reflex knocking his arm aside. He swung again, by which time I was on my feet and the green bottle of Holland's finest brew was upside down in my hand, its amber liquid pouring over my shoes.

He snarled and I managed to block and trap the blow that would have sliced off half my face. As I held his fighting arm I brought the Heineken bottle hard up into his chin. I would have preferred the time to smash the bottle over the kitchen counter because the jagged edges would have ended the fight then and there but it was still a useful thrust that had him staggering backwards. I then backhanded him across the chin with my makeshift truncheon. That sorted him out. He popped right down onto his arse, dropped the cleaver and stared at me with goggly eyes. To make sure, I booted him forcefully in the side of the head. David Beckham, who had just got the Number 10 shirt, would have been proud of that kick.

Quickly I checked that there were no other men in the corridor then asked the girls: "Do you know him?"

They both shook their heads, both still trembling and holding on to each other although I noticed that El's sister had grabbed the giant dildo in an attempt to arm herself. Not that it would have been much use unless the man was bending over and dropping his pants.

"Who the hell is he?" I said again. "Have you had any problems with your manager?"

I knelt down and felt for a pulse. The carotid artery can be frustratingly hard to locate when you really want it. My own pulse was racing from the sudden exertion and adrenalin from the battle was coursing around my veins cleaning out all the mellowing effects of the booze and smokes I had earlier.

He was still alive but I'd given him a good hiding. The right side of his face was burgundy pulp and his nose was smashed. I removed pieces of broken teeth from his mouth and put him into the recovery position. Usually I know whom I'm fighting and I know how far to go but this was something out of the blue. It could have been a case of mistaken identity but I doubted it.

My suspicions were fully raised when I noticed a blue mark barely visible under the man's cheap Casio wristwatch. I removed the watch and found the same crocodile style tattoo on his skin as I'd seen the day before on Brigit Nguyen's wrist. It looked like the Lacoste logo but faced the other way. Curiouser and curiouser. Something strange was going on around me and it had nothing to do with a grinning Cheshire Cat.

3

I trusted the girls to keep my identity a secret. There was no point in getting involved with the police and as long as I was careful not to be seen exiting the rooms it was unlikely anyone could describe me enough for the police to track me down.

El knew that if she got me into trouble I'd manage to find her back in Thailand. But there was no need for threats. We agreed on a story of me being a mysterious punter who had been attacked by the equally mysterious Chinese guy. We called the ambulance and I slipped out into the night having pressed some large denomination bank notes into both of their hands. They'd have something to natter about for the next few days.

I made my way back to the hotel keeping a wary eye over my shoulder in case anyone else wanted to tangle with me. There were still many groups of men milling around the canal streets but most of them were drunk and bawdy and could barely walk.

Back in my room I checked the bathroom, cupboard and windows carefully, placed the chair against the bolted door and managed to get a peaceful night's sleep until it was time for breakfast. No dawn knocks woke me up and no uniformed men dragged me from my bed for interrogation.

I ate a continental breakfast and checked out of the hotel stashing my suitcase with the concierge and then made a call to Jeremiah's number. His answering machine picked up. I decided not to leave a message.

I killed the next few hours reading the paper and drinking coffee then called again. No luck again. I was starting to get irritated. After last night's incident my instincts were starting to itch. I began suspecting that things were not in order. Jeremiah was a strange businessman but it was unlikely he'd simply ignore his main contact number especially since he didn't carry a mobile.

I went shopping and found that European fashion was substantially different from that found across the Channel. There was nothing that took my fancy but it killed the time. I had a steak in an Argentinean restaurant and tried to reach Jeremiah again. By now I was getting angry. I had no intention of hanging around in Amsterdam for much longer.

The taxi driver knew the address but it was out of town and the drive took around half an hour. Everything is flat in the Netherlands which is why the windmills and power turbines get plenty of wind all year long. The drive was monotonous. We reached the suburbs and went beyond. All the buildings were decent bourgeois houses with pristine, curtain-less windows and neatly tended gardens.

Finally the driver turned down a side road and stopped in front of a large, nondescript house. A dog barked. A group of uniformed men were loitering in the front garden conferring while my taxi parked directly behind the ambulance.

I didn't like what I saw.

"What's happened here?" I asked and noticed the small brass plaque which was attached on the wall next to the heavy front door. It said discretely 'Rosenstein & Levin, Importer'.

It would have been nice if there was a Mr. Levin to talk with but he'd passed away ten years earlier and it became rapidly obvious that Jeremiah Rosenstein had followed him down that prickly path to oblivion.

"He was attacked by a burglar," the policeman said to me in perfect English. "Are you a friend?"

"No, I've come for business. From South Africa."

"Your name." I gave him the name in my current passport and a fictitious address.

"Is he… you know…?"

"Yes, dead. He was shot in the heart. Two times and they stole some things but we don't know what. The housekeeper is trying to make a list."

"When was this?"

"Last night sometime. We were only alerted half an hour ago when the woman came to clean."

"That's terrible. We had an appointment."

"Have you known him for a long time?"

"Yes, but not very well. I used to sell diamonds to him. We would meet once a year perhaps."

I made my exit as soon as I could and departed in my waiting taxi. It was time to go back home. To leave Europe behind. It had been an interesting few days. Now it was getting a bit too messy. I pulled the handphone from my pocket and called the airline. There was an SQ flight to Singapore leaving in three hours and if I hurried I could still make it. No point in hanging around.

When I strode into the hotel lobby, an elderly couple from the north of England were making a big deal out of checking in. I didn't have time to dick around so I yelled at the young lad behind the counter and he got flustered for a while until the key for the security room was found.

I was half way out of the door with my case when the lad called me back.

"Are you Mr. Jedburgh?"

"Yes, of course." I was wary but it had been the name I used to check in.

"There was a package delivered this morning after you went out."

I frowned and put my gear down. Outside the taxi meter was ticking over and I didn't want to get hung up in any traffic.

"Where is it?"

"Will you sign for it here please." The lad handed me a shopping bag emblazoned with the brand name Tumi. Inside I found, wrapped in thin paper and protective plastic, what appeared to be a Tumi wash bag. It felt empty.

"Who is it from?" I demanded.

"There is a note with it."

I tore open the envelope and found a brief letter from my recently deceased business acquaintance. A quick glance told me what I needed to know. I took the washbag over to a corner and ripped open the protective plastic. In one of the zippered internal compartments I found two small packages each one slightly larger than my thumb. They were wrapped up in duct tape. One was marked with my name. It wasn't the entire consignment I'd ordered but felt like a decent quantity. The other one I assumed contained the special Vietnam delivery and was marked M.G. There was also a roll of US dollars held together with an elastic band. I saw the face of Benjamin Franklin glaring at me. I reckoned twenty of those would cover my travel expenses.

I opened my Samsonite and then slotted the wash bag into a space, closing the hard shell-like case and spinning the combination lock back to a random pattern. If I took the bag in my hand luggage it would be questioned. So I had to risk putting it into the hold.

Five minutes later the Surinamese taxi driver was flooring his accelerator and assuring me we'd be well in time.

After take-off I ordered a glass of the Business Class plonk and re-read the note from Jeremiah Rosenstein, toasting him a fond farewell and promising myself I'd find out who and what was behind all this.

Bill,

An urgent business matter has arisen that means I will have to leave town immediately. I do not know exactly when I'll be back and assume you do not have the time to wait for me. Therefore I have sent you this small consignment. It contains some of what you requested yesterday. My apologies if I could not manage all in the short time. I will hold you to credit and my poor father will be turning in his grave if he knew of me extending such terms to a client.

The other box is the special delivery I had mentioned to you. I trust you to take great care as it is of the utmost importance and must be delivered to a man (I deliberately do not refer to him as a gentleman) named Milford Grosvenor, one of the partners at the law firm of Huntley, Mason & Mason whose Ho Chi Minh City office should be easy to locate.

Good luck and I will be in touch as soon as I can.

Sincerely
J.R.

I folded the note and replaced it in my jacket pocket. On the whole I had done well out of the transaction. Jeremiah had funded my airfare and it was unlikely he'd be demanding payment for the diamonds he'd just supplied to me.

Something had frightened the old trader last night and he had obviously made hurried arrangements to get out of town. But not fast enough. He must have upset somebody, who later came around and exacted the ultimate payment.

Besides being a huge entrepôt for the diamond trade, Amsterdam was also known as an international drug trading hub. The laxness of the authorities with regards to softer recreational drugs allowed gangs to move freely when dealing with more hard-core product. I could image that some drug dealers may have been using diamonds to pay for transactions and Jeremiah could have been part of such arrangements. A raging Russian or a swivel-eyed Armenian would not think twice about murder if he felt he'd got a bum deal from the canny Jewish merchant.

It was only speculation but it was a valid theory given the environment. I did not want to be around when the Dutch police went through Jeremiah's client records. I knew he'd been a cautious man and it was unlikely he'd keep detailed files that would point investigators in my direction but being on the other side of the world was a fine idea today.

"We've got a lobster bisque soup or an Italian salad for starters, sir," the kebaya-clad stewardess explained bending over so I could appreciate the swell of her breasts under the thin garment. It was a long way back to Asia so I might as well keep myself busy with food, drink and lascivious thoughts.

After dinner and two glasses of port I felt tired enough and dropped off into a fitful sleep. There was turbulence over Siberia and it filtered into my dreams. However by the time the cabin lights came on and the crew busied themselves with breakfast I was feeling fine and looking forward to getting back to the condominium I owned in the Lion City. I'd been away for a while and it would be nice to sit on the balcony and gaze over the greenery, then catch up with some old friends.

When I got to immigration my new-found tranquility was ruthlessly shattered by the sight of one of those old friends already waiting for me with a crooked grin. He was by himself, so that was a positive sign.

I said: "I hate it when you pop up unexpectedly. Couldn't you have waited for my call once I was back home, at least given me a chance to shave and shower and we could have gone for a few beers?" I scowled at Larry Lim while the Malay immigration lady examined my passport and chopped it quickly knowing that I was being met by this official who was standing on the other side of her booth.

"I would have had to wait days for your call," Larry said.

"Anyway, what the hell do you want? No, don't answer that. I know the answer. How about why? And what's so damned urgent."

Larry shook his head sadly and clasped my hand. He was wearing a red tie and white shirt that framed his broad shoulders and chest. Around his neck he wore an official identity badge permitting him entry to secure areas of the airport. We walked over to the baggage reclaim. I scanned the hall and found Singapore as pristine, efficient and modern as I'd left it some weeks ago. I split my time between this city and a beach house I owned several hours south of Bangkok.

"We got a message from Interpol featuring your name."

"Amsterdam?"

He looked puzzled for a second. "Something bad you did in Amsterdam?"

"Not if the girl didn't complain to her parents."

"We're not interested in Amsterdam."

"Good because that's the only bad conscience I have."

"You have no conscience. You are as cold as the Antarctic, Bill."

"Hey, I have feelings. I'm good to my friends and those people who have saved my life in the past."

"It's good to see you again, Bill," the Singaporean said with genuine feeling. We had had a few adventures together in his capacity as an operative of Singapore's Security and Intelligence Department, their version of the United Kingdom's MI6 and SAS rolled into one.

"Do we have a problem?" I demanded.

He shrugged. "Nothing major but I have to bring you in for questioning." He grinned when he said this, so I suspected it wasn't as bad as it could be.

"How is the old bastard?"

"I didn't tell you this and will deny everything: but he's very pleased."

"So he should be. I wish he'd just leave me alone."

Larry sighed. This was Singapore and any citizen or permanent resident would never get away entirely from the benevolent shadow of the government and its maternal ministrations.

My bags arrived and we cruised through Customs. It helped being in official custody because I would have been uncomfortable explaining my wash bag with uncut diamonds if the young girl in uniform had chosen to stop me.

My escort pointed to the exit towards the car park and we found his black Toyota where he'd left it. It was seven in the morning and although daylight was telling me I should be energetic my body-clock felt it was being conned.

"Set a wedding date yet?" I asked as Larry steered the car in the direction of Changi Village. At night this was a notorious hang-out for Chinese and Malay lady-boys and contrary to the world press Singapore was not as uptight and conservative as it liked to appear. If you knew under which stone to look there was much sleaze to be found in the Lion City. It's just that the stones were neatly arranged and highly scrubbed.

But this was also the area of the army camps and one of these had the distinction of quartering the activities of Brigadier Wee. We passed through a number of security check-points and finally entered the barracks building. A pretty Indian girl led us upstairs and we waited on a leather sofa for a while until the great man was ready for us.

He sat in his usual chair, behind a vast desk, looking for all the world like an Asian Churchill without the cigar but with the same bulldog scowl. His head was bald and, as were his hands, covered in liver spots. Through the window behind him one could see a training ground where young uniformed men and women jogged, leapt, crawled and assaulted each other under the watchful eyes of stern-faced sergeants.

"Do they ever get a rest, the poor kids?" I said.

"Not while they're in this camp," the Brigadier said. "Welcome back to Singapore, Bill Jedburgh." I thought for a second that I detected a slight upturning of the corners of his mouth that could, in an ordinary man, have been construed as a smile but I was probably mistaken.

I shrugged by way of reply, not sure in which direction the conversation would move.

"So he is dead then?" the Brigadier said, squinting at me.

"That's what the papers say." I assumed we were not talking about Amsterdam but I didn't want to say too much. Best to let him do the talking.

"And you happened to be in town at the same time as he got killed?"

"Well, there were a lot of people in town at the same time. It's a popular place, London."

"Not for men like you, Bill." He gave me one of his long, soul-searching looks and I tried to meet it steadily without being offensive. One tried not to offend the Brigadier. There wasn't much I feared between heaven and earth but this man could bring sweat to the forehead of the bravest warrior.

He had no soul or compassion. He manipulated circumstances and situations without compunction. His duty was to protect the safety of the state of Singapore and he pursued this mission with a single-minded ruthlessness that bordered on the psychotic. I knew this because I'd occasionally had a glimpse into his game plans and been part of his machinations in the past. I was an unwilling knight on his chequered board and whenever it took his fancy he would reach for me as he was doing now to protect his king or more likely to destroy an opposing queen before she manoeuvred into a position of advantage.

And, he had the ear of the Senior Minister, Lee Kuan Yew, the father of the nation.

"You're not suggesting that I killed him, are you, Brigadier?"

He made a noise that was a chuckle for him. By now I knew that our conversation had nothing to do with the incidents in Amsterdam. That was off the radar so far, I assumed.

"Larry, this ang-mo friend of yours is very convincing," Brigadier Wee said.

It was our little charade. As a matter of principle I would not admit what I had done, even though there was no doubt in my mind that Brigadier Wee had intended this to be the outcome right from the beginning. But assassination was still a crime in all civilised countries and so admission was unprofessional. Although I had a shrewd idea that the Singapore constitution did permit government-sanctioned assassinations as a foreign policy tool. I really had to look that one up one of these days.

"Bill, I sincerely hope you were not involved in the appalling murder of this man, however despicable a creature he turned out to be. We don't condone that sort of activity in Singapore or by Singaporeans. If I were to suspect that you had committed such a crime I'd be forced to hand you over to the police department immediately." He enjoyed the irony of our conversation. But I suspected that this was only his foreplay.

"Of course there is no record of you having been on that plane. No description of anyone looking like you, but somehow you turn up in London...," Wee let the accusation dangle for a while. I kept on looking him straight in the eye. It was more honest than the schoolboy phrase, 'It wasn't me, sir'.

"What are your plans for the next few weeks, Bill?" he asked.

"Take it easy. I thought I'd go over to Thailand and Vietnam. Catch up with some friends."

"Vietnam? Any particular reason?" he appeared intrigued.

"Nothing special. I haven't been there for a while."

"Coincidentally we have a small job for you in Vietnam. Nothing special, if you must know. But if you are going there we won't have to send someone like Larry."

I stroked the stubble on my left cheek and placed a mask of indecision and lack of interest on my face. Not that it would help much. "I'd rather not do any job, special or not for a while. The Hong Kong thing was depressing and I want to get away from all that for a while."

Brigadier Wee stared at me without expression for a while then nodded slightly. "It's a shame. We'd be willing to pay you. But you do what you have to do. We'll be in touch next time we have a job for you."

Was he really letting me off the hook that easily?

"I'd be more interested if you paid me the going rate next time," I said.

"SID has always paid you fairly."

"Not at my normal consulting rates."

"We don't agree with your normal rates." He made the strange chuckling noise again then said something strangely heart-warming. "You're a good man, Bill. Now go and take a rest and remember that when I want you, you'd better well be there, fit and ready to go."

That was his mild way of reminding me that although I thought I was a free man, he actually owned me and anytime he wanted to yank the chain, I'd have to come running.

I pursed my lips, shook his proffered hand knowing that it was his way of thanking me for a good job done and turned to leave the office still accompanied by Larry.

"What was that all about?" I said to Larry as he drove me home to my condo.

"I thought you weren't interested?"

"I'm not. But I'm curious why he just dropped the matter."

"He was going to tell you that we've got intelligence that Lavender Daai is working on a project in Vietnam. She's teamed up with a major local drug dealer and helping him to set up a distribution network in the United States. We've been keeping an eye on them and sharing data with the American DEA because these drugs have been turning up in the dance clubs in Singapore."

"Ah-ha," I commented. "What sort of drugs?"

"Mostly MDMA, what they are calling 'Ecstasy'."

I nodded because I was no stranger to what people did around me.

"They mix it with other shit like ephedrine, amphetamine and methamphetamine," Larry went on as he took the car off the highway, "and then our Ah Kong gangs sell it around the clubs."

"I thought you'd cleaned up the Ah Kong. Who runs it now?

"A guy called Nor Du. He won't be around for much longer," Larry said with some satisfaction. "We've made him an offer he can't refuse to move to Amsterdam."

"So Lavender Daai is in Vietnam?"

"We believe she is, so keep your eyes open in case you bump into her."

"I'll shoot first and ask for a dance later if I bump into her," I said grimly. The girl had caused me enough trouble. And her father, although a Triad big boss, had been such a nice man.

"I'm sorry I can't help you guys on this one. But I need a break."

Larry pulled up in front of my condo. "No worries. You'll be back." He gave me a knowing smile which disconcerted me. I slapped him hard on the bicep by way of thanks for the lift and went around to the boot to get my suitcase out.

My apartment smelt clean and fragrant. The maid must have been there earlier in the day. There were fresh sheets on my bed; there was milk and bread in the fridge as well as cold beers.

I dumped my suitcase in the guest bedroom, grabbed a beer, stripped off and ten minutes later slipped into the hot, scented water of my Jacuzzi on the balcony.

As I lay letting the bubbles soothe my aching muscles I thought about my meeting with the Brigadier. Why did he always make me feel like he was the boss?"

"Fuck him," I said out loud. Then I repeated it a few times. Two times now he'd set me up for a job in Hong Kong. Now I really wanted to keep my distance from Brigadier Wee and his manipulations.

As I studied the bruises on my shins, I recalled the case of The Hairy Filipino, as Larry Lim always enjoyed calling it.

That had been about five months ago.

4

"Do you like dimsum?" said Brigadier Wee.

"What do you mean when you say dimsum?" I answered. "I rather like spring rolls but not those chicken feet and shrimp balls. They're just too greasy and tasteless for me."

"Dimsum," replied Brigadier Wee, a man of few words.

"Are you suggesting that I must go to Hong Kong?"

He nodded curtly and, taking hold of the bottle of Clos de Vougeot, began pouring the last of it into his glass.

"One should do what one can to mitigate the rigours of life," remarked the Brigadier.

"In my youth, I was always taught that one should take a woman by the waist and a bottle by the neck," I said.

Wee fixed his hard, dark eyes on me and replied, "I am glad you told me. I shall continue to hold a bottle by the waist and give women a wide birth."

I shrugged, being rather partial to both wine and women, even given to a spot of song when the occasion so required. We were just at the tail end of a fine dinner in a private room of the Raffles Hotel, and I'd been wondering all evening what was on the old boy's mind. We didn't dine often, but when we did, he usually prevailed on me to do difficult favours for him, which

I could not refuse since he always came armed with the right incentives. It was his habit to keep my genitals in a tight vice-like grip — metaphorically speaking — although in a sense, it hurt just as much.

"I'm expecting a fellow to join us," he said once he'd lit his Romeo y Julieta with a small blow-torch-like device. He took a glance at the slim time piece on his wrist. "He's known as the Hairy Filipino."

"Why?"

"Because," he paused to see if the end of his Havana was glowing suitably, "he's hairy, and because he's a Filipino."

"That explanation seems perfectly satisfactory, sir," I said.

"He'll tell you all about himself. He talks the hind leg off a donkey. Like they all do. Pretends he's not Filipino at all but really a son of a Spanish nobleman who fell in love with a woman from Manila. You know the sort."

I frowned and made no comment as none was required.

"He was some type of colonel in their army. But during the last coup under Aquino, he was booted out. He insists that he'd be a general by now, and that they confiscated his lands and farmhouse." Brigadier Wee waved his cigar in small circles to indicate the unspoken 'etc. etc. etc'. "That sort of thing," he concluded.

"So, you want me to go to Hong Kong with him?"

He nodded.

"And do what?"

"Well… you're a bodyguard by profession." He regarded me stoically.

"I used to be. I wish you stopped reminding me of that fact, so I could get on and earn a decent living doing a proper job."

"I should think you're rather good at what you used to do." He smiled with barely noticeable humour. "Otherwise, why would I keep on making use of your services?"

He had a point. There was a whole company of fit, young Singaporean commandos ready, willing, and able to lay down their firm young bodies for Brigadier Wee and the protection of their fresh young nation. What I suspected was that Wee only used me for those assignments that were best done by someone far removed from him by race and background. One could be forgiven for thinking that he used me only for the dirty work, but it seemed now he'd found someone else for his sordid tasks, and I was to be there only to play second fiddle. In a way, I was disappointed, although I knew in my heart it wasn't like that at all. He just hadn't got around to explaining things properly yet.

"What does he have to do, this Hairy Filipino?"

"It's best you don't know too much. Just go along and keep an eye on him. He's a nice enough fellow but, like all his race, terribly temperamental and prone to fits of passion and violence. He rather fancies himself as a ladies' man and he won't think twice about shooting another bloke in the back. Just last month he was in a bar in Angeles City and gunned down an American sailor who had picked up the wrong bottle of San Miguel."

"I get the picture. So how come he isn't behind bars?"

"You know how it is in the Philippines. If you know the right people — and he seems to be well-connected

— you slip them a few thousand pesos, and all witnesses are struck down with amnesia."

I smiled politely, because I was no stranger to that country or its customs.

"Now don't mess things up like you did the last time in Jakarta," Wee reminded me. "Here he is."

The door had opened and in front of us stood the Hairy Filipino.

"I have arrived. Good evening, Brigadier. I am enchanted to see you."

Both of us stood up to shake hands.

"Had a nice flight, Fernando? This is Bill Jedburgh. He'll be going to Hong Kong with you."

The Hairy Filipino was a short, squat man with a bull-dog face, but there was a subtle grace about the way he moved. His grip was as firm as a jailhouse mattress and it was true: he was as hairy a man as one could imagine. His eyebrows met over his slightly squashed nose, reminding one of a Russian politician, and there were great growths of black hair protruding from the cuffs and collar of his fancy, yellow silk shirt. His head, however, had been closely cropped, giving him a rather mean, military look. And, of course, there was a dark shadow around his jaw. One could imagine that he shaved several times a day because he gave off a strong reek of an effeminate perfume which didn't seem right for a man who looked, to all intents and purposes, like an ape dressed-up.

We sat down again at the table, and Wee offered the Filipino a Havana.

"Well, Fernando, have you been breaking any hearts today?"

The man laughed with a self-satisfaction that he didn't try to disguise. He spoke English well but with that lilting accent that could have been very appealing indeed had it come from the mouth of an attractive raven-haired Filipina temptress.

"Since you ask me, Brigadier, I don't mind telling you that I got a phone number from the stewardess that served me in business class. She agreed to meet me for drinks sometime."

"Let's get to business." Brigadier Wee jumped the conversation forward once the social banter was concluded. We talked for twenty minutes, then stood up to go our separate ways.

The last thing that the Brigadier said was, "Now remember, Fernando. You do the job and when it's all completed, then Bill here will give you the money. We are clear on that?"

"I am a man of honour, Brigadier. You, as a military man, should know that."

Wee smiled coldly and turned away.

"What will you be doing later tonight?" I asked as we stood outside waiting for a cab. The Brigadier's driver had already whisked him away in the direction of Changi where he lived in a well-appointed flat in the middle of his regimental barracks.

"You?" the Hairy Filipino wanted to know.

"I'm going to go home and get an early night. I have a girlfriend who lives with me."

"I shall take a walk around Orchard Towers. I am interested in life. Lend me two hundred dollars until tomorrow, Bill. I have no change on me."

I grinned and took out my wallet, because it was no big deal; it would go down on expenses. I had no idea what the Hairy Filipino's preferences were, but around Orchard Towers, one could get pretty much anything for that sort of money. The ladies of the night in this city were versatile. You could be on top or below, whatever took your fancy.

The next day, we flew to Hong Kong. I'd checked in earlier at the airport in order not to sit next to him during the three airborne hours. I had a feeling that he liked his drink and would rattle on once he'd downed a few Armagnacs. I wasn't in the mood for conversation with a man I probably would never see again after this assignment. On arriving, we took a red Toyota taxi all the way from the new airport to the Grand Hyatt Hotel.

We got our rooms and arranged to meet in the Champagne Bar an hour later. I found him there leaning against the black leather counter-top, chatting away in rapid Tagalog, his native tongue, with one of the waitresses. She had a slit in her skirt that ran all the way up to her waist and a glint in her eye that implied she was rather impressed by this perfumed ape-man.

"My friend, Bill. And this is Rosalita, the most beautiful waitress in the hotel. She tells me they have a famous singer from Manila in town."

The waitress nodded shyly and then slipped away before the wrath of the Chinese manager could descend on her for pausing to chat with one of her countrymen.

"I heard this singer once in Manila. Her name is Kuh Ledesma. She sang like a nightingale, and everyone in the audience was crying. Including President Marcos."

"He was there?" I pretended to be impressed.

"I knew him," he said, "before he forgot our country and thought only of himself."

"That's what usually happens with dictators. They lose their sense of reality."

He didn't reply, simply looked into his glass and frowned as if he'd thought of something unpleasant but still wanted to consider it for a while. He quietly said to himself: "Ako ay Pilipino."

The audience was mostly composed of men and women in their thirties and forties who were well-dressed and had that air of executive importance about them. The singer turned up soon and began charming us with old songs performed with a refreshing, modern energy. She embraced the entire room with her melodies and spun a mood from wall to wall that entranced us all. Then she shyly bobbed her head and scurried off for a brief break and a glass of water.

"She's marvellous. Only the Filipina can sing like that. It is the gift of our nation," the Hairy One said. He finished his drink and asked for another one.

"I liked the way she handled 'Funny Valentine'," I said.

He nodded, looking sombre again. "So where do we have to go?" he wanted to know.

"Not far from here. We have to walk across the street and then a flyover."

"This is a nice hotel. Have you often worked for the Brigadier?"

"More often than I'd like to."

"And before you became a bodyguard, what did you do?" he asked.

"I was here, in the Royal Hong Kong Police. Inspector."

"Ah, a policeman," he looked at me with a slightly different expression suddenly. Perhaps he'd thought of me as a runaway squaddie who couldn't find any other job.

"And they made you leave the police, yes?"

"Not really. They made me leave by boring me to tears, perhaps. The job wasn't fun any more, and with the run-up to 1997…"

He didn't seem to comprehend what I was implying, so I completed the sentence with, "there weren't many career opportunities for non-Chinese after the handover."

"Oh," he nodded rapidly, "I understand."

"What are you drinking?" I asked.

"Madeira. It is so rare to find it these days," he said, twirling the little glass of tawny liquid.

"What is it, a Blandy's?" I tried to show off my rudimentary knowledge.

He shook his head gravely. "A Twenty-five-year-old Rutherford & Miles."

I grinned. That too would go down on expenses, like all the rest.

We had two more drinks and then moved off, crossing the marble lobby and down past the Immigration and Revenue Towers, twin sentinels of oppression in a city that had up to recently been one of the freest societies in the world.

"They say he killed Esteban Ramirez but I know that's not true," the Hairy Filipino said. He had his hands in the pockets of a pale, cotton suit and looked at me speculatively.

"Who's Esteban Ramirez?"

"You don't know. He is dead now, of course." The Colonel took a silk handkerchief from his pocket, and

I caught the whiff of his customary scent. He blew his nose in short, sharp bursts.

I asked, "Who killed Ramirez?"

"They call him the Reliable Man. He is a killer by profession. Nobody knows what nationality he is or where he came from. But he is good. He has a reputation."

"He does? And who is this Esteban Ramirez fellow?"

"Was. He owned Pampanga Airlines and much land."

"And now he's dead, killed by this Reliable fellow?"

We were just walking up the stairs that led to the flyover across Gloucester Road. The air was humid as always in Hong Kong.

"And tonight, we will kill The Reliable Man," the Colonel said grimly, although, in the neon-lit evening, there was an ironic smile on his face as if he knew more than he was letting on.

"You will. I'm just there to watch your back."

"I've never worked with a partner before. This Brigadier Wee has strange ideas."

"He's a Singaporean. They're all a bit anally retentive. You get used to it."

"Do you like women?"

"I have a girlfriend. She's nice. Keeps me out of trouble. Mostly."

"It is not the same, my friend," he said mysteriously as we began coming down the stairs on the other side. We walked past some places called 'La Bamba' and 'Big Apple', then turned left past a club called 'Neptune II' and carried on until we reached the entrance to a small hotel marked 'Villa Victoria'. All this time, the Hairy Filipino hadn't spoken but he'd mopped his brow repeatedly with the perfumed silk hankie. Perhaps the exercise was making him hot.

"What is this place?" he asked.

"It's a love hotel. You can rent rooms for an hour or two. It's very clean."

He nodded. "We have them in Manila. But not as nice as this one."

"He's in Room 305, but we have to go up the back stairs to avoid being seen."

I found the fire exit door and levered it open, then stepped aside to let him go in first. We went up two flights and emerged onto a small, corridor decorated in fake rococo style. Little statues stood on alcoves. There was a faint smell of lemongrass in the air. It was silent as a graveyard. One would have thought that a love hotel at this time of the evening had a certain amount of background noise: bedsprings and the stifled sounds of sweaty passion. But there was nothing. The sound proofing must have been excellent.

We proceeded cautiously. Outside the door, he stopped and gave me an enquiring look. I pointed my index finger in confirmation at the plastic number tag. We both checked the corridor.

He produced from under his linen jacket a large automatic. I was surprised to note that it was a Walther P99 — the latest model - which I'd heard was good but heavy in the hand.

For myself, I eased the tiny Colt Detective from its Bianchi holster at the small of my back.

I handed the Hairy Filipino a keycard, which I'd been told would open the door. He hefted his Walther in one hand and pushed the keycard into the lock with the other.

Slowly, he turned the knob while leaning close against the wood in order to anticipate any movement inside. The door swung open, and he leapt into the room. I was close behind him.

Lying on the bed was a young man, fully dressed, watching a porno movie on a small TV, which was suspended from the ceiling in one corner. He looked startled as the door burst open, and he began moving away from us. From the bathroom came the sound of a shower running.

"Stop. Your time has come, Reliable Man," the Colonel yelled melodramatically as he ratcheted the round into the breech and brought the weapon to bear on the young man who had just begun rolling off the edge of the bed. Three bullets thudded into the young man's chest and then he flopped down onto the floor out of sight. There was no further movement.

"Fernando," I said.

I tapped the Hairy Filipino lightly on the shoulder and as he turned, a questioning frown on his face, I shot him twice in the heart. He toppled backwards, his eyes wide-open in horror at this strange volte-face.

Bending forwards, the muzzle of my revolver against his nose, I checked cautiously that he was indeed dead, then kicked the door shut behind me. A face peeked over the counterpane from the other side of the bed. The young man rose hesitantly. There was no blood on him, only the vicious rips in his shirt, which the hot lead had made as it struck his kevlar vest.

"You okay?" I said. He nodded, pale in the face.

The noise of rushing water stopped and Brigadier Wee emerged from the bathroom.

"Good work," he said curtly. "Vile man." He touched the Hairy Filipino's body with the tip of his shoe.

I slid the snub-nosed Colt back into its hiding place.

"This is the man who killed my father?" asked the young guy.

"Yes," Wee replied.

"This is the one they call The Reliable Man?"

"That's what we believe. He's got quite a record. A notorious fellow," Wee said, almost jovially now. "We've been trying to put him down for a while. It's what the American police call 'zero tolerance' these days. No messing about, just a couple of bullets in the back. Much better than a long jail sentence and early parole for good behaviour. Isn't that right, Bill?"

"I can't disagree."

"This is Ramon Ramirez, by the way," he indicated the young man.

We smiled politely at each other. The Brigadier raised his eyebrows and disappeared through the door into the room across the corridor, from which emerged a young girl dressed only in a wrap-around towel. Wordlessly, she slipped under the covers of the bed without giving the corpse on the floor a second glance.

Five minutes later, the police arrived. At first, a duo of startled beat constables who had probably never seen such a strange tableau, later a detective-inspector and his team followed by Simon Foxcroft, the Assistant Divisional Commander-Crime, a chief inspector now, with whom I'd been at Police Training School.

"What a mess," he said, stepping around the room with a distasteful expression on his bearded face. "What's the story, Jedburgh?"

I said, "I was body-guarding Mr. Ramirez here, because we'd had a tip-off that The Reliable Man was coming after him, having just killed his father a few weeks ago. A family vendetta, or something. Ramirez here was taking some time out with his newly acquired girlfriend. I was down the corridor having a cigarette. I heard some noises, saw the deceased letting himself into the room and came after him. He'd just plugged three rounds into Ramirez who happened to be wearing a vest. I did my thing to stop the matter getting further out of hand."

"Couldn't you just sock him over the head with a blackjack or something, Bill?" Foxcroft growled.

"Would you have?"

"So, this is The Reliable Man?"

"Apparently. Don't think he's got a calling card on him, though."

"Well, nobody is going to shed any tears over him. You'd all better come down to Wanchai nick for statements. Tell the girl to get some clothes on. I assume she arrived with some?"

One of the constables went into the bathroom and found the girl's handbag, high heels and little black dress, then we all trouped out so she could get dressed. As we stood in the corridor, the door opposite opened two inches and I saw Brigadier Wee's liver-spotted face. I winked at him over the chief inspector's shoulder.

Wee was a ruthless, calculating bastard but you had to admire his style. Not only had he just got my services for free but for the next few months I'd be operating with a clean bill of health. After all, everyone now believed that the Reliable Man was dead when in fact he was just stepping down to the police station to give a preliminary statement and was hoping to catch Kuh Ledesma's final set at the Champagne Bar.

5

My skin had gotten all wrinkly from staying too long in the jacuzzi. I was still doubtful about what the Brigadier was up to this time but I was just going to ignore him and get on with my own plans.

It was time to examine what posthumous gifts Jeremiah Rosenstein had bequeathed to me. In my black towelling bathrobe I sat at the dining table and opened up the packet addressed to me that had arrived in the Tumi wash bag.

My own pile of diamonds was not very impressive but nor was it insignificant. They were of a uniform size, all uncut and large enough to be turned into decent engagement or ear-rings. Using a magnifying glass which I'd screwed into my right eye socket I could not detect any particular flaws. Overall I had to admit that Rosenstein had chosen reliably. Whatever other failings the man had carried about with him, there had never been any doubt that he had been an expert in his trade.

The minor moral dilemma I briefly addressed was whether I should pay for them. If there had been a partner it would have been fair to transfer the money to the Liechtenstein account but since Rosenstein was dead, what was the point of paying the bill? There had been an invoice in the TUMI wash-bag for 32,000 US dollars.

I left the sparkling stones on the table and poured myself a generous slug of Absolut Citron. I toasted Jeremiah and wished him well wherever he was now, amongst the glittering gemstones in the sky.

It was the other packet that aroused my curiosity but since it was destined for someone else I resisted the temptation to cut it open. I hefted it in my hand. It wasn't heavy. I felt the contents through the outer plastic which had been tightly wrapped in black duct tape. The texture indicated a standard box for a diamond ring perhaps. I shook the packet, but that didn't tell me much. After staring at the item for a minute or so with X-ray vision that I did not possess, I put it aside and proceeded to wrap up my lot of jewels.

In the spare room, behind a book case was a wall safe that I had installed when I bought the apartment. I spun the dials and opened the door with the special key. Nothing was amiss with the safe's usual contents so I shifted everything around and placed the diamonds on the bottom shelf.

Next, I contemplated what to do for the evening. Sitting around at home was not so appealing but there was no woman I felt like calling. The previous one had long gone. Of course there was a girl in Thailand, sitting in my beach front property making sure the gardeners were watering the grass. I'd get back there in a few weeks once this trip to Vietnam was done and after selling my diamonds in the Philippines.

So I felt like going out.

I had not been bar-hopping for months in Singapore. The scene changed quickly around town so I'd have to get some updated information on what was hot and what was not.

I looked at my Rolex and was surprised to see it was 8 p.m. already. It felt earlier.

Going into the other bedroom which served as a study, I booted up my Compaq Contura laptop and connected through the phone line into a server in Norway. I listened to the beeping and then the hissing sound that told me my computer was shaking hands with the one in Norway. There were two separate sets of passwords I had to enter and then I could check my messages. This e-mail service was a cut above AOL and CompuServe because it ran over a proxy server dedicated to absolute personal privacy. It was a new experimental system that had not been officially launched yet and was called Firemail. This was cutting-edge hacker technology and Sabeer, the Indian fellow who'd set it up for me, had never met me face to face. An annual donation to a bank account in Delhi kept my e-mail address active without messy credit card numbers or any other need for direct contact. Communicating with my customers had been so much more complex and time consuming in the old days prior to the World Wide Web.

There were two messages. The first one came from a CompuServe e-mail address that was a jumble of numbers. It simply said 'Job well done, expect more business in future.' I had a good idea who that was from.

The second message was infinitely more intriguing. It came from an AOL email address. The sender signed himself 'Thanatos' and there was a name and several lines of background on a man whom somebody wished to be killed. At the bottom of the email, downloading slowly at the speed of the phone connection, was a picture of a middle-aged Asian man. I studied the information for a while, saved the email and the picture to a special folder and then deleted the message from my inbox which also made it vanish from the original server.

For added security I had a clever little program on my laptop which my hacker friend had called 'Destruktocom'. If anyone powered up the computer it would not ask for any password but simply go to the main screen. However if one didn't blind-type in a set of numbers twice within the first 20 seconds 'Destruktocom' would silently kick-in and reformat the entire hard-drive. Once I'd gotten the password wrong and it had been a pain to reload all my programs. The price of personal protection.

I chose a pair of linen pants and a cream shirt, sprayed some Obsession around my chin which would soon fade in the sultry, tropical night and found my car keys in the drawer by the front door. It had been nearly two months since I'd last driven the 323i and I was strangely looking forward to giving it a spin. You can't road race in Singapore but traffic jams were virtually unheard of.

I went the long way round and by the time I pulled into the park house near Boat Quay it was close to half past ten: a civilised time to be stepping into the bar scene. My first port of call was a place called 'Buzz' because that's what I wanted to catch up on. The latest info from an old mucker.

Tommy Doncaster was a canny Northern lad who had made heaps of money in the late eighties running a disco in Hong Kong called Hot Gossip. On a normal Saturday night the queue of punters waiting to be let in had stretched half a mile down Canton Road and Tommy had negotiated himself a profit share that was highly geared.

Besides being in the right place at the right time he was also an astute and seasoned nightclub manager, with eyes in the back of his head and a wicked right hook that regularly dropped a misbehaving customer flat on his back before the bouncers knew anything had even started. He'd always reminded me of Humphrey Bogart in 'Casablanca', leaning against the bar nursing a Southern Comfort & Seven Up, a cigarette dangling from his lower lip, carrying on a conversation with a regular while nodding or shaking his head at the doormen as people presented themselves at the lobby hoping for admittance.

'Buzz' was more of a fun pub concept and Tommy had graduated from doing the real work himself, now that he owned most of the shares. A couple of gregarious Scotsmen kept the waiters in check, the customers happy and the ladies dancing. Most of the time Tommy sat in the back room and played computer games or watched the monitors. If he spotted someone interesting he'd come out and walk the floor for a while.

There was a new man at the door, a Malay bodybuilder with shoulders courtesy of Schwarzenegger, so I paid my entrance fee like the rest of them. Three tall Indian guys pushed past me, without showing the green but getting a welcome nod from the doormen. They would have coughed up an annual membership fee for the privilege, up front cash that Tommy would have reinvested quickly.

I found a spot at the bar between two Aussies who were discussing cricket and a Chinese lad who had gone bright purple in the face from the Kamikaze shooter his mates had just forced down his throat.

My Absolut and soda arrived within a minute. It took Tommy Doncaster not much longer than four minutes.

"You should have called. I was thinking of taking the evening off," he said in his broad Lancashire brogue.

"You never take the evening off," I said pumping his hand.

"I was thinking of it."

"The road to hell is paved with bad intentions."

"You should have told them you're a mate of mine instead of paying to get in."

"Watching the door were you?"

He nodded knowingly. "New doorman. Want to see how he's behaving himself. His girlfriend works on Till No. 2, been with us for a while but she's been ripping off small amounts for the last month."

"What you going to do about it?"

He shrugged. "See if anyone else is involved and then call the police eventually." He pondered the question a bit longer, then added, "Or maybe not."

Tommy had always been a bit of a control freak and any new employee who misjudged his boss' understanding of the nightclub business was in for some sore and savage surprises.

"You've been away long," he said circling his finger at the nearest barman indicating another round for us.

"Thailand and a job I was doing in Hong Kong. McAlistair sends his regards, we just met up in London recently."

"How is the old wanker?"

"We had a great night out and he got laid."

"So not a wanker anymore?"

"I didn't ask the girl."

"How long you staying in Singapore this time?"

"Not too long. I've got some other stuff going on. Might go to Vietnam. What's new here? Business good?"

"Been consistent the last few weeks. No new places have opened recently to take the crowd away. You know how fickle the party people are in this town."

"Well, you know how to walk the tightrope between cool and burnt-out."

"Won't be doing it for much longer," he said, a serious note creeping into his words.

"What do you mean?"

"I'm planning to sell up and leave Singapore."

His words surprised me. "But things are going well here. And you just bought that new apartment off Meyer Road."

"Tired of Singapore and this business."

"Not sure I believe you."

He laughed and then went on to explain what it was all about:

"I've applied to become a copper back in England."

I smiled politely. "Why would you want to do that?"

"I've always wanted to be a policeman. Since I left the Marines the idea of going back into a disciplined service has been at the back of my mind."

"Tommy, you're 45 years old, you're a self-made millionaire. You won't fit in. They'll never accept you."

He shook his head, a serious frown on his face. "Yes they will, they're short of good recruits and they've extended the minimum age. I've been given a preliminary interview date in a month."

"Why would you want to leave all this behind to go back into training school with a bunch of kids half your age only to end up as PC Doncaster pounding the beat on a freezing cold winter morning?"

"That's exactly why. Seems worthwhile." He smiled because I wasn't the first or last guy who'd been telling him he was crazy to walk away from the life he'd built for himself.

"Mind you, you'd be a damn good copper. You wouldn't accept bribes, and you wouldn't take any shit from the pissed bastards trying to start a fight after closing time. I admire the sentiment. But I still think they won't accept you. You don't fit the profile. They're looking for local lads with three kids, a mortgage and a wife who dyes her hair blonde."

"If they need men on the street they'll take me."

"You'll write and let us know how it goes?"

"Been running 5 miles every morning and swotting up on my maths and English grammar."

I patted him on the arm and our conversation moved into another direction. With any other man I would have said it was a manifestation of a mid-life crisis but with Tommy Doncaster he really wanted to do something worthwhile and fulfil a dream that had remained unattainable while he'd been making a name for himself in the night club business.

"Who are those three little honeys?" I asked nodding at the dance floor.

"The Sin sisters, we call them," Tommy said. We both watched as the three girls bopped around the dance-floor provocatively. No normal man could fail to get horny watching their performance: moving their long, brown legs, tossing their long, black hair in time to the beat of Ecuador by Sash!

"Sin by name or sin by game?"

"Family name. And they really are sisters. The two on the left are twins."

"They're gorgeous. I feel sorry for their father."

Tommy shrugged. "I bedded them all together one night last month," he said and waited for my response.

I rolled my eyes, because it was better than gnashing my teeth. If Tommy said he'd bedded them then that's what had happened. He was the Pied Piper of Boat Quay. All he had to do was say he was going home and they followed him to his German motor.

"Trouble with Singapore," I said, "is its such a boring strait-laced place."

"If you believe the American press."

"Long live CNN."

We watched the dance floor for a while and I tried to imagine what it would be like to wake up with all three of the amber beauties on a bright Sunday morning. I decided it was best for Tommy Doncaster to leave for England immediately and disappear in the shadows of the dark satanic mills.

"Tommy, you ever come across a tattoo of a small crocodile, something like the Lacoste insignia drawn on the arm or wrist?"

If anyone knew about that sort of stuff it would be him since he'd had to deal with most of the local gangsters in the course of his work. It paid to know them, respect them and occasionally pay them.

"Crocodile? A buaya?" he said.

"A buaya. That's the Malay word for crocodile, right?"

"Yeah, like you and me are buayas. Reptiles hunting female flesh."

"I saw this tattoo on an Asian girl's wrist and on a Chinese guy's."

"The same design?"

"Yes, about one and a half inches long, the fangs facing the opposite direction to the Lacoste logo."

"Wait here," he said and disappeared into his office.

I continued to enjoy watching the Sin sisters who by now had come off the dance floor and were drinking Tequila shooters without using their hands, getting their lips around the rim of the glass and then tipping it back and up, a move that made their breasts jiggle and jut all in one. Men were lining up to buy them shots. Oh, to be young, female and gorgeous.

When Tommy returned he had some information. "1950s Malaya Secret Society, probably pro-communist called the Buaya Brotherhood. Not much known. Founded by a Chinese Malayan called Ong Bing. When he was killed in a gun battle with the colonial police the society seems to have disappeared." He handed me a print-out from his computer with a picture of the crocodile tattoo. It seemed to be the same design and was placed on a wrist in the same position.

"Useful thing the Internet," I said.

"If you know where to look." Tommy smiled. "I plugged into a website run for Singapore police officers. Someone gave me the password."

"Useful things passwords." I inclined my head. "Now look at that. Sin is alive and well in Sin-gapore." Tommy and I watched as one of the Sin sisters licked salt and lime off a man's nipple and then downed her tequila with practised glee.

At the corner of the room I noticed two Chinese guys who did not seem to be impressed by the antics of the girls. They were standing with disapproving looks, far too sober and poorly dressed to be really part of the party crowd. I got the feeling they had been watching me talking with Tommy but I chalked it up to my usual paranoia. This was my home turf and I'd already concluded my business with Brigadier Wee.

An hour later I had all the latest information on the Singapore bar scene but was starting to feel tired. The long flight was catching up on me. The bar had begun to thin out as the right people moved on to the next trendy venue for that time of the night. Liquid Room was red hot, I overheard someone say. But for me my king size mattress with linen sheets sounded like a better destination.

Tommy had left me for other customers but returned periodically for short conversations. I made my decision to cut and run aided by the stealthy approach of a jet-lag headache and wished him a good night.

"Good luck getting into the police in England."

"I'll get in."

"We'll see each other before you leave."

"You're the one who comes and goes like a night-stalker," he said pleasantly.

We shook hands and I left the bar, noticing that the liquor had hit me harder than expected. It might be a thought to get over to the Philippines and spend a few weeks scuba diving, having early nights and cutting out the booze.

I trudged down the road towards the park house. There were groups milling around trying to get taxis or walking in the direction of food stalls which was where one ended up after clubbing. My car was parked on the third floor so I took the lift. As the doors opened I stepped forward hearing and sensing a movement which translated instantly into a sharp pain on the side of my head. It sent me staggering forward, my knees buckling and my arms flaying for support as I tried to work out where the danger was coming from.

Out of the corner of my eye I saw a sweeping arm and what could have been a stick or cosh. I had enough consciousness to drop down on my knees and roll. A burst of adrenalin removed some of the fuzziness from the earlier blow. A few more rolls brought me far enough from my attackers and I forced myself to my feet, faced off and got my hands up in a defensive position.

There were two of them and I recognised them. The two grim Chinese lads, the ones from 'Buzz'. One was holding a truncheon, the other a long carving knife. It was tough to get hold of a gun in Singapore.

We eyed each other in a wary stand-off. One of the two would try and slip around the side of me while the other kept me busy. The one with the truncheon was the weaker link. If I could get at him and wrestle it from his hands without letting his buddy cut me up, there was a chance.

The one with the knife moved but it was a faint. He smiled coldly.

The other one spoke suddenly, "Where you put the diamond?"

I didn't reply. He repeated his words, this time louder.

"Fuck you," I replied to be sure we understood each other.

"You got the diamond. Just give to us - we don't cut you or kill you."

"Try it, shit-face."

That got the reaction I wanted. Asians are easy to goad. With the exception of a well-trained Kung Fu fighter who understood that there was more to battle than a precise movement of arms and legs, a lot of Asians could not remain cool and detached enough.

The one with the truncheon stormed at me, his eyes glazed in fury. I deflected the blow with a Wing Chun block then swept his feet from under him. The truncheon clattered on the concrete. But at that moment my shoes slipped on some oil. It would have worked but for my losing control. The carving knife was all over me. I threw a punch at Knife-man's throat giving me the second I needed to get disentangled. But the knife was fast and he was all over me, slicing into the shoulder padding of my jacket.

This was looking bad and my body was not responding to my commands at the speed required. I managed to get away, slipping again on the concrete garage floor.

Knife-man was breathing hard and taking stock. He was confident he had the initiative. His buddy was groaning and the truncheon lay on the floor too far for me to reach.

Suddenly, from behind Knife-man, a figure emerged and a voice spoke with calm authority. Relief hit me because I knew the fight was over now.

Tommy Doncaster had come up the staircase and was strolling towards us with a casual glint of subdued violence in his eyes.

"Okay fella, now drop the knife and fuck off home to your mummy. This has gone far enough."

Knife-man turned slightly and stared at Tommy with a mixture of astonishment and confusion. He could see no weapon in Tommy's hands, yet the lanky Lancastrian kept bearing down on him at a slow, steady pace.

"Diu lei, ang-moh," Knife-man yelled and charged at Tommy. I got to my feet, puffed deep breaths into my lungs and watched as Tommy brought 25 years of brawling experience to bear. He sidestepped the arc of the knife, trapped the attacker's wrist with a left-hand grip and brought up a right fist that landed hard under the chin of the Chinese fellow. I flinched as I heard the sound of cracking bone and hoped for Tommy's sake it wasn't the neck that was snapping.

Knife-man's body went floppy and he dropped his weapon even as Tommy let him go and the man fell to the concrete floor. By now I'd stepped over to Truncheon-man and picked up his weapon, in case its owner wanted to be tapped on the head with it. He was trying to get to his feet. Giving in to my anger I gave him a vicious swipe on the side of the face that fractured his cheekbone and knocked him out.

"Saw them following you, as you left," Tommy said, standing over his victim and prodding him with a steel toe cap. He always wore functional shoes. He had his mobile phone out already. I waited until he'd completed the call to his manager telling them to call the police and get them up here to sort out a mugging.

"He's still breathing," I confirmed.

"Yeah, well he's lucky to be, after having a go at me with a knife," Tommy said. "Let's get the hell out of here. No other witnesses."

I knelt over Truncheon-man and checked his pulse at his carotid artery. Still beating. Then I grabbed his left wrist. Under the watch was the same Buaya tattoo we'd been talking about earlier. It was starting to dog me. I didn't like it at all. I showed it to Tommy. He nodded grimly. Knife-man had the same tattoo.

We got into my BMW and I pulled out fast from the garage.

"Drop me off at Meyer Road and I'll fix you a cup of coffee," he said as I floored the accelerator. I was angry with myself that they'd been able to jump me so easily. I was grateful that Tommy Doncaster had shown up instead of anyone else. He'd be sorely missed once he left Asia.

6

It was three thirty by the time I got back home but the night was not over yet.

As I stepped into the apartment I got a sense that someone had been here. There were no marks on the front door but something smelt different and when I went into the bedrooms it became immediately obvious that furniture had been moved and not rearranged to the same alignment. I was particular about that sort of thing.

I checked the entire place and found nothing missing, nobody hiding. I went to the laptop and verified everything was in order. Nobody had booted it up and the hard drive was still intact. Finally I went to the wall safe. The dial had been moved but when I dialled in the right combination and opened the armoured door there was nothing missing. Burglars but not safe breakers. That was odd.

I did not keep guns in my apartment because it was too easy for the police to find them. Instead I had some other useful but more legal weapons. At the back of the clothes cupboard, behind the rack of sombre Hugo Boss suits was a seventeenth Century Samurai sword that I'd been given by McAlistair for my birthday a few years back. I'd never used it in anger but had practised assiduously for a while at a Kendo Dojo I'd found in Bangkok. Then I'd got bored of it. Guns were so much more disposable. This sword was an antique. It had sentimental value. It was worth a fortune. In an age where lopping arms and heads off was frowned upon it was not a convenient weapon of choice but good to deal with any unexpected home invasions.

I placed it next to my bedside, hoping that the burglars would be back and I could rediscover my slashing techniques. Then I locked all the doors, drank a pint of water and crawled into bed where I slept soundly until the phone rang six hours later.

"Listening to the radio I had this distinct feeling that you must be back in town."

"What?"

"Muggers viciously beaten up in Boat Quay. Sounds like something to do with my old mate Bill Jedburgh."

"What?"

"Are you tired or something? It's nearly eleven in the morning and I'm on my second cup of Columbian here."

"Hello, Harry. I'm jet-lagged."

"That's not what I heard from Tommy Doncaster. He said you were drunk."

"Hung over, jet-lagged. It's all the same."

"Got coffee and two nubile young Thais perfectly willing to give you a wake-up massage. No naughty stuff of course."

I opened my eyes and contemplated the offer for a few seconds as the long hand on my Rolex moved smoothly around its face. "Half an hour."

In the bathroom mirror I studied my unshaven face. It could stay that way for the moment. A quick, freezing cold shower got my eyes wide open and wearing baggy cotton pants and a ragged T-shirt I left the apartment. I did not have far to go. The lift took me up to the penthouse where Harry Bolt's door was opened by one of his four live-in girlfriends, Summer. She hugged me and led me into the main room where my friend and officially my employer was reclining on one of four Brobdingnagian sofas watching a football match on a flat plasma screen that covered the entire wall. He muted the sound.

Harry Bolt had gained some weight in the last two months but his head remained as bald as a baby's bottom and his pale blue eyes still glinted with sharp amusement. He was dressed in a navy blue silk dressing gown and one of his other girlfriends, Autumn, was massaging his feet with a pungent green ointment.

"How come you've been talking with Tommy Doncaster?" I said, throwing myself into the sofa which stood at right angles to his. The sunlight filtering in through the open French windows seemed indecently bright for my jaded soul.

"Coffee?" Bolt suggested, pointing at a large silver pot on the table between us. Summer was already pouring me a cup. It smelt rich and heart-warming and made one think of rain-forests and flying Dutchmen.

Bolt considered me for a while, a tiny frown creasing his gleaming forehead. "He and I have been discussing a little business deal and he just happened to mention your bloody encounter with a couple of thuggees last night."

"It was good that he turned up when he did."

"He said you were doing fine but he needed to get some practice in for his upcoming police interview." Bolt smiled mischievously.

It suddenly clicked. "You're the one buying his bar from him."

"Correct in one. If we get the small matter of price sorted out."

"How much does he want?"

"More than I'm willing to pay."

"Nothing astonishing about that."

"We'll reach an agreement. I'm thinking of turning it into a lap dancing bar."

I decided to ignore the comment. However enlightened Singapore had become, that would never happen. "What do you think of him wanting to become a copper?"

"Admirable. Laudable. Amusing. Madness. None of my business," Bolt said.

I sipped my coffee for a while and gave Summer a smile. She was sitting on the floor cross-legged working on a cross-stitch. Bolt's four companions were all equally gorgeous. They had come to him in their early teens from a remote village in North-Eastern Thailand and he'd sent them to school and turned them into wonderfully, refined young ladies.

"Where are the rest of the gang?" I asked.

"Italian class. We're going to spend a month in Tuscany."

"Any reason?"

"I just bought a vineyard in Tuscany. Thought it would be nice to stay there for a while. You know. Watch the vines grown."

I nodded sagely. Knowing Bolt, there would be some other, more practical business reason. He'd tell me if he wanted to.

"Here's a clever clogs question," I said. "What does the word 'thanatos' mean to you?"

Bolt enjoyed the affectation of being a wily wheeler-dealer who had risen from the ranks of Peckham barrow-boys to become a self-made millionaire or media mogul. But the fact was he actually came from money and had the benefit of an expensive, public school education.

"Should I know the answer to this conundrum?"

"It's not a conundrum. I assume it's Greek."

"And I speak Greek?"

"Humour me, Harry."

He stared at me for a full minute but I knew his mind was shifting through old memories.

"You didn't tell me about the Hong Kong adventure. I assume from reading the 'Times' that it was concluded in London?" he asked.

"You want to hear the full story?"

"Sure, I love your stories."

I glanced around the room and asked, "Is it safe to talk here?"

He nodded and pointed at a small device that hung in a corner. It was a black box with a miniature antenna and a green light blinked periodically.

"Safe from bugs and any kind of electronic surveillance. Summer ran the program just half an hour ago."

"Well, it's a long story and it starts once upon a time…"

"Get on with it, Bill."

Along with Julian McAlistair, Bolt was one of the few people whom I truly trusted with the secrets of my occupation. It had been Bolt who got me started and set me up and if I ever went down he'd go down with me. But Bolt was not a man who went down, he was too careful for that. I told him the story and then he told me a few of his and suddenly it was lunch-time.

We had lunch in a Vietnamese restaurant on Killiney Road after which I spent two hours in the gym which was within walking distance. It was a quiet afternoon and there were only a few bodies working out. The girl at reception gave me a funny look when I asked her to turn the loud music down but she knew me as a regular and was happy to comply.

I drove back home and checked everything carefully but there'd been no more unauthorised visitors. At six thirty the messenger arrived with my plane ticket for the nine o'clock flight. Originally I'd planned a few days' break in Singapore but recent events made me want to get on with delivering my package. Something was going on and only by making myself a moving target could I get a better idea of what it was. Moving targets, as my training sergeant had constantly drilled into our heads, made harder targets.

Back on the laptop I considered the e-mail that had come in the previous evening. As we were parting, following lunch, Harry Bolt had said to me, "You were asking about 'thanatos'. It's the name given by the ancient Greeks to the god of death."

"You knew all along," I accused him.

"No, Summer remembered reading about it in a book of mythology."

"Useful to have well-educated concubines." He'd winked and climbed into his Mercedes.

So somebody thought he was being clever calling himself Mr. Death. Somebody with a classical education perhaps. I reviewed the attached file. I hadn't paid it much attention the first time around apart from noting that I had not come across the name and face before.

The target was a man called Wing Cam. He was in his fifties and he lived in Vietnam. He was a drug dealer and the leader of a criminal gang that controlled brothels in Ho Chi Minh City as well as Danang. He appeared to be short in stature, not more than five foot two, with a bland but vicious Vietnamese face, a receding hair-line and a growing paunch. He glared grimly at the camera. It seemed to me that this was an individual who possibly deserved to be killed. I'd shot half a dozen men like him and never felt any remorse or pangs of guilt. They were the vultures of modern Asian society, often glorified and even glamorised in movies and television but in reality cold, heartless men who murdered in the course of their business for both profit and pleasure.

The key question was of course: would I take on this job? And who was trying to commission me? A rival gang leader or some representatives of law enforcement? My instincts told me it might be Brigadier Wee trying to be coy, even wanting to catch me out by giving me an assignment and then having me followed. There was something that did not feel right about this job. Wing Cam appeared too good a contract. A man obviously deserving of a violent death. And the name Thanatos was also too clever by half. It felt like the Brigadier. If it was him, he'd be paying full rack rate this time for my services.

I pondered the question for a few minutes then shut down the laptop, shoved it into my carry-on bag and packed the rest of my stuff. I was planning to be gone for only a few days.

Singapore Airlines had a direct flight into Ho Chi Minh City, the former Saigon. Everybody still called it Saigon. The new name was too much of a mouthful. It was late by the time we landed but immigration and baggage claim were swift.

Outside the small airport stood rows of new white taxis and polite drivers waved at arriving passengers to get their attention for business.

Unlike Bangkok or Manila, there was no haggling over the fare. The driver turned the meter on and began practising his English. It was a half hour journey and all around us young men and women were out riding their Honda Dream motorcycles. Affluence had come quickly in the last few years. Traffic would get worse eventually, if things continued like this, and they would have to start investing in toll-ways and fly-overs.

The hotel was located on what was now called Dhong Khoi Street. In Graham Greene's time it had been called the Rue Catinat. In recent years it had regained its former hustle and bustle and even some of its colonial splendour after two decades of grey communist decay.

The hotel manager was obliging when I informed him I had valuables that needed storing in the safe. I deposited my package in the monstrosity they kept for the purpose in the back room and received a plastic ticket in return.

"Please do not lose," the manager named Nguyen warned me. Half of Vietnam was surnamed Nguyen.

It was getting late but I'd slept on the plane and, outside, Saigon was waiting. I could almost hear the city calling, enticing me siren-like to seek out its seedier delights.

Half an hour later I was strolling up Dhong Khoi Street, ducking out of the way of little boys who wanted to polish my shoes and grave shopkeepers who were still peddling their wares, mostly antiques such as GI Zippo lighters or very fine art which was locally painted. It was nearly midnight.

A few hundred metres up the road I found the establishment I'd been looking for. A discrete sign on the door read 'Gecko Club' but the raucous revelry emanating from it made it obvious that this was a place of drunken debauchery and fine, masculine companionship.

It was not a large bar and it appeared even smaller, since all the tables were busy and everywhere else was standing room only. The only women were the waitresses which meant the place had to be popular for its atmosphere and not its hostess girls. There were other bars full of ladies of negotiable affection, but not this one. This was an expat hang-out and the speciality of the house was the tequila with a dead gecko lodged in the bottom of the bottle. I chose beer this time and found a small space at the end of the counter-top.

It was not long before I got into conversation with the group of men standing near me.

"New in town?" said an American who I later found out was called Terry.

"Up from Singapore. Haven't been here for a while."

"Ah," he intoned sagely, "town changes faster than the broads in Philippe's bed." He pointed a stubby finger at his neighbour, a lean Frenchman judging by his thick Gallic accent.

"Of course this is not Bangkok or Manila. This is only poor boring Ho Chi Minh City. But we like it," the Frenchman said holding aloft a bottle of red wine and proffering it to anyone who might want another glass. He nodded in welcome at me.

"When was the last time you were in Ho Chi Minh City?" Terry asked. He was not yet slurring his words but it would not be long.

"About a year ago."

"Business or pleasure?" Terry asked.

"Pleasure, pleasure, what else should bring one anywhere."

He looked puzzled, his forehead creasing. "Sounds like a quote?"

"No, it's a lifestyle statement." I gave him a warm smile. "Actually I'm lying. Yes, business. I do financial consulting."

"Plenty of that needed here. I'm in the courier business. Philippe here, he does some crap with quality. Shit Good Shit, I think his company is called."

The Frenchman rolled his eyes disdainfully. "I work for a prestigious Swiss company. What we do is important. We ensure that the rice is good before it gets shipped. That bicycles don't collapse when they arc

- 93 -

manufactured, that shirts don't shrink when you wash them…"

"Don't listen to that pompous ass. He has people that open boxes and count what's in them. Likes to make it sound more glamorous than it is."

"At least I don't work for a company called 'American Express' who take five days to get a box to a city that is only one hour's flight away."

"It's not 'American' it's …" Terry shut up because he knew the Frenchman was teasing him.

"This wine, it's not bad. I just found out last week they make wine in Australia. It's amazing isn't it?" Philippe said joyously.

We passed an hour or so in easy banter and I was introduced to a few more fellows. There was an Englishman who sold printing machines, and a small Belgian who was the regional sales representative for a famous chocolate manufacturer. He kept on insisting it was time to go to 'The Gossip' but everyone would jeer him down by saying there would be no girls there yet and, by the way, it was his round again.

"You know, Bill," Philippe said to me, "this is still a small town. It is how an expat lifestyle should be. We all know each other, we don't hate each other because of our nationality. We stick together and fight the bureaucracy and exchange stories about how difficult our day in the office has been." He gave a Gallic shrug of his shoulders. "I have worked in Hong Kong before and everyone is cold and does not help each other. It is a big, cold, crappy city. This place… it is warm, it is difficult, but it has style. Of course that is the French colonial influence. You can put your arms around this place and feel the heart…"

He went on in this vein for a while explaining where one could get the best baguettes and croissants, baked by bakers who had been trained before the first Vietnam conflict and before the Americans even found the place on a map and spoilt it all with their French fries.

Over the wooden bar hung a large picture of a crawling gecko and as I studied it, the creature reminded me of the tattoo that had been haunting me the last few days. What did a miniature crocodile mean? Who had chosen this as a symbol of their secret society and what did they have to do with me?

The crowd began thinning out. Some of the men in ties and dishevelled shirts were probably going home, others had begun to move on to other places.

"What is 'The Gossip'?" I asked.

"It's the only disco in town," Terry explained.

"Is it good?"

"It's damn hot for this town."

"No air-con?"

"Okay, Brit. Stop this wise-cracking. We Americans have a patent on it. Stick to being serious and pompous."

"Not possible, the French have a patent on those two already."

"Did you hear that Philippe? He was bad-mouthing your culture. He was saying the President of France is a cross-dressing fag and that the Marseillaise is barely fit for a funeral procession."

A small German who had joined us was stamping his feet and insisted that we go to the Q Bar first. He had heard that Robert de Niro had been spotted there.

The rest of the United Nations ignored the Kraut and finally we all made our way to 'The Gossip'. Everyone seemed to have a car and a driver. I got a lift with the Frenchman whose refurbished 1953 Renault was an impressive antique, right down to the perfectly burnished leather upholstery.

"The rule eeze. No barfing on ze backseat." His accent seemed to get thicker as the night progressed. "If you have to barf. It is out ze window of course."

I nodded.

The disco was only a ten minute ride away and could be recognised from the line of locals that were waiting to be admitted.

The expats strolled to the front of the line and after being relieved of ten American Dollars were waved in. It was not a fancy club by London standards but it had a certain updated music hall charm. One could imagine this place full of weary GIs and rouge-faced dancing girls in skin-tight Ao Dai – a traditional Vietnamese dress - fox-trotting to Jimi Hendrix, the air thick with smoke from Camels and Lucky Strikes. Tonight the dress code was jeans and mini-skirts, the smoke was from Marlboros and the DJ played the staple Top of the Pops fodder. The speakers were blaring out an older song telling me: "From Westwood to Hollywood, the one thing that's understood, is that you can't buy time but you can sell your soul, and the closest thing to heaven is to rock and roll."

On stage a four-piece band were tuning up and closer inspection revealed that they were all girls and only the drummer was ugly.

"The Four Cats," said Terry noticing my staring at the stage. "They're pretty good. But if you come here as often as we do, you start to hate every one of their songs."

"Should stay at home more often," I said.

"Are you drunk?" he asked and toasted me with his beer.

I walked the club a while later. Upstairs were karaoke rooms and a balcony that gave a good view of the dance floor. I watched the action for a while. All the Western guys were with local girls and the only Western women present were fat and mean looking. Probably British Airways cabin crew.

The band started up and did a good rendition of 'Smoke on the Water'. There was something enticingly erotic about the bass guitarist as her fingers worked the big musical axe that hung over her shoulder. I found a pillar half-way down the dance floor and leant there sipping my vodka. My attentions focused on the keyboards player who seemed to be exceptionally well-endowed but it was hard to concentrate as she bounced up and down behind her Korg synthesiser. They segued into Rainbow's 'Since you've been gone' and the lead singer, cute as a button with short, cropped, spiky hair tried her best with the lyrics.

Over by the bar I noticed a group of men dressed in dark, pinstripe suits. It seemed unusually formal for this city.

"Who are those guys?" I asked Philippe who was busy talking with two local girls who kept declining his offer to have some of his bottle of wine.

"Oh, English guys, lawyers. They are here a lot."

"You know them?"

"Just a little bit. One recognises peoples' faces."

"Do you know an English lawyer; a man called Milford Grosvenor?"

Philippe stopped giving his attentions to the two girls. He frowned and stared at the men in suits then said to me, "That's him, I think. The one in the middle with the longish grey hair. The one putting the cigar in his mouth."

We watched the group for a short moment. This was useful. Saigon's social circles were smaller than expected. Everyone ended up in 'The Gossip' unless they were forced to stay at home by their expat wives. The Four Cats cranked up 'Pretty Little Thing called Love'.

I went to the bar and got another drink. Terry was still nursing his first Budweiser and deep in conversation with the Belgian chocolatier. It was two in the morning and the air was near impenetrable with cigarette smoke. I forced my way through the crowd towards the end of the bar where Grosvenor and his cronies were congregating.

"Excuse me, I believe you're Milford Grosvenor?" I said.

He turned and eyed me with interest. "Yes, and you are?"

"My name is Bill Jedburgh and I've just come into town today. I have a package for you that someone asked me to deliver."

Grosvenor didn't look surprised. He nodded and took another puff from his cigar letting the blue smoke curl around his podgy lips, obscuring his face.

"A package? From whom?"

"Jeremiah Rosenstein in Holland."

"Right, I've been expecting you." For an instant an expression of concern fleeted across his patrician features. "How is the old trader?"

"Not well I'm afraid." I hesitated. "He died shortly after we spoke. Some sort of an accident."

Grosvenor expressed regrets then asked me where the package was.

"It's safely locked away. When can I bring it over? Any time tomorrow morning?"

"Oh, yes absolutely, Bill. Tomorrow. Just before lunch and we can go out and get a bite to eat." He shook his head. "Really shocking about Rosenstein. Brilliant diamond dealer." He handed me a simple, engraved calling card with his contact details and we shook hands.

"I just had a call from him yesterday. He told me someone would be bringing me the stuff. He didn't provide any further details. I'm glad you made it."

I paused. It took me a moment to think it through because of the time zones. "Yesterday? That couldn't have been. He wasn't alive yesterday."

Grosvenor stared at me, and there was a flicker of irritation in his eyes. He let his cigar travel to his mouth one more time before replying. "I could have been mistaken. It might have been two days ago.

"You sure it was him?"

"I'd say so."

"That's very odd."

"It must have been shortly before he was killed," he said and gave me a shifty smile. I decided to leave the matter. There was nothing to be gained from pursuing it now. This was the man I'd agreed to deliver the package to and that would be the end of the matter.

"Tomorrow then," I said.

He nodded and excused himself saying he had to take care of his customers. They were in town from London and wanted to cram as much fun into one night as was humanly possible.

Half an hour later I found myself at the bar again, this time in conversation with an interesting woman Philippe had introduced to me. The Four Cats had gone off to drink their milk or whatever they did in between sets and the DJ was rolling out an astonishingly mediocre selection of old hits.

The girl's name was Wai Lin and she was French but of Vietnamese extraction. She had been born in France and just recently moved to Saigon. Her mannerisms, her dress sense, her poise were pure Parisian. But her face and her figure were as local as the 333 beer which I'd moved onto by now.

"I'm a marketing manager," she told me. Somehow I felt that I'd been set up by Philippe but did not yet know why.

"Selling anything interesting?"

"Oh, yes," she smiled and lit one of her cigarettes with a plastic Bic lighter. She offered me one but I declined.

"And do you like the country of your forefathers?"

"Oh, yes it has charm and subtlety." Her French accent coming from the Asian mouth reminded me of someone else and I felt a stab of pain in my chest that was nearly physical. There had been someone like her … before.

"Sorry, you didn't say what it is you are marketing?"

"These," she replied, waving the paper-covered tobacco stick in front of my face.

"You work for Marlboro?"

"Yes, you can say that. Vietnam is our fastest growing market. First they can afford beer, then they can afford cigarettes and at last the Honda motorbikes."

"I've noticed." We talked about the cultural dichotomies she had grown up with and I watched her short-bobbed hair and wondered what the back of her neck looked like and if there was any chance of me nuzzling it that night.

Another half-hour and we had a dance and then the place began to empty. I got the feeling she liked me and when she suggested we move on to 'Apocalypse Now', it was easy to say yes.

In the short taxi ride which went past my hotel she rolled down the window, lit another cigarette and said, "Most of the men here don't feel comfortable with me. They are all looking for shallow fun with the simple girls. It's mostly about sex and money."

I nodded sagely. One could not argue with that assessment.

"I'm an educated French woman but everyone looks at me and sees an Asian chick."

"Well, they are being shallow. I'm an educated Englishman and everyone looks at me and sees a drunken expat."

My attempt at humour fell flat because she was busy obsessing about her position as a single, successful career woman without any romantic attachment in a city that was littered with foreign bachelors.

"You are a very attractive girl, Wai Lin," I said.

"That's your English style. If we were in France and you were a Frenchman you would be trying to jump on me by now."

"We Englishmen only jump on ladies when they invite us to."

"Ah, that is your country's problem. You are not relaxed about relations with the opposite sex."

Before I could think of the right reply the taxi had stopped and she was handing over a fistful of Dong, the local currency. I followed her fine figure up the stairs and into the club. This had been one of the first places to open when Vietnam relaxed its communist stranglehold and now it was firmly established as a late night hang-out. The main room was packed with the same type of crowd that had been at the Gossip. Out the back was a patio and there were still some tables unoccupied. The action was in the front room. I went to get us some drinks and cast my eye around. There was a high proportion of obvious 'working girls' and they were rolling their eyes and hips with lascivious enthusiasm. To get into the place they would have had to pay the gangster bosses 50 US dollars and a night without a customer could hit their pocketbooks hard.

Wai Lin was already firing up her next Marlboro Light. There was nothing like endorsing your own product.

"And you were in London last week? I love going clubbing in London."

"I'm surprised. A French person saying something nice about England?"

She shrugged. "It's not Paris. I was not saying it was better than Paris. I said I enjoyed going there. The shopping is fun. Regent Street, Oxford Street, Knightsbridge and Soho."

Suddenly a yawn came over me and I had to move quickly to stifle it. The last few days were still catching up on me. I thought it might be time to make a graceful exit and get a phone number for a civilised luncheon rendezvous.

"You are tired, Bill." She stabbed out her white cigarette in the red ashtray and fixed me with an earnest expression. "Let's go to your hotel and have sex. I'm in the mood."

7

The security guard in the lobby hesitated for a moment when he saw us enter through the glass doors and walk towards the lifts. I had my key-card out and was ready to get angry with him if he gave us a hard time but Wai Lin was ahead of me. She barked something at him in Vietnamese and waved what appeared to be her French passport at his face. He retreated with profuse apologies.

"They don't let the local putes come in here. It's a government-run hotel."

"That seems reasonable," I said.

"It is hypocritical. Down the street they have half a dozen mini-hotels where everyone takes their whores and the police do nothing about that."

"Moving towards a free market economy."

"What floor?" she asked. I pressed the button and the old lift rattled upwards reminiscent of similar contraptions in her country of birth. Although the hotel had been renovated, many original fixtures remained as part of the neo-colonial charm.

We walked along the deep carpet until we got to my room and I slotted the card into the door. I was curious and excited. It would be like making love to a Western woman although she had the type of Asian body to which I was accustomed. What had shocked me was her French forwardness. I felt her presence close behind me and the Bulgari perfume she wore wafted into my nostrils.

As I opened the door expecting nothing but a dark, empty room I was greeted by lights and the sound of the television. Instantly my senses rang alarm bells and my muscles tensed but Wai Lin was behind me practically pushing me into the room.

The room was not empty. There was somebody in my bed and it was the last person I would have expected.

The television was muted. It was the BBC and somewhere in the world there had been another earthquake.

"What is this?" Wai Lin demanded and took the words right out of my mouth. All I could do was stare with a rising sense of irritation mixed with a shot of resigned amusement. Here I was, dead tired, in a city I rarely visited and there was a girl wearing pyjamas in my bed and another one was ready to throw a tantrum of Gallic proportions.

The girl in my bed opened her eyes at the sound of voices. The remote had dropped from her hands onto the floor. She looked pleased to see me, then confused at the sight of Wai Lin.

"Brigit. What the hell are you doing here?" I said.

Wai Lin said, "Is this your wife?" An angry, dark thunder cloud had gathered over her features. A woman slighted, led on by a man, only to be humiliated.

Brigit Nguyen pulled the sheets up to her chin. "Hi, surprise." Her mouth turned down as she added: "Not a great idea I see."

"What are you doing here? In my bed. In my bloody room. In Vietnam?" was all I could say at that moment.

She gazed sheepishly at me. I heard Wai Lin let out a long, sharp exhalation of breath. "Ca suffit, quel con." She shifted her body and slapped me hard on the side of the face, a blow I should have anticipated. Then she was on the way out. I stared at her retreating figure, shrugged and closed the hotel door.

"Seems like I spoilt your evening," Brigit said contritely.

"No, not really. I was being frog-marched back here to fulfil her desires not mine. All I really want is a good night's sleep." I was exaggerating a bit but the tableau had shifted and it made sense to adjust to the new circumstances. I sat down on the sofa and began undoing my shoe-laces.

"Not much chance of a good night's sleep," Brigit said. "It's four in the morning."

"Explain to me again why you are lying in my bed, ten thousand miles from where you live?"

"I'm not wearing anything under these pyjamas," she said coyly.

"I hope you're at least wearing Chanel No.5."

"Come in and find out, stranger." She seemed curiously happy that she had scared away the competition and that I was not in the slight bit bothered by it. "Are you pleased to see me?" she asked with a concerned frown.

"I'm pleased," I said. "It's lovely to see you. Admittedly the circumstances are unusual and the timing is unfortunate."

"Unfortunate?"

"Sorry, that's not what I meant. I wanted to say that you have a knack for the unexpected. Now, I'm going to have a quick shower and then you can explain precisely what you are doing here."

Brigit had no intention of letting me fall asleep for the next hour. Once she had explained that she felt duty-bound to come to Saigon and look for her brother she grabbed me by the crotch and proceeded to kiss me fervently until my flaccid friend woke up and revelled in her attentions.

Finally I could stand it no longer and finding an unexpected reserve of testosterone-induced energy, rolled her over and pausing only briefly for the obligatory prophylactic from the wash-bag, pushed into her with a simultaneous gasp of pleasure from both of us. We thrashed around with the intensity that comes from being comfortable with each other's bodies but still delighted by their novelty.

Exhausted I collapsed onto her chest twenty minutes later. Despite the air-con, I'd dripped sweat from my forehead over hers and we looked like a pair of marathon runners flopped in the grass at the finish line.

"I'm glad I flew all this way. That was worth it," she said with a cheery grin, pushing me off gently. I studied the stucco in the ceiling while my mind remained blank.

I said, "You kill me." My breathing has slowly returning to normal and I felt the chariot of sleep sidle up alongside my weary bones, ready to whisk me off to a deep, dark place.

"Hey, don't fall asleep."

"I can't stay awake. Haven't you had enough?"

"I'm jet lagged," she pointed out.

"That's a frightening statement." I stroked her face and then ran my index finger down her arm until it came to her wrist. I'd forgotten about it, of course, but there it was. She'd removed her Longines watch before slipping between my sheets. The mocking crocodile tattoo lay on her wrist reminding me of recent events and concerns.

"What is this thing again? And don't give me that story about it being a fun girl's night out. I've seen this tattoo on other people's wrists. It's a Triad thing."

Her eyes took on a sudden, frightened cast and she hurriedly asked, "Where have you seen it before? Did you see it recently?"

"Just yesterday. Two guys tried to mug me. They were both sporting that same tattoo on their wrists."

"You were mugged by two guys?"

"No. They tried to mug me but someone helped me and so they weren't successful."

"But who were the guys?" she said in a puzzled voice.

"That's the question I was asking you. Who are these people who wear the crocodile tattoo. It's called a Buaya, right?"

"It must be a coincidence. It can't have anything to do with you knowing me."

"Yes?" I prompted her.

She frowned, searching for ways to avoid the issue. "It's embarrassing. I don't want to tell you."

"You have to tell me or I'll pick you up stark naked as you are and throw you out of my room and lock the door."

"You wouldn't."

"I will."

A look of panic came into her eyes now. She was debating what to tell me. Finally she said, "You're right. It's a gangster thing. I've had it since I was a little girl. When my parents left Vietnam it was with the help of some Triad gangsters. They had to pay a big price for our freedom and part of that was owing loyalty and allegiance to the gang."

"And what did that allegiance entail?"

"We had to pay money. A percentage of everything our family earned had to be paid. And we were all forced to have the tattoo to remind us that it was a life-long commitment."

"So you still have to pay now?"

"No. I moved and escaped the influence of the gang when my parents passed away. So did my brother. I think. But maybe he got involved again. That's what I'm so worried about."

"So that's the whole story?"

She nodded and tears appeared, rolling quietly down the side of her nose and cheek. Brigit bowed her head and I gave her a long hug. The story made sense but my instinct warned me that there might be some bits still missing.

"There is a man whose name frightens us. He was the boss of the gang. The last time I met my brother he told me this man had contacted him again," Brigit went on in a low voice. She was sniffling a bit now and wiping her face with the back of her hand.

"And this guy is still running the gang in Britain?"

"No, he left a long time ago. He came back to Vietnam. He was the man my father feared more than anything. I'm sure he drove my father into an early grave. The man who had all of us branded with this ..."

She touched the crocodile on her arm. "I'm worried that bastard might have got his claws into Stephen again."

"You should have told me this before."

"It's such a stupid story. It's such a cliché. Poor Asian immigrants under the control of the Vietnamese Triads. It's something I've been trying to escape from all my life. But it's hard when every time you take a shower you look down and are reminded of your past."

"It could have been worse. They could have mutilated you, chopped your fingers off, put a brand on your chest or your pubic bone. The wrist is a reasonable enough place."

"You have no idea," she said, "how much evil this tattoo has done in my life. Losing a finger would have been more pleasant."

I chose to end the conversation there. Giving her a gentle kiss on the cheek I stood up and took a shower. As I was soaping myself it occurred to me that the obvious question had not been asked.

When I came out, drying myself I said, "What was the gangster boss's name?"

Brigit stared at me for a few seconds, then whispered, "His name is Wing Cam. He is the most sadistic bastard I have ever come across. If I had the ability and the opportunity I would kill him without a moment's hesitation."

I laughed because I should have seen this coming.

"Yes, I thought it would be something like that." I studied her for a while wondering if she was really good or if someone had cunningly dealt me the Joker in the pack of cards again.

Brigit said: "Three days ago I got a letter from my brother saying he was in Danang working on a job. But there is nothing in Danang. It has a big airport left over from the war by the Americans. There is a university but not much industry. Unless he is working for Wing Cam who has a factory there making toys. That's why I had to come out here. Do you see?"

"Versatile character. Human trafficker, all round gangster and toy manufacturer," I said.

She gave me a long, hard stare and turned over in bed. I sighed, my attempt at humour inappropriate. A few minutes later I had turned off the bedside lamp and Brigit was snuggled up against me. Her hair smelt of camomile and the rest was a mingling of our more feral perfumes. All I wanted now was to drift off and forget everything until a few hours had passed and my mind was sharper, my body stronger again.

But it was not to be.

A hand clamped itself over my mouth and I sensed rather than felt the cold, hard pressure of gunmetal against my left temple. For a moment I thought it was a dream because there had been many in the past that were vivid and violent. Then I came awake and realised there were people in the room.

"You say nothing," a voice told me harshly. I could feel Brigit thrashing around as she was similarly held down. Someone switched on the light and the situation became clearer. Five men stood in my room. They were all hard-looking, squat Asian individuals with close-cropped hair and mean vicious eyes. All the men wore a similar uniform: jeans, cowboy boots with pointed toes, black or blue T-shirts and a type of navy-blue blazer on top.

I could not make out the type of weapon that was being pushed into the side of my head but peripherally it appeared large enough to rip out a big chunk of my brains so there seemed no point in fighting it.

The man who'd spoken stood behind the one with the gun. He said, "We are here for the diamond, you know what I mean." He spoke with a curious mingled accent that blended Vietnamese with hints of Geordie. He was short like the rest of them. His nose had been broken a number of times and there was scar tissue under both his eyes.

I gazed blankly at him. Brigit was making whimpering noises and on first assessment there appeared no room for manoeuvre. How had they got in, I wondered? In all the excitement we must have forgotten to latch the room door and it would have been easy to force someone in reception to hand over a master key card.

"Where you put the diamond? In this safe?" the man was asking again and he thumped a gloved fist against the small room safe where I'd placed my travel wallet and passport. I shook my head slowly. There was no point misdirecting them. They would find out anyway.

He didn't believe me. "Get up and open this safe. Move slowly." None of them trusted me and they watched cautiously as if I were a rabid bear that could leap at them any minute. Brigit had fallen silent and I gave her a comforting nod as I slipped out of the sheets.

It didn't help much to alter the terrified expression on her face.

I said, "The diamonds are not in there. They're in the downstairs hotel safe."

"Open this box, now!" the leader insisted, so I punched in the code: the first four digits of my former Army number. By now the muzzle of the gun had moved to the back of my neck and I could smell the gunman's poor dental hygiene. Why did they all have bad breath, the one's that stood too close?

The leader tugged open the small armoured door and pushed me aside roughly. He unzipped the travel wallet and riffled through its contents, stopping to study my passport and my personal details on the last page.

When he was done he tossed it all on the floor.

"Where is the safe downstairs?"

"Behind the reception."

"You come with us and don't try to be funny," he said in his curious Geordie-Vietnamese accent. "Or we will cut the girl and I'll let the boys rape her." He indicated with his chin and one of his men laughed and pulled out a long kitchen knife from a sheath concealed under his cheap blazer.

"Are you okay, Brigit?" I asked.

"Yes, I think so."

"I'm ready to go downstairs. You have to bring my wallet."

The leader stared at me fiercely then issued some orders in Vietnamese. He picked up the leather wallet which I'd left on the bedside table.

Two men stayed with Brigit and three came with me. One holding my right arm while the other now kept his gun pressed hard into the small of my back. There were ways to get out of a tight situation like this but the training generally assumed you were only being controlled by one armed man and not three.

They seemed to have no qualms about showing off that they were armed, strutting down the hotel corridor, shamelessly threatening a guest. Perhaps they did this all the time and the hotel staff were used to it. I thought I'd come to Ho Chi Minh, not Dodge City.

We waited for the rattling lift and took it downstairs. As we came out, the lone security guard gave a sudden start of shock but the leader barked at him and produced an automatic from under his jacket making it crystal clear that a security guard armed only with a brown, foot-long truncheon should not entertain any ideas of heroics. The guard got down on his knees and then lay face down with his hands behind his back. The man who'd been holding my arm let go and stepped back to keep an eye on the security guard.

My other captor pushed me forward. There was nobody visible in reception but once we moved into the back room a young fellow started up from the armchair in which he'd been dozing.

The leader saw the man-sized safe in the corner next to a wide mahogany manager's desk. He began yelling at the young receptionist. The receptionist replied, shaking his head repeatedly as though trying to make the point that he did not have a key or authorisation to open the big, steel doors. I watched passively for a minute until the leader suddenly leapt forward and grabbed the receptionist by the throat. He kicked the boy's feet out from under him and then slammed his head hard against the side of the desk.

Surprisingly the receptionist did not lose consciousness. He slumped on the floor, a bloody gash over his temple, then tried to struggle back to his feet.

The leader yelled at him again until the receptionist muttered quietly and reached for the phone. A minute later the same manager who had locked my diamonds into the safe appeared. He was in a T-shirt and shorts, his hair messy from sleep. His eyes were terrified but in his hand he held a large bunch of keys. There was an exchange of sentences and the leader produced my wallet with the identification card I'd been given earlier. They opened the safe and rummaged around until the packet was found.

This was the moment I'd been waiting for. There was a glint of triumph in the leader's eyes and the man guarding me was distracted. The hotel manager was still busy with the safe while the receptionist was holding tissues to his head, slumped in the chair he'd been occupying earlier.

I twisted my body and knocked the muzzle of the gun aside while stamping hard on my man's instep. By this time we were facing each other so my left hand grabbed his wrist with the gun to keep it controlled and my right palm drove hard upwards against his chin. His eyes rolled away under their lids while I tugged the weapon from his loosening fingers.

I'd calculated that the leader would hesitate long enough for me to gain an advantage. He had to drop or stow the precious package he was holding and that would give me time to turn and meet him.

The leader was already coming at me and I barely had time to get into a stance. His first one was a long kick and I took it on my left elbow, then he was whirling, his foot high, impressive, fast and I just managed to duck. I didn't recognise the style he fought but he liked his kicks and they gave him range and power. When the next assault came I was ready for it, trying to trap his leg rather than block it. But he was too fast.

I'd dropped the gun of course because I'd had no time to grab it properly and had no idea if it really had a round in the chamber. Cocking an automatic takes two hands. You don't have the luxury of free hands when a trained fighter is coming at you hard.

The leader didn't pause for an instant. He'd taken into account that I had some martial art skills and now he was hammering away trying to force an opening. Four more kicks came my way and I could not get past them. I was kicking too but our legs clashed in mid-air. It would have been better if he used his hands because my arms were longer.

From the corner of my eye I saw a movement. Already the leader's next swing was coming. He pulled back the kick at the last minute telegraphing that he was switching into another stance and I was ready for his left arm jab, trapped his elbow for an instant, landed a blow on his unguarded sternum. I saw the pain and the wind come out of his mouth and then something unexpected hit me hard on the side of the head and this fight was over for me.

8

Sometimes I wonder how many brain cells there can still be left given the times I've been hit hard over the head. How many fights does it take for a boxer before he starts losing coordination and his speech becomes slurred?

When I woke up it was in the comfort of my hotel bed. My eye sight was blurred and my head hurt like hell. Little demons with sledge hammers were running around inside smashing all they could find.

A pretty girl wearing her hotel uniform was sitting in a chair reading and when she noticed that I was awake she asked if I needed any water or wanted me to call the manager.

I felt my head and found an enormous welt under a large plaster but otherwise no damage. She assisted me out of the bed and things were somewhat wobbly. I was relieved to find that someone had put a robe on me.

"The doctor say you okay. Only have a small knock but maybe you want to go to the hospital for a check-up once you have enough sleep?" the girl said. "Check for concussion."

She left me to go downstairs while I rummaged in my wash-bag until I found the box of Alka Seltzer. They might banish some of the satanic orgy that was taking place.

The hotel general manager turned up five minutes later and did an excellent imitation of a fawning eunuch at the court of a Ming dynasty emperor. They could not believe that such terrible events could have happened in their hotel and their apologies were profuse. Of course the room would be free and my entire bill would be waived and did I want to report the matter to the police? It was always complicated once the police became involved, he suggested, and waited for me to take the hint.

"Where is the girl?" I asked.

"Which girl?"

"The girl that was here in my room. Brigit. She is a friend from London."

He looked puzzled. "We don't know of any girl. The security guard mentioned you came back with a woman who had a French passport but she did not stay."

"That's right. But there was another girl. She had the key to the room and when I went downstairs with the gangsters she was still here waiting for us."

"There was no girl in this room," he said and I began to feel sick in the pit of my stomach. They had taken her. "One minute please," he said and went to the phone.

After a longer conversation he explained that the gangsters had been seen by a member of staff leaving with a girl, that was true. Nobody knew where they had gone. Once I'd been knocked unconscious the night manager had woken up his boss and all the other security guards while the young lad who'd taken a beating was sent off to hospital.

"So you haven't notified the police of the incident?" I asked. The Alka Seltzers were not kicking in yet and I had to sit down on the bed.

"No, Mr. Jedburgh. It is a very bad thing for our hotel's reputation and will scare a lot of the guests if many policemen come here and ask questions." He hesitated before going on. "If you insist we call the police, we will. It is only eleven in the morning." He smiled an ingratiating, pleading smile and nervously adjusted the black tie on his white collar.

"So what we have here is a burglary, a robbery, a wounding and probably an abduction and you suggest we keep this matter to ourselves?"

"If that is the way you are putting it. It is so bad for our hotel this thing. We will pay all your hospital bills of course. Is the thing that the criminals have stolen very expensive? Why do they come and steal this from you?"

He was trying to turn the issue and insinuate that it was my fault the gangsters knew about the package and had come to cause havoc in his hotel. He had a point. It could be argued.

"Perhaps they were sent by your business associates?" he suggested, driving away from the theme of whether the police should be called.

Frankly I was the last person who wanted the police involved. It was a relief that they had not done so. There would have been too many questions already and too much of a spotlight on me. I hated any kind of undue attention.

"The package contained samples, some electronics, a new design. I was just delivering them. They are not mine and I will have to discuss with the real owner what   he   wants   to   do."

A light of relief went on in the General Manager's eyes. Apart from the main consideration of anonymity I simply did not want to continue this conversation until I'd rested a few more hours, filled myself with more painkillers and could consider all the angles with some degree of objectivity. I had no idea where they would have taken Brigit. If they had taken her, I assumed she would either be released once they felt safe or they would contact me with some kind of demand. There was nothing I could do in my present condition.

I dismissed the manager, made a phone call to the office of Milford Grosvenor to ask for an appointment at the tail end of the working day and having chained the door went back to burrow between the pillows. Something was going on and I had no idea what it was. But I was going to find out.

The Law Offices of Huntley, Mason & Mason were located in an old colonial mansion in District One. The gates were open and the guard waved me through. I admired the manicured garden and the neat arrangement of several antique automobiles, then found my way to the reception.

"He is expecting you," the girl said with the mellow sing-song of the Vietnamese native speaking English. She was wearing a pale, blue Ao Dai and I fancied that her knickers were visible on the sides where the material was thin enough to be practically see-through.

It might just have been my imagination. There seemed to be no shortage of pretty girls in Saigon.

She knocked deferentially on the open, latticed door that led into a large chamber, with a parquet floor, that might have once been the dining room. The man himself was on his mobile phone, standing staring out of the window while he held a sotto voce conversation. He turned and glanced at me, motioned for me to sit on the sofa set that was arranged a few steps from his imposing desk.

"No, Frank, it's not what we decided. It needs to be prima facie evidence, not some bollocks that nobody will take seriously.... I'm making my position plain.... Working in Cambodia is not black or white. We all know that... Sure I have full confidence in your approach on this. You've got more experience than we all have. But don't make it wishy-washy.... You understand. I'm glad."

I could not help overhearing the conversation but it was meaningless to me. When it came to the law, I had always been an ass. Handcuffs had been my thing. Grosvenor put the phone down, frowning, then came over and shook my hand.

"Good to see you again. You had an accident?" he asked, indicating the plaster on the side of my head.

"I had an accident," I confirmed. It was late afternoon, nearly six o'clock and I felt surprisingly better for having spent the entire day in bed. Part of my travel kit which I always had with me was a small box of medications and bandages. The Alka Seltzers were just a hangover cure so eventually I'd gone for an Oxycodone, a more heavy duty painkiller. Now I felt as if the outer extremities of my body were made of marshmallows and there was a rosy tint to the world which I knew would wear off as the evening progressed. As I sat and began talking with Milford Grosvenor I had no idea how badly the rest of the day would turn out.

"What kind of accident? Problem with a cyclo driver? Or fell down the staircase at the Gossip?" He sounded sincere in his concern and sat down in the other leather Chesterfield opposite me. He shucked up his black pinstripe trousers to reveal burgundy socks over glossy brogues. The receptionist came in with a china teapot and cups on a tray.

"Slightly more dramatic, I'm afraid. I was robbed at gunpoint in my hotel and they forced the hotel manager to open the safe."

He frowned when he heard the news. "And the package was in the safe?"

"Yes, it's what they came for."

"Who were they?"

"A team of Vietnamese gangsters. Nasty, short and brutish fellows. Any idea how they might have found out I was carrying this stuff for you?" I watched his face carefully because it was important for me to know if he'd had anything to do with it.

He appeared puzzled. "Why would I know anything about the theft of something that's supposed to be delivered to me?"

"I'm just the suspicious sort, Grosvenor. There've been some odd things going on lately and I can't make a lot of sense of them."

"Odd like what?"

I shook my head. There was no apparent pain when I did this. There was no feeling at all in fact. "It's not something I want to go into. I was asked to deliver a package of diamonds to you. I suppose my bringing them into the country constitutes some kind of smuggling but that was acceptable to me. Now it seems other people knew about me coming with the package, even before I got on the plane in Singapore.... I hate letting people down."

"It's unfortunate that you were attacked and robbed. Nobody is blaming you for that. I assume you took all the necessary precautions and were discrete about what you were carrying?"

"I was. I'm careful when it comes to things like that. I'm not a professional courier but my background is in the disciplined forces."

He smiled a bleak smile, "I assumed as much when I first saw you. It's not your fault. I'm not blaming you," he repeated. "Did you report this to the police?"

I shook my head again. "The hotel was reluctant to contact the police. In fact they asked me not to, so I said I had to speak to the owner of the goods first. And that's you. Is there any point in involving the police?"

Grosvenor pursed his lips and leaned forward to work on the tea pot. Finally he said casually, "Things get complicated once you involve the authorities in this town."

"You're echoing the words of the hotel manager."

He acknowledged this with a movement of his head then glanced out of his fine windows into the gardens with a far-away look in his eyes. I bent forward and sipped some of my tea. It was Earl Grey and probably the best thing to drink in my condition.

Grosvenor said, "Not much we can do if these guys have run off with the package. Did you know what was in it?"

"It came from Rosenstein. I assume they were diamonds."

"Hmm." He gave a tight, mirthless smile.

"They will try and sell them locally or do you think they will contact you and try to sell them back to you?"

"That's most likely. Let's wait and see." He seemed curiously unmoved by the loss of his valuable package. It bothered me because either he had so much money that it wasn't important, or he knew who had stolen the package from the hotel. But why rob himself? It didn't feel right but I could not put my finger on it. We sat in a pensive silence for a while. He obviously was considering what else could be done and I was trying to reach a conclusion on how much I trusted him.

What the hell, I thought. It wasn't my package and all I knew was that it should go to Milford Grosvenor. I reached down to the laptop bag which I'd carried with me and unzipped it.

"I owe you an apology, Grosvenor. I wanted to see your reaction when I told you the hotel safe had been robbed yesterday. I don't like what's been going on around me and I'm not inclined to trust anyone these days. But the package I was asked to deliver is still with me. I put a decoy into the hotel safe."

He looked at me with astonishment as I took out the Compaq Contura 400 laptop I had been toting around with me and flicked the releases that allowed me to slide the battery out. Inside the battery housing was a hollow space and it was large enough to store the package of diamonds which I shook out into my hand, then passed to him.

"This is the real package?" he asked, weighing it in his palm as if it were a small fish he'd caught.

"It's the real one, the one I was requested to deliver by Rosenstein. I've never opened it so I hope he hasn't conned you."

"You're quite a character, Bill." He studied me with some level of approval. "I get the feeling you don't feel comfortable with me in this affair," he said astutely.

"Not entirely but that's another matter. You've got the real package there and if the gangsters turn up and want to sell you the package they stole yesterday you can laugh in their faces. It still leaves the matter of the missing girl."

"What's was in the other package?"

"Some pebbles from my car park in Singapore."

There was a movement at the door and I turned to see Grosvenor's assistant ushering in somebody whom I never expected to see again.

"Didn't I tell you that this man would not disappoint us? What a brilliant stunt, Bill. Congratulations." Jeremiah Rosenstein, living and breathing slouched into the office, beaming from ear to ear. If I hadn't been so astonished I might have stood up and twatted him on his prominent nose. "You're not dead," was all I managed to say.

"Not ... dead. Very much alive, old fellow. And is there a cup of tea for me?" He came over to the sofas and Grosvenor stood up to give him a quick, friendly handshake. Like two conspirators they smirked at each other and enjoyed my confusion.

I cleared my throat and spent a few moments thinking things through.

Rosenstein said: "Sorry for the Lazarus act, Bill, but as the story goes, the reports of my demise were somewhat exaggerated. I did make a dramatic exit though."

"Do you mind explaining all this to me?" I finally said keeping my tone as neutral as my anger would permit. "I find it offensive being taken advantage of. Do you know what happened last night?"

Rosenstein nodded his head from side to side, still beaming with amusement and said, "I'm fully aware of what you've been through and I'm very, very sorry you were injured. We'll make it up to you."

"There is a girl missing. Do you know about that?"

"Missing or has she run away? I believe you'll find it's not as sinister as you think."

"Tell me the story from the beginning, Jeremiah, before I beat you to death properly, with this laptop here."

He sighed. "Very well then. Grosvenor here and I have been doing business together for a few years and very lucrative it has been. We started a relationship with a big buyer here in Vietnam, someone notorious for his obsession with diamonds and his habit of cheating anyone with whom he does business. It was a bit of a dilemma. He's got the deepest pockets but it's like doing business with Lucifer himself. He has every customs official under his control. The police won't move against him. He has no compunction about resorting to violence and if he can avoid paying he always will. So we devised a little plan that would distract his attention and you were part of that plan."

"And this man's name, your buyer, is?"

"Oh, that's not so important. You don't need to know too much. He's a bastard of the first degree as you found out last night."

"His name wouldn't by any chance be Wing Cam?"

Rosenstein hesitated for a moment and Milford Grosvenor busied himself with the teapot. "You are well informed. Bad to ever underestimate you, old fellow. Yes, his name is Wing Cam and he's a powerful gangster in these parts who gets away with murder when he wants."

"You really are playing with fire doing business with a man like him," I suggested.

"It's a risk we have evaluated carefully. The profits are attractive."

"I can't imagine why he's so besotted with diamonds and how come a package like this can be worth that kind of risk to you?"

Rosenstein smiled blandly indicating that he wasn't going to say more about his motivations. He nodded at the package on Grosvenor's desk. "That of course is not the real package. We were using you to bluff Wing Cam and it seems you then worked a double bluff on him as well. He certainly will be fuming. But he'll have to pay out."

"So what's in that package?" I asked.

"Oh, diamonds... but pretty shoddy ones. Not what he was specifically interested in. Those diamonds are in another location. And it's money up front."

"You think you've been very clever. If he lives outside the normal rule of law he might just turn around and shoot you for pissing him off."

Rosenstein turned to Grosvenor and said, "What do you think about that, Grosvenor? You know the Vietnamese bastard better than we do."

"Yes, it's a possibility but he's a businessman first and foremost and he won't go about killing the goose that lays the golden eggs," the lawyer said, hiding partially behind his tea cup. His eyes considered me with the same mild approval of earlier. It angered me again that they'd taken advantage of my willingness to help out. From what Grosvenor was saying this wasn't the first bunch of diamonds they had sold to Wing Cam but there must be something special about this lot.

I said, "Right, so my job is done, Jeremiah. You've risen from the dead. You've got your buyer sufficiently distracted and I've got a bang on the head for my pains. Now I want to hear your suggestions for compensating me for my troubles." I paused for an instant then added, "And no deals on future purchases. And I'm seriously thinking of buying diamonds from someone else in future for this shitty trick you've played on me."

He said quickly, "Ten thousand US dollars. In cash. Later today."

I didn't think I'd ever hear this man come up with a cash offer so rapidly. It bothered me because it meant that whatever deal they were hoping to conclude with Wing Cam was dazzlingly lucrative. I stared at the two men for a while, trying to make them uncomfortable, then I said, "I'll take it. Not later than tomorrow morning. And believe me, as Grosvenor here is our witness, if you don't come through with the cash I'll track you down and break all the fingers on your right hand so you'll never be able to wank again." I stared fiercely at the old Semite and waved my right hand in the air, wiggling the fingers to make sure there was no misunderstanding. The money was simply to assuage my anger. There was no point in haggling. I wanted them to know that I didn't like being played for a fool.

"I'm going now," I told them, standing up.

"No, you're not, Bill," a woman's voice said from behind me, sending a jolt of pent-up anger through my entire body. What the hell was that bitch doing here?

9

The trouble with Lavender Daai was that she could look so damn good when she wanted to. It totally distracted any man from the real evil that lurked below the surface of her flawless skin and behind the apparent innocence of her fine, almond eyes.

There was only one woman I'd ever met who could match her for pure and cruel malevolence and I'd killed her on an island in the Indonesian archipelago.

Lavender Daai was the dissolute daughter of a retired Triad boss. A man who had loved her even when he knew that his genes had become twisted into something far worse than he'd ever been himself. I'd come to like him in the short time we knew each other. But his daughter ... I hated her like the plague and she hated me back with a vengeance that I was only just starting to appreciate.

She was manipulative and without any sense of conscience. She pursued her passions with a single-minded drive that did not allow for one ounce of normal human morality. I was not a standard bearer for morality myself but I tried to do good by the people that were good to me. Lavender Daai only did good by herself. Everyone else that came into her zone of influence simply became a pawn to her plans and ambitions.

And now here she stood, in tight black leather leggings, two-inch heeled boots, a white blouse and a vicious little smile that played around her crimson lips. In her right hand was a Sig Sauer P225 and I was the last person to doubt that she knew how to use it and would take pleasure in doing so.

"Who the hell are you?" Grosvenor barked at her, ignoring the weapon. "How dare you come into my office threatening us." He was on his feet as was Rosenstein. The tension was palpable.

Lavender advanced a few steps and without taking her eyes off our group kicked the doors shut behind her.

"I'm an old friend of Bill's. He'll tell you who I am."

"You've got no right to come in here with a gun," Grosvenor blustered but that's all it was. He could tell already that this was a lady who meant business.

I stared at her, willing my own passion to go away, so I could be rational and react rapidly. I said, "This is Lavender Daai. We've crossed paths before and let me warn you that she is not to be underestimated."

The last thing I wanted was for Grosvenor or Rosenstein to do something rash and for our gathering to turn sour. If anyone was going to do anything dramatic it would be me. I had some measure of the lady and a healthy respect for her abilities. I tried to communicate these thoughts by my body language but telepathy was not part of my skillset.

"What is it you want, Lavender?" I asked, moving my body so we faced each other directly. She was still five metres from me and I was not going to jump her unless she got closer.

"Sit down, all of you. You all look tense." Lavender spoke with a Filipino-American accent because her Chinese mother had come from the Philippines and part of her education had been overseas. She was an attractive woman despite the little Sig in her hand and she looked as fit as when we'd last met - and fought - in my friend's flat in Hong Kong.

"Now, Bill you didn't think I'd just disappear from your life after all the trouble you caused me?"

"I had hoped perhaps...," I said.

"I thought you understood me better than that. You screwed up a nice little scheme we had going. I should have let the fat American rip all your fingernails out and tear out your eyes while we had the chance."

"Nice thoughts."

She smiled icily and took a few steps closer. She addressed the others. "Yes, Bill here has been a frigging large thorn in my side and he's been pissing me off even more lately."

"How's that?" I asked.

"I've had people following you trying to kill you and somehow you keep on getting away. So what is a woman to do? Best do it yourself if everyone else is just too incompetent."

"You sent people after me in Europe?"

She nodded coolly. "Amsterdam, Singapore. You are a hard man to kill."

"I'll take that as a compliment."

"It's just dumb luck, asshole. Don't pride yourself."

"And the Buaya Society. What's your involvement with them?"

"Oh, that's clever... but it's none of your goddamn business." She let the menace hang in the air and I was

- 132 -

still wondering what she was doing here. Was it simply to kill me? Surely she'd want a more protracted revenge. And why hadn't she turned up yesterday?

"I want that diamond packet," she seemed to read my thoughts. "And then you and me, Bill, we are going to walk out of here nice and politely."

"Who are you working for, Lavender?" Grosvenor demanded. "Did Wing Cam send you?"

She just gave him a tight smile, no teeth.

"You, pass me the packet from the desk." She waved at Rosenstein with the compact semi-automatic. The old man stared at her angrily but slowly began to turn and do as he was told.

I was watching the girl, trying to work out at which point I could get away from her and the gun. I'd experienced captivity and torture at her hands once before and had no desire to dance down that path again.

As Rosenstein reached for the packet it occurred to me that these were the worthless diamonds so if Lavender took them it would be no great loss.

Rosenstein asked: "Where do you want them?"

"Toss them over here at my feet," the girl instructed.

He made as if to throw them but at the last instant seemed to stumble and drop the packet. The next second a revolver had appeared in his hand and there was an exchange of shots. Grosvenor dived for the carpet and I threw myself down and sideways.

What the hell was the old geezer thinking? Too many John Wayne movies? He couldn't reach for his gun faster than the girl could drop him with two rounds in the chest.

On the floor, Rosenstein lay in a dead shabby heap, all his ambitions and deals turned to dust in the split second it took for Lavender's bullets to find their target. He'd not even got his revolver up to the horizontal before she'd gunned him down.

I watched her face as she finished, ready to pull the trigger one more time. There was a grim pleasure across her features that seemed to imply she'd been waiting for something like this and had enjoyed the gun play. But she was also annoyed. It had been a hell of a noise in the small room. The Sig is a 9 mm and it has a distinctive snap, crackle and pop when it's fired. There were shouts from outside and somebody called for help and another voice screamed for the police. Lavender looked irritated.

"Don't fucking move, you bastards," she yelled at us, jumping forward like a panther, recovering the packet of diamonds from where they'd fallen and then turning to make a quick exit.

I knew what she'd do next. A sixth sense seemed to tell me in advance. She wasn't going to leave me just like that. I was ready for it.

When she got to the door, she pivoted, she sighted the Sig and in the instant that she squeezed the trigger I rolled to the right, partially behind the sofa. A hard, mule-kick in the upper arm told me I'd not timed it as well as I'd hoped. My vision started going and I hoped she wouldn't come back to finish the job.

"Fuck you, Bill," she yelled and her booted heels clattered out on the wooden floor then down the stairs.

The last thing I saw was Grosvenor leaning over me, his face becoming only a white blur. Then I was sucked into a dark, distant pool of nothingness.

This time I did wake up in hospital. It wasn't an impressive place but I got the sense that I was being given first class treatment. There were four other patients in the room, our beds discretely hidden from each other by curtains. A strong smell of bleach pervaded the room.

My throat felt parched but when I reached over to the glass of water on the bedside table I found my right arm strapped and bandaged. A cursory inspection revealed that no other parts of me seemed to be damaged, however my brain still felt as scrambled as before. Events had not been kind to my body these last two days. Using my left hand I helped myself to water and noticed a piece of paper lying under my Rolex. Someone had removed my expensive watch and thoughtfully not stolen it. It was seven in the morning. I'd been sedated all night.

I picked up the paper and read a note from Milford Grosvenor to call him when I felt better. It was unlikely I'd feel better for a while to come knowing Lavender Daai was on the prowl. So I had no intention of waiting that long to find out what was going on.

A piece of string over my bed turned out to ring the bell that summoned the nurse. She explained to me that a bullet had taken a chunk of flesh out of my upper bicep. Doctor didn't think it was serious. She managed to find me a mobile phone with which I contacted the lawyer. He said he'd be around some time after lunch. He was working on sorting out the mess and I'd be best off resting. Things were under control.

I took his advice and drifted in and out of sleep until suddenly I was aware of other people standing around my bed.

"You are very accident prone. You must be more careful," a familiar voice said.

My eyes flew open. It was the man who'd come to my hotel room and then forced the manager to open the safe. He wore the same outfit and the same grim expression. This time he was accompanied by only one of his men. He came around to the side of the bed. My hand moved towards the string above my head.

"Don't call the nurse. She can't help you," he said menacingly in his Geordie-Vietnamese accent. "They call me Mr. Ven, by the way. I work for a person who is very powerful in this country and I can tell you that my boss is not very happy today."

"And why would that be?" I said coolly.

"You know what I am talking about," Ven pointed out.

"I have an idea. What have you done with Brigit?"

He dismissed my question with a shrug of his shoulders. "The package we took from the hotel safe was not the real one. It was rubbish. There was a girl, you know her from before, she said she could find you and get the real package, but she hasn't come back yet."

"You mean Lavender? Does she work for your boss as well?"

Ven shook his head. He grinned menacingly. "No, they have some business dealings. I can tell you something: I don't really care about you either way. You seem an okay guy. But this girl, she really hates you. Did you fuck her and leave her pregnant?" Ven pulled up a wooden chair and sat down next to my bed while his partner stood watching by the door.

I shrugged. What did Ven want? The real diamonds or a bit of revenge for making him look stupid? Probably both.

"Maybe the girl took the real diamonds and is selling them somewhere else," I suggested.

"People who know my boss don't try to trick him that way. Has she got the real package?"

I thought about it for a while and decided it was best to tell the truth here. They'd find out soon enough.

"No, she doesn't have the real diamonds."

"Diamonds?" Ven appeared puzzled for a second, then shrugged. "Where is the real package? You know don't you?"

"I have no idea. I delivered a decoy package. The real package is somewhere else. The girl came and shot the only guy who knows where the real package is." This was as much as I wanted to say without getting Grosvenor into trouble. He might know where the real diamonds were by now.

Ven was stumped by this. He said, "Stupid bitch," then fell silent for a while as he processed this information. His eyes lit up when he reached what seemed like a workable conclusion. "Okay, here is what we do. You find the real package or I will come back and kill you. And you know we have the tart that was in bed with you. We will kill her too."

"What have you done with her?" I snapped.

He laughed. "Oh, she is fine. You know her brother works with us. He is a chemist and he is doing some quality work for us."

"You've taken her to Danang, haven't you?"

"Oh, what a clever boy you are…. Now you bring the real package to me by tomorrow evening or the girl is in trouble."

"I have no idea where the real diamonds are. I've just told you."

"I don't give a shit. You go and find it. You're a smart guy. And don't play any tricks." He gave me a hard, cold stare, then pointed a finger at me in a gesture of intimidation. He turned to leave the room. His side-kick followed closely on his heels.

Staring at the ceiling I watched a small gecko scurry from one corner to the other. Things were a bit clearer now. I still had an option to walk away from it all. It made no difference to me who got the real package.

Except for Brigit and my own offended sense of pride.

I wasn't going to let Lavender or Ven get away with this kind of shit. And I was starting to suspect that the package contained something more valuable than simply high quality diamonds. And Rosenstein, for all his foibles, had not deserved to die at the hands of that bitch. He deserved revenge.

I lay back and gave the whole matter some serious thought. Running away was not my style and the best form of defence was attack.

Two hours later Grosvenor appeared. He was in his usual pinstripe suit and corporate look, not sweating at all despite the outside heat and marginal air-conditioning.

"Treating you well? I made sure you got the best Saigon has to offer."

"I've seen nicer hospitals but I'm not complaining."

"Most people still fly out to Bangkok if they've got anything serious."

"So it's not too serious?" I said. The nurse had been vague and the doctor was not due to make his rounds until early evening.

"Gunshot wounds are pretty routine. The older doctors all learned their trade during the war. They can patch you up faster than you can say 'rural revolutionary guerrilla warfare'." He chuckled at his turn of phrase.

"Any long term damage?"

"They can't say but they believe the bullet just took a big slice of flesh out of your arm and didn't touch the bone at all."

"A flesh wound."

"You'd still get the Purple Heart if you were an American soldier. You'll be up and about playing tennis again in no time."

"What about Rosenstein and how come there are no policemen bothering us here?"

Grosvenor sighed and reached over for the same wooden chair Ven had used. Once he'd sat down and crossed his legs, he explained: "He was dead even before he hit the floor. Crazy old bastard. There was no need for any heroics at all. That wasn't the real package and the girl wouldn't have found out until hours later. I don't know why he did it. He wasn't normally an impulsive man."

"No, greedy and calculating are the only adjectives that come to my mind."

"Exactly, so what got into him? Strange, wild behaviour." He paused and frowned. "Unless he knew something I didn't. But where was the sense in that? Are you sure you weren't carrying the real package?"

I snorted derisively, "How would I know which was the real lot and which wasn't?"

"Exactly. Well, I searched his body before the police arrived and later I went to his hotel and searched everywhere there and I couldn't turn up the real package. That's what makes me wonder." He stared at me pensively.

"So you're stuffed. Rosenstein dead and no idea where the real goods are?"

"Yes, Bill, you can say that again. We're a bit up shit creek without a paddle."

"What do you mean 'we'? It's your deal. I was just a courier and my bit is done."

He smiled at me knowingly. "That's right but I thought you had this great passion to go and rescue your missing lady friend?"

"I've no idea where she is," I said, not ready to tell him yet about my visit earlier from Mr. Ven and friend.

"I'd wager money on it that Wing Cam has her nicely tied up somewhere, waiting for a deal. Those thugs that hit you over the head in the hotel were his men. You can bet money on that."

"But we've got nothing to bargain or bet with, now that the diamonds are gone."

Grosvenor chuckled. "Yes, but Wing Cam doesn't know that."

"What about Lavender Daai? Do you think she was working for Wing Cam or running her own show?"

"You know her better than me. Never set eyes on her before," he commented.

I considered the issue. "Could be either way. Perhaps she had something to do with Wing Cam and then decided to double-cross him. It's her speciality."

"I got the impression she was interested in getting revenge on you as much as she wanted to get hold of that package. By now she'd have found out that the package is worthless." After a while of studying his manicured fingertips he added, "If it really was worthless."

Changing the subject, I asked: "Tell me what the police have to say about all this?"

He said, "It was awkward at first. Foreign law firms are not supposed to be the scene of murderous gunfights but after a while and some pulling of strings they settled for the fact that it was a robbery gone wrong. Our Vietnamese senior partner is very well connected at the highest level." He wore a devious smile. "We have some very good contacts at the Interior Ministry in Hanoi and our firm contributes regularly to the local Chief of Police's personal charities. We do keep large amounts of money around the office."

"That means they won't investigate too much?"

"They have Lavender's description although they had some issues with it being a woman all by herself. But the office staff got a good look at her and that gun she was waving about. With luck, the police might catch her at the airport or trying to get across the border somewhere. My personal feeling is, she seems too smart for that. Her father was a Hong Kong Triad boss, you were saying?"

"Yes, and a fine ball room dancer. One of the nicer career criminals I've met."

"Deceased?"

"Yes. He who lives by the sword, dies by the sword, as the good book has us believe."

Grosvenor found this amusing. We sat in silence for a minute or two while he tapped a finger on the side of his shoe.

Finally he said, "So, Bill. What are we going to do? There's a damsel in distress... You strike me as a knight errant."

"And you're casting yourself in the role of King Arthur?"

"No, I rather fancy myself as Merlin."

I nodded at him. "You obviously have an idea of what you want to do or you wouldn't be here."

"You know Bill, I wish we'd met before. I'm starting to like you. There are some great opportunities for business out here as you know. We could work well together."

For a moment there Milford Grosvenor reminded me of Harry Bolt. They shared the same manipulative mindset. They both had an eye for the off-chance and they could sniff out a deal better than a bloodhound with its nose to the ground. However Grosvenor subtly disguised his entrepreneurial ambitions under the suave exterior of the measured master of jurisprudence.

"I'm listening, Grosvenor," I challenged him.

He smiled. "Only you and I know that the package wasn't the real one. We'll ignore our mild suspicions that Rosenstein was not entirely honest with us. Wing Cam bases himself up in Danang, about an hour's flight from here. He owns a large toy factory up there and probably has some other shady deals going on. Danang has a large airport built by the Americans during the Vietnam war. It's a convenient location, both remote and accessible if you have means. Not much industry there and an hours' drive from the jungle. You and I go up to Danang and arrange a meeting with Wing Cam and negotiate a deal on the real package. Trust me, he is very keen to have this stuff. Part of the deal is that they release the girl."

"And her brother," I said, "He's the reason she came to Vietnam."

"Whatever," Grosvenor said lightly. "I'll have my people keep on looking for the real package - I have a few ideas about its possible location - and in the meantime we'll make up a new fake package."

My face obviously showed doubt in the plan. Grosvenor stared at me with expectation. If I wanted to track down Brigit there weren't many alternatives. And by now I thought it likely that she was up in Danang and that Wing Cam was anxious to get his hands on the package.

"What's to stop Wing Cam shooting us the moment we hand over the diamonds," I said.

"We'll be clever about it. I'll negotiate and you stay in the background with the package. I've got a few ideas on that but we can discuss it in detail later. Are you in or out?" He suddenly looked like a public schoolboy ready for a big adventure. But this was more dangerous than sneaking over the walls for a night out in the local pub.

"We'll need some weapons. We can't face up to a guy like Wing Cam without some way of protecting ourselves."

"I guess you are familiar with guns?" he asked.

"I spent several years with the Royal Hong Kong Police's Special Duties Unit which was trained by the SAS. Before that I was in the Army for a while."

"Splendid then. Our very own mercenary. I know a man who can help us with the hardware. In Vietnam, all things can be had at a price."

"If we have guns we can't fly up to Danang."

"I'll get a car. It's a 17 hour drive unless it's raining."

"When can we get the guns sorted out?"

"Later this afternoon. You won't be of much use with your right arm like that so I'd better get some extra bodies. Plenty of veterans around. Do you think you'll be up to travelling tomorrow? We'd have to leave by around 3 a.m. No traffic around then."

"It's just a flesh wound as you said. It's a wonder what modern drugs can do. So you really want to go up against Wing Cam?" I said.

"As Rosenstein said, it's always been a calculated risk."

"Yes, and then he went and did something rash."

"We can't dwell on that. Let's not make the same mistake."

"And all this for a bunch of diamonds?" I said ironically.

Grosvenor looked at me for a long hard moment and his mouth was about to open. Then he changed his mind.

"Grosvenor, before we go ahead with this I want you to tell me what is really supposed to be in that package.

Wing Cam can't be that crazy about a few diamonds."
I told him about Ven's visit.

Grosvenor listened without interrupting.

"Still don't really trust me, Bill. Do you?" he said
after I'd finished. "You're right of course. The package
isn't just a bunch of ordinary diamonds. It's a very
particular diamond that Rosenstein managed to acquire
and Wing Cam is obsessed about getting it into his
collection."

"What is it then, the Koh-I-Nor?"

The lawyer shook his head dismissively. "Of course
not. But it's a particularly nice diamond. It just became
available and it's what they call a fancy red."

"What's it worth?"

"I can't say. Rosenstein wouldn't tell me how much
he'd paid for it. Maybe half a million? Depends on how
crazy Wing Cam is to get his hands on it."

"He sounds like the sort of man who'll have people
killed for five hundred bucks let alone half a million,"
I said. "Things are starting to make a bit more sense
now." I gave him a speculative look. "How did you get
into this diamond smuggling racket?"

He looked angry for a second. "Bill, understand here.
I'm a middleman who knows how to get business done
in Vietnam. I help people with their legal problems,
which are not always black and white and I put buyers
and sellers together. It's irrelevant to me what the
product is. If it's whisky, an engineering component,
washing up liquid. It makes not difference. It's just
product. I'm an agent in this matter. Sadly my principal
Rosenstein dropped out so it makes sense to complete
the deal. Why throw away an opportunity to make
cash?"

We looked at each other for a while and I came to the conclusion that I didn't really care after all. I dealt in death.

"You do know that Wing Cam is a major drug dealer?" I said.

"He's a gangster. It's what they do. How else could he afford to buy fancy diamonds?" he said.

"I've heard his name mentioned before. He manufactures drugs. I guess that's what he is really doing at his site in Danang."

"Is that a problem for you?" he asked.

"Not really. My priority now is to get that girl back, so let's come up with a solid plan for that."

He seemed relieved and replied, "I'll be back in a few hours so get some more rest."

After he'd gone I thought it all over and wondered again if this was really my affair. Whichever way I looked at the facts I came to the same conclusion: Lavender Daai was out there somewhere and I couldn't relax as long as I knew she had me in her sights. Certainly I wanted to find Brigit; I didn't mind helping Grosvenor - although I didn't trust him further than I could throw a cricket ball with my right arm - and I wanted to revenge Rosenstein's death even though the old Semite had pulled a fast one on me.

I had to go up to Danang but the only way to do it was with circumspection and a lot of firepower. I touched my right arm, feeling the tender parts. It was a good job I always practised shooting with my left hand every time I went on the range.

10

Grosvenor came back in the late afternoon. I'd been dozing lightly most of the time, a concern at the back of my mind that Lavender might track me down to the hospital. I was looking forward to finding out what Grosvenor's plans were for getting us weapons. It's always a problem in my line of work and although I had a source in Saigon I didn't want to tap into it until I'd seen what the lawyer could come up with.

"What did the doctor say?" he asked.

"He said I'd be a fool to check myself out of hospital and go on a long bumpy car journey. But he was happy to give me enough drugs for two weeks."

"Are you still up for it, Bill?"

"He said as long as I'm careful with the arm and don't let the stitches rip I'd be okay. He suggested I avoid getting shot again."

"We'll try our best on that count."

"I can shoot with my left hand nearly as well as with my right."

"Good for us." He was about to pat me on the shoulder but I ducked.

I struggled out of bed with some help from Grosvenor. Getting the bandaged arm into my shirt took a bit longer than normal. In the end we succeeded. We always take it for granted when we have the use of both hands. Doing mundane tasks in other ways focuses the mind and reminds us how fortunate we usually are. A debilitating injury gives us a good dose of humility. It's surprising though how fast one could adapt if one had the will power.

Cursing my limitations, I stepped gingerly forward and left the ward. Grosvenor had told me earlier that he'd take care of the hospital bill and so he did. Producing a gold card which was rapidly swiped through their card reader he smiled at me genially. "My obligation for getting you into this trouble."

"I appreciate that."

"Ready to meet a man about some guns?" he said as we stepped into the sultry night. The motorbikes were out. Exhaust fumes hit my nostrils. It was rush hour in Saigon. Grosvenor indicated his car, an older model Mercedes parked up on the curve. His skinny Vietnamese driver opened the door for us and we slid into a clubby, rich leather smell that insulated us from the pollution of the street.

"So you're an old Hong Kong hand, Bill?" Grosvenor said conversationally.

"Yes, I left a few years ago. With 1997 coming up I didn't have much confidence in the future."

"It'll be interesting to see what the Chinese do with the place. It will all be softly-softly for the first few years. You know how they are. I spent ten years in Hong Kong myself." He mentioned one of the more famous law firms. "More and more of our partners were locals and it changed the way we did business. I thought coming to Vietnam and working the Indochina beat was the next great challenge."

"You seem to have established yourself well."

"I like to think so," he said, not without a hint of pride in his voice.

The driver seemed to know where he was going. He threaded the big beast through the two wheelers, leaning on the horn from time to time, keeping the ride at a steady speed.

"And why did you leave the police?" Grosvenor asked.

"The same reason you probably left your law firm. It wasn't fun or challenging any more. Minor things were being blown out of proportion. And I had the chance to do some private work. I've been a security consultant for a Singaporean firm for several years."

"Looking for any other jobs?"

"Not really. I like to think I'm semi-retired. While I was in the police we had great gratuities and unlike some guys who invested them in Carlsberg beer I bought properties and built up a share portfolio. For a while I worked as a financial adviser but that wasn't my thing. You need to be aggressive for that industry and have no compunction about hitting on your friends for business when they're trying to relax over a beer."

He laughed at my assessment and it sounded as if he was comfortable with my tale. It was mostly true but matters had not been as simple as I made them sound. Money wasn't a problem but lately I'd been caught up too often in other people's schemes. For a second I had a vision of Brigadier Wee's face and his bald, liver spotted head. Somewhere out there the old strategist was sending out missives and pulling strings. I wondered, as I sat bullshitting in the Saigon traffic, if unknown to me he was yanking my strings at this very moment. It wouldn't be the first time. A cold shiver of foreboding ran down my back. I'd just have to play the game through to its conclusion if I wanted to know. Meanwhile Lavender Daai was out there. I'd have to find her before she found me.

"It's not far now," Grosvenor said.

"Where are we?"

"Somewhere in District 2," he explained, although that meant nothing to me.

We drove down a darkened road. The buildings on either side probably hadn't changed much since the seventies. They were traditional shophouses, four stories high. The large shuttered gates were left open in the day-time while at night the family would park its Honda scooters downstairs amongst other items of common storage. The driver pulled up at the curb and shut off the engine. He got out and opened the door for us then pointed at a dark alleyway, before heading off towards it. We followed him in silence.

I was wary. It was a quiet part of town and a good place to get into trouble. I kept my senses alert although I felt dizzy walking. I'd have to ease up on the medication if I wanted to stay sharp in the next few days.

"Who lives here then?" I whispered to Grosvenor as we stopped in front of a side-door.

"Retired general."

"Makes sense."

The driver was rapping on the door and it was soon opened. We were led into what was a cross between a garage, a storeroom and a shop filled with an assortment of hardware. In the middle of the space, at a folding table on folding chairs, sat a group of six people, all men in their forties or fifties. They were eating with chopsticks. The driver made the introductions. Everyone stared at us suspiciously but the oldest of the men put down his bowl and got to his feet.

He gave a hollow smile of welcome and led the way into a similar room further back. Boxes were stacked up here and linen sacks of what smelt like rice were piled against the walls.

The older man turned to us and said a word that we all could understand: "Money."

Grosvenor nodded and pulled out a stack of US dollar notes. I could only see the top one briefly but they were hundreds with Benjamin Franklin's face on them and the old man looked pleased. It all seemed highly amicable but just in case, I edged back from them and kept my eyes on the door. If we were robbed here there was no running to the police.

The driver spoke in Vietnamese and explained what we were looking for. In an ideal world I wanted four General Purpose Machine Guns with enough ammunition to blast Wing Cam and all his henchmen to kingdom come, but that was barely practical. What we needed was small, concealable, reliable and with enough punch to get us out of any difficulties that might arise. We were not planning on storming Wing Cam's operation. We simply wanted to ensure we were given an appropriate level of respect in any negotiation.

The old man opened a crate labelled in Cyrillic letters and displayed what I would have expected: a dozen or more AK-47 Kalashnikov assault rifles wrapped in waxed paper. It's still the most popular weapon in the world: unbelievably rugged, simple to maintain and manufactured in a standard calibre. It was the mainstay of most terrorist armies and if its inventor had been an American with a patent, he would have died a billionaire.

"What do you think of these, Bill?" Grosvenor asked. He stood over the crate and gazed at the rifles with interest but limited understanding. I stepped forward and pulled out the top Kalashnikov. Gently I unrolled the waxed paper and inspected the quality of the product. There were many copies in existence, both Chinese and Eastern European and most of them were equally good. But this was the genuine Russian product. Along with beluga and vodka this piece of kit defined modern Russian culture. I found a serial number which told me the manufacturing date. They'd been made six years earlier. I removed the banana shaped magazine and worked the action. It moved smoothly and the grease still glistened in the dim light of the single overhead bulb. I put my finger inside the chamber to check for any traces of rust. My finger came out rust-free and greasy.

"They look in good shape. We could do with two of these for starters," I said. "Any grenades?"

The driver translated but the old man shook his head. No grenades. Shame.

"What about handguns?" I said.

The old man moved to another part of the room and uncovered what looked like a steel trunk. It had a padlock and he took out a key. When he threw back the lid I found a treasure trove of revolvers and automatic pistols. All of the weapons were wrapped in oily cloths and I gave the old man a thumbs up sign to show my approval of his storage techniques. This was the nearest thing to a gun 7-11 store that I'd come across. I took out a Ruger and played with it for a while. Then I unbundled what turned out to be a Smith & Wesson revolver, nice, solid and dependable in .38 calibre. My preference was for something in nine millimetres. It's the most common standard for handguns and one can get a good variety of ammunition for this calibre. I often used the illegal Deformationsgeschoss. Bullets that ripped your target to shreds. They were only illegal for civilians because some of the specialised units, like the German GSG9 used them. My particular favourite was the Dynamit Nobel Action 1 which had been designed for them.

Finally I found what I was looking for. A pair of Beretta Brigadiers. Both were in excellent condition although there was some wear and tear on the grips. It was a fine combat gun and was favoured by many US Special Forces until the Glock and the new Walthers appeared on the market.

The old man had plenty of nine mill ammo although none of it was the high powered stuff I would have liked.

"Let's not scrimp on the bullets," Grosvenor suggested when I began counting out the small brown boxes.

"How much money do we have?" I said. "Enough for the two assault rifles and the two Berettas?"

He smiled. "Let's begin the negotiations."

Initially the old man wanted two thousand US dollars for the whole lot but the driver bargained him down to just over a thousand and I thought that was a great deal. I spent some more time checking out what we were getting. I field-stripped all four pieces of hardware and checked the internal workings and the condition of the firing pins. When I was satisfied, I nodded at the driver and we had a deal. Grosvenor pulled out a stack of dirty, green notes and the old men's eyes beamed. The greenback was still the currency of choice in this country.

"Shall I shoot them all and take the money back," I said toying with one of the ammunition cartons.

For an instant Grosvenor looked horrified until I laughed and he saw the joke. We'd never get past the men in the front room if we tried to rip them off. They might be on the mature side but the glint in their eyes hinted at vicious jungle battles fought in their younger years.

As we stepped back into the alleyway, I marvelled at how simple things had been. A part of me wanted to ask the old man for a calling card. Of course he wouldn't have one. It would be tough to remember the exact location of his shop. It was an excellent resource.

The guns had been wrapped in old newspapers and then placed in a big mesh holdall which the driver carried to the car and locked away in the boot.

As we shook hands with the old man he winked at me and said in heavily accented American, "Death before Dishonour". I patted him on the shoulder and nodded pleasantly. Death wasn't the intention but honour certainly played a part in our plans.

It pleased me greatly that Grosvenor had let me keep one of the Berettas and 50 rounds of ammunition. It meant I would sleep well in my hotel room. If Lavender turned up she'd get a load between her eyes.

The hotel manager had upgraded me to one of their suites. In fact this was only two rooms placed together but it was the sentiment that counted. I locked and chained all the doors, cleaned my new tool with a cotton cloth and WD40 – not the best gun-oil but better than nothing - which I'd requisitioned, then eased myself into bed. I thought about Brigit and hoped she was doing okay. If they had mistreated her there would be hell to pay. I'd started to develop a soft spot for the girl and there wasn't anything I could do about that feeling except let it fester for now.

We'd planned for a 3 a.m. start the next morning but when the wake up call came, it was altogether too early and my body expressed displeasure. I didn't bother with a shower, just put my head under the cold tap and ran a toothbrush across my teeth. My bag was all packed and I was out of the door within ten minutes.

The night manager was there to bow me out. They were happy to see the back of me because I was nothing but trouble without a penny of profit. I was beginning to wonder what I'd let myself in for with the ride up to Danang. By plane it was a straight hour and a half and the train took twelve hours. I dreaded to think how the roads were and what suffering they would inflict on my battered carcass. My left hand curled around the plastic bag which contained all my drugs. I'd have to go easy on them.

Grosvenor looked dapper, as usual, with a tropical bushman's hat that shadowed his face and a tan jacket that boasted many pockets and hid many mysteries – one assumed.

"Sleep well, old boy?" he asked cheerily and helped me with my bag. It was a roomy 4 x 4 Toyota which inspired me with hope although it implied the roads were less than smooth. In the front sat the same old driver from the night before and riding shot-gun – literally – was a guy called Jake, who had a bundle on his lap that looked suspiciously like one of our Kalashnikov AK-47s with its stock folded back. His features were craggy and his accent was Australian when he wished me a 'g'day'.

"Jake's our getaway pilot. Cunning plan, you know," Grosvenor winked when I gave him a puzzled frown. "I'll explain it all later. We've got to get out of town before the morning traffic hots up."

That sounded fine by me. I settled into my corner and squashed a purple pillow - which I'd found on the back shelf – into the side of my neck.

I don't recall much of the first hour and nothing of the next four hours. Saigon was not on the list of the world's top traffic nightmares – Bangkok, Jakarta and Manila are certainly in the top ten and I'd hazard the rest are African capitals – so we slipped out pretty fast at this time of the night and found ourselves weaving past trucks and motor scooters with ever increasing countryside visible. The roads were still flat and wide but this was no highway. Top speed was an urgent forty miles an hour.

Nobody bothered me for a long time. From time to time I woke up from drug-induced dozing, aware that Grosvenor was mumbling into his mobile phone, that Jake was staring keenly at the rice paddies and water-buffalos and that the driver was humming the latest hit by TLC, 'Don't go chasing waterfalls ..." Did he know something we didn't?

Somehow the road was getting bumpier and I felt myself floating upwards towards greater consciousness again. I opened my eyes and felt drowsy, my joints were sore and there were pins and needles in all my limbs.

"Where are we?" I asked.

Grosvenor raised his eyebrows at me and said a Vietnamese name. It could have been the main course from a menu for all I knew.

"How long have we been driving?" I tried.

"Five hours, time to pull over and get some petrol and tuck into our sandwiches if you are hungry."

"Yes, food sounds like the preferred option." I groggily studied the landscape outside the vehicle and found nothing that reminded me we were in the twentieth century. There was jungle, and there were peasants and there were wooden huts and there were those funny big straw hats you always see Vietnamese people wearing in war movies. "The land that time forgot," I commented.

"Yes, communism hasn't changed much of life out here and the cunning capitalism that has re-emerged in Saigon is just a dream to these villagers."

I looked out of the rear window and noted a few trucks following us. "The road is not as bad as I thought."

"It's the major artery between the North, Central and South of Vietnam."

"It could do with four extra lanes, perhaps."

Grosvenor chuckled. "It will come. By 2020 you won't recognise this country."

He produced a cool box from the footwell. He handed it over and I found an assortment of sandwiches, mostly cheese and ham. There were also Mars Bars and small bottles of Evian water.

"Rations," I said with appreciation and grabbed what I liked.

Ten minutes later the driver pulled over into what masqueraded in these parts for a petrol station. A fellow in olive-green overalls slouched over and filled the Toyota with fuel. We all got out to stretch our legs and pee in the bushes. The world here had a moist, succulent smell. Behind the petrol station was jungle and at any moment I expected Mowgli and Balou Bear to stick their heads out of the dense verdant greenery.

Grosvenor smoked one of his cigars, spoiling the outdoorsy odour with a man-made stink.

"How far from here?" I asked the oldest question in the book.

"Far, still damn far," Jake replied. He'd strolled over and was slugging from a tinnie of Fosters. It was the locally brewed stuff but I assumed he knew what he was doing and had the vaccinations.

"Been in Vietnam long?" I said, making conversation. He didn't look old enough to have been part of the conflict although life had not been kind to him: two scars ran across the side of his face – the sort of tracks left when one is at the hurting end of a broken bottle neck – and there were big bags under blood-shot eyes.

"'Bout four years. Came to help them set up at the airport and moved on to charter flights."

"Jake here is a certified, qualified, authenticated, real-life, down-to-earth, genuine bush pilot," Grosvenor said redundantly, squinting in the smoke of his tobacco.

"Nah, I used to fly jets in the Aussie air force," Jake said.

"Then he moved on to puddle-hoppers across the wide expanse of the Australian bush," Grosvenor added.

"This here is Vietnam," Jake said by way of ending the conversation which was getting too personal for his liking. I nodded and decided he was a good man. There didn't seem to be any vanity or posturing there and although he looked a hard-drinking, hard-living geezer that came along with the other qualifications.

I looked at my watch and thought it would be late and dark before we got anywhere near Danang. The driver gave us a nod of readiness once he'd killed the butt of a cigarette under the heel of his boot.

"Mount up, chaps," Grosvenor said. We continued on our interminable journey. This time Grosvenor was dozing so I had no chance of asking him any questions. I took out a yellow sliver of diazepam which I knew would both relax my muscles and make me feel warm, loving and drowsy. In this way another four hours passed. The next time I woke, Jake was driving and the other feller was snoring his head off.

"What's the plan when we get there?" I finally got around to asking Grosvenor the next time we stopped for bladder relief.

"There's one decent hotel," he explained, fumbling with another of his cigars. "It's the Furama. Just been built, usually empty because they don't have groups of tourists coming in yet and it sits just on top of what used to be called China beach. Very pleasant in fact."

"Ah-ha," I said, wanting to interrupt his tourist guide speech.

"So we'll check in there and get comfortable and if we feel like it, we'll go down to the only decent expat bar in town, which is Christie's, for a few wet ones."

"And what happens at Christie's?" I said.

"Well, sadly, old boy, bugger all happens in Christie's. It's just one of those pokey old joints where gin-sozzled expats sit around griping and telling each other tales about the spunky little native tarts they knocked off the previous night."

"Bit of a shit-hole then," I ventured.

"Judge for yourself. But good for our requirements. Whatever is happening in Danang, we'll be able to find out. Every white man in town, and there aren't many, who likes a bit of company turns up at Christie's at some point in the evening."

"Okay. So we do a recce by gossip and then…"

Grosvenor shrugged. "We'll see what we hear and how best to get in contact with Wing Cam."

"A highly complex plan," I said mockingly.

"Keep it simple stupid," he said tapping his nose.

"I see you had the same training sergeant as I did somewhere in your career."

"Oxford Officer Training Corps," he replied.

"What about the pilot then?" I said.

"We will have a plane in Danang which means we can get out fast if we want to."

"Well at least the exit strategy impresses me."

"Trust me, old fellow."

"I trust mainly that piece of Russian precision engineering which Jake is toying with."

Grosvenor smiled, patted me on the uninjured shoulder and suggested it was time to get going again.

Around 7.30 p.m. we finally reached the outskirts of Danang. It was a singularly unimpressive city. They said a million people lived here but it looked more like a large village and hardly any building was over three stories. As usual most of the visible transportation was motorbikes or scooters. Nobody wore a crash helmet. Occasionally a truck squeezed past and even more rarely a car such as ours.

The population went about their business as in any other Asian conurbation. There were stalls on the side of the road selling meat, vegetables and fruit. Shop fronts which revealed dismantled trucks, basic electrical goods such as fridges and televisions and occasionally a place that sold mobile phones. It was easier to buy a mobile than to bribe a government official for the installation of a land-line. We passed restaurants and beer-bars, although none were imposing – just little establishments servicing the local middle-class. After all, everyone has a right to rest and relaxation in the form of a bowl of noodles and some cheap brew.

We drove along past the airport. The big sign on the roof read 'Danang International Airport' which amused me. Grosvenor noticed my frown and said, "They have one flight a week to Macau. So that makes it an International airport. They're trying to get regular direct flights with Hong Kong and Bangkok to start bringing the tourists in. I can't see it happening though."

I nodded and looked at the single, terminal building. We were still in the seventies here and on the runway I could see an antique Tupolev TU-134 taxi-ing for take-off. That was a piece of Russian workmanship I wouldn't trust with my life. I watched for a while with morbid fascination as it struggled to lift its small body on stubby wings off the tarmac, finally managing to cut loose and wobble up into the grey, cloud-speckled sky.

I let out my breath with a sigh of relief, surprised that I'd been holding it. The miracle of flight has always baffled me.

"Where is this top-notch five star hostelry you have promised us, Grosvenor?" I said, suddenly noticing how much better I felt for having spent the day bumping along in the back of the well-padded Toyota.

"Not far," he replied and picked up his mobile to make a call.

11

After all that I'd seen of Danang so far, the Furama was a revelation, a welcome oasis of civilisation.

We were greeted by the Swiss General Manager as if we'd trekked along the Silk Road and were Italian royalty. Grosvenor was upgraded to a suite and the rest of us were given deluxe rooms. It seemed the place had only opened six months ago and bona fide, quality guests were still a rarity. Beyond the lobby was a magnificent patio. On the left was the obligatory French restaurant and on the right a bar area with colonial style wicker furniture and a selection of single malt whiskies – as we found out later. There was hardly anyone to be seen: an old French couple relaxing with aperitifs, a lone American engineer who was buried in a pile of papers. Otherwise it was just the bowing and scraping of the hotel employees dressed in immaculate white linen outfits with high collars and – for the girls – short skirts showing a pleasing length of stockinged thigh.

"What's the industry here in town?" I asked the general manager while we were filling in our forms and having our passports checked.

"Oh, not much. Mainly agriculture, a few big Taiwanese and Hong Kong owned factories making garments or toys and there are some rice and timber projects being developed." He smiled with the smarminess of his profession. "We are hoping to get the tourism industry moving. Look at that beach." He pointed at the sand which encroached onto the hotel veranda. "Isn't it wonderful? We even have a dive shop starting next month. Do you scuba dive, sir?"

I nodded. "Haven't had much chance lately. What's the coral like?"

"They say it's excellent. Up in Nha Trang they've been very successful with their dive shop and we hope we can get the same level of interest."

"Most people still only think of Danang as something to do with the Vietnam war," I said.

"That's true. It was the airport. Do you know the runway is so large they could easily land a Jumbo Jet? During the Vietnam war it was the busiest airport in the world."

I smiled politely and accepted my key from the pretty girl behind the counter. There was something about Vietnamese girls. They were all so well endowed. The next moment I was thinking of Brigit and that made me angry and reminded me we were not here to enjoy the beach or admire the airport. We were here to fix a problem.

Grosvenor suggested we shower and meet again half an hour later. Jake wasn't going to join us and the driver would find a local restaurant once he'd fuelled up the car.

My room was as pleasant as I expected it, right down to the mini-bar which held the usual assortment of liquors as well as some I hadn't seen for a while. There was a thin balcony which gazed out over the pristine beach and an aquamarine ocean that reminded me of my beach-house in Thailand. This was the South China

Sea and out there somewhere, about a thousand kilometres across the water, was Hong Kong.

The chill-out effect of the drugs had worn off so I felt more energetic. There was no pain in my arm and the dull ache in my head had also nearly gone. I might be ready for a beer or two. Grosvenor appeared fresh and sprightly when we met downstairs.

"I have no idea how I survived that road trip," I said while he hailed a taxi.

"Long journey, I've got to admit," he replied. "It'll be faster on the way back if things work out."

"Lots of ifs in our plan."

He grinned. "Where's your sense of adventure, Bill?"

"There's already been way too much adventure in my life, Grosvenor. Whoever doles the stuff out up there just loves slapping it all over me."

"What a load of bollocks," he said cheerfully.

It didn't take long to get to Christie's nor did the taxi driver have a problem with the address. In most respects, so far, Danang was nothing but a one-horse town.

Christie's was as impressive as an old shoe-box. It was a clap-board building that stood on the edge of what could have been called a promenade. The inside windows faced out onto the sea but part of the view was spoiled by a fleet of manky fishing vessels hauled up nearby. They were rapidly vanishing from sight as dusk encroached.

Even Grosvenor, who knew what to expect, viewed the place with an expression of dismay on his face. The best way to describe Christie's would have been to call it a Wild West saloon transported through time into an Asian back-water. A pitted, timber floor set the stage, along with tired wooden tables and chairs and a long bar presided over by a sallow faced fellow in a scruffy old apron. A jaded pool table was surrounded by a foursome of pot-bellied white men who took turns in thwacking the balls and supping their beers.

About twenty people were dotted around the room with a few regulars occupying the bar. A small television set was suspended over the bartender's head, tuned to CNN, thankfully without the sound.

"Y'all want some food there? Kitchen's bout to close in twenny minutes," the barman said.

"What's on the menu?" Grosvenor asked, daringly.

"Burgers, burgers and burgers," the barman said, then added in the same neutral tone, "and French fries with 'em."

"Steak?" Grosvenor wanted to know.

The barman shook his head. "Mondays, Wednesdays and Fridays only. Imported from the US and New Zealand." He handed over a small, laminated card which told us what selection of condiments we could elect to slap on top of the burgers.

Grosvenor hummed to himself for a moment then said, "When in Rome... I'll have the Christie Burger with extra mushrooms."

"Same," I said, noticing all of a sudden that a large hunger had crept up on me and that American comfort food might just be the cure. "Extra grease," I added but the barman didn't find it funny.

We pulled up two stools at the bar and ordered draft beer. I leant on the counter-top with my good arm and carried on my examination of the other customers. There were no girls. It only struck me then. If this had been Saigon they would have been fluttering around the place like butterflies. Not that the men were much to vie for but the expats were no more impressive in the big city than here in the back of beyond.

A movement beside me made me start. Someone had pulled up their stool close to mine.

"Had yourself an argument with a staircase there, son?" the man said. I could smell him before I had fully turned to look at him. He was tall, probably strong when he was young, but he'd gone to seed. What was left of his fair hair hung from just above his temples and his face looked like a Sunday paper that had been scrunched up, then unfolded again. The smell of stale beer hung around his clothes and blended with the general atmosphere of the bar. As close up to him as I was, the pong made me wrinkle my nose. For a second I came close to asking him if he'd had a bath in the last week and did he need a few dollars.

"New in town," he said because I hadn't replied to his first sentence.

"Just arrived," I said, "and you've been here, wearing that same jacket since President Nixon's second term of office?" I hadn't meant to say it but once it was out, the words hung in the air ready to cause offence.

Instead he gave me a mellow smile, as if I'd just told him he had a pretty daughter. He said, "The name's Hank Petersen. And sorry to disappoint you. I wasn't old enough to be drafted for the Vietnam conflict." He held out his hand and, not wanting to be churlish, I shook it. After all we were here to meet the locals and glean useful information. Grosvenor seemed to have started a conversation with a small fellow whose strong Yorkshire accent drifted over to my ears. Petersen, of the alcoholic odour, was American and, although not an expert, I thought his accent was probably from the South.

"What part of the States are you from?" I asked as the bar-tender placed a large, frosty beer glass in front of Petersen. A moment later he set a tiny shot-glass of clear liquid next to the beer. My eyes must have stared because Petersen said, "It's vodka. Got me the habit when I was doing pipelines in Tajikistan."

"I like a good vodka myself. But beer and vodka makes my head explode."

He thought that was funny and began to laugh for nearly a minute, coming very close to slapping me on my back. I held up a hand and he got the message.

"Here's to vodka blowing your head off," he said jovially. "Which is what the damn stuff was invented for." He jerked the clear, sharp liquid into his mouth, then wiping his lips with the back of his hand. "Fuck me, brother. If that don't sting, the world is my oyster."

I took a steady sip from my own beer and found it neither good nor bad but at least cold. "So you do oil or what?"

"I do me a bit of this and a bit of that. And yes, fella, I've been in oil some before."

"What brings you to Danang?"

"There's this big US corporation and they have it in their mind they want to do some big corporate business up here. Trouble is they need to find some friends up here first. And that's my line of work. Making friends and influencing people."

"Tough profession."

"Ah, you grow into it," he said and tapped the counter-top with his index finger which the barman seemed to understand.

"Now, Mr…

"Bill."

"Now you'll be drinking with me, Bill, won't you? All this talk of heads exploding has got me thinking that I haven't seen anything exciting in this darned honky-tonk bar for a long time."

I considered his invitation for a while. "What's the vodka?"

"Ah, it's the real stuff. They bring it down from Siberia and you can taste the gasoline in it. The fact that it's genuine don't mean it's good for you."

"I once knew a guy who was always putting pepper into his vodka."

Petersen nodded, "You can still see the old Rooskies do that. But heck knows what the hell for. Won't take the oil out proper. You might as well live with it."

We held up our shot-glasses to inspect each other through the curved glass, then chucked the hard stuff down the hatch. It burnt like an ulcer and probably left scorch marks in my oesophagus as it rolled down.

"Guess you're not sight-seeing in this fine piss-hole of a town?" Petersen asked. If it wasn't the standard question that everyone always starts with when talking to a stranger in a bar in Asia, I would have thought he was checking us out.

"No, just come to use the toilets and move on," I said. Grosvenor still had his back to us, deep in conversation regarding the latest football results. I studied Petersen some more and he took my silence for acquiescence. Another round of Siberian vodkas appeared.

Once again the liquor hurt like someone had slashed my throat with a razor blade. I downed a few quick mouthfuls of bland beer.

"Ever heard of a man called Wing Cam who runs a factory around here somewhere?" I asked as casually as possible.

Petersen studied me with his blood-shot eyes. Somehow I felt he was a lot less bedraggled than he made out. He nodded and reached into his jacket pocket for a pack of red Marlboro. He flipped back the top and offered me pick of the sticks. I declined. The last time I'd smoked one of those was when I was a teenager. I made do with the light ones from time to time.

"As Neil Young said in one of his songs 'He plenty bad man'."

"So you know the man?"

"By reputation only," he growled, flicking his Bic lighter at the cigarette. "Around town they talk about him in hushed whispers. As if he were a god descended from the mountains. You stay here for a while, you hear about him. Sometimes you see his Mercedes powering down the street." He studied me for a few seconds, pushing out a cloud of smoke from between his pursed lips. "Like I said: he plenty bad man."

"Beats his workers and rapes their wives, I assume? Just another feudal landlord." I was trying to sound like a man who'd heard some fascinating gossip and wanted more of the juicy bits.

"He has a big toy factory over on the other side of the airport. Suppose he has some big name customers like McDonalds. Makes those Happy Meal toys and that Disney stuff. Cinderella and the Seven Dwarfs or whatever the latest movie is."

I smiled blankly not wanting to correct his fairy tale general knowledge. He didn't look like a man who was going to appear on a television quiz show. "So what makes him such a mean son of a bitch?"

Petersen shrugged and his eyes turned to the empty shot-glasses. It didn't take much deduction to know what was on his mind. I caught the barman's eye and used my index finger to give a rolling sign.

"Wing Cam - what makes everyone think he's such a bastard?" I repeated.

Petersen glanced around the room as if considering the question and wanting to formulate the answer with care. He picked up the newly delivered shot-glass and toyed with it for a while, rolling it between his chubby fingers, then saluting me with it and making it vanish like all the other ones before. I pushed mine over towards him. I'd reached my limit for the night.

"They talk about him. The locals," he said. "He's a man of power, with connections and you don't cross him. That's the word. And if you do cross him, that's the last anyone hears of you."

"Sounds like a cross between Count Dracula and the Hound of the Baskervilles," I said, not meaning to be flippant but it came out that way and Petersen started choking up with laughter again.

Grosvenor turned back to us and wanted to know what had been happening. I introduced them and said we'd just been discussing a well-known local character named Wing Cam.

"Yes," the lawyer nodded sagely, "he's a big shot around here. Bit of a warlord."

Petersen shook Grosvenor's hand and after a while we moved on to other topics. I had a suspicion that Petersen knew more about Wing Cam than he was telling, but to pry more would have been too obvious.

It wasn't much longer before Petersen began slurring his words and conversation became harder. I checked my Rolex and decided we'd done enough reconnaissance by banter. When the large, washed-out American shambled over to the gents, I suggested to Grosvenor that my batteries were running down and a few hours of kip were in order. He nodded in agreement. By the time Petersen had re-emerged our taxi had arrived. I shook his hand and told him we'd hook up again for drinks the following evening. He gave me the kind of sly look that again belied his level of intoxication.

"Now don't be going anywhere near that Wing dude. He'll eat you all alive and then shit you out for breakfast."

"Won't be in town long enough to either have or be had for breakfast," I said foolishly and gave him a few blunt thumps on the side of the arm with my good hand.

Back in the hotel I feigned a higher level of exhaustion than was the case and agreed to meet Grosvenor in the coffee shop at eight for breakfast. The vodkas had left me light-headed and over-confident but otherwise not incapacitated. I got back into my room and had a few bottles of Evian and a cold, brisk shower holding my bandaged arm up in the air.

The fact was: I had a cunning plan to get closer to Wing Cam much earlier than Grosvenor envisaged. I wanted to recce the facility where Wing was doing his deals and before we officially went anywhere near it offering the diamond for sale. I wanted to get an idea of the lie of the land.

Petersen had mentioned roughly where the toy factory was and I was convinced there wouldn't be many other similar facilities in the area. All I needed now was a car with a driver.

I snuck downstairs and strode through the lobby. I'd changed to dark clothes and sneakers so I looked as if I was either on the way to a trendy new nightspot or planning to crawl mischievously around in the shadows.

Outside the hotel a doorman asked me if I needed a car or any other help. I nodded. It didn't look like I could rent a bike at this time of the night nor did I think I could ride one with my damaged arm, so I had to risk taking a driver along. I suggested driving myself but the hotel employee shook his head sadly and explained that simply wasn't possible. I admired his devotion to duty: while he was saying this I was fingering a large wad of US dollar notes and probably his sadness came mainly from seeing the money that could be his, while knowing he'd lose his job if he agreed.

It was the same driver we'd had before. He didn't seem surprised to see me again and began by enthusiastically suggesting a place called the Royal Hotel where they had many beautiful girls in the Karaoke lounge. He grinned happily for a while until I told him I wanted to drive out towards the airport. This puzzled him for a moment, then he shrugged.

We set off and in less than twenty minutes were back near the airport. I told him to keep driving on down the road. I wanted to know if there were any factories out here. He nodded but there was a cautiousness in his face all of a sudden. I was on the right track. There was a whiff of fear in the air. We must be near Dracula's castle. As we passed the airport and motored down the dark road he slowed the limousine down.

"Why you want to come here, sir?" he asked, glancing over his shoulder as his foot became lighter on the accelerator.

"I want to see a big factory here. How many are there?"

"Not many, sir."

"What's that?" I said, pointing at a long white wall that seemed to stretch off into all directions of the night.

"Cleaning station," the driver said.

"Cleaning what?"

"Water, I think. For drink."

"Drive on."

Another five minutes went by and more walls appeared. "And this," I said. "Who's building is this?"

"Toy Factory."

"I think we're getting warmer," I said to myself. "Slow down." By now he was sweating, beads on his forehead visible in the amber light of the dashboard.

"Who owns this factory?" I said softly, leaning forward over the back of his seat.

"A big boss," he said and his tongue licked his dry lips. You had to admire Wing Cam. His influence was nearly as tangible as the Beretta Brigadier that was gouging into the flesh at the small of my back.

"Where's the entrance?"

"I think far, sir. You cannot go there. They close. It's night."

I tapped his shoulder with a crisp 20 US dollar bill – half a month's salary for a factory worker - and whispered, "Drive on. I want to see how big the factory is."

The headlights swept over sections of the four-metre high wall. Three strands of barbed wire stretched across the top of the grey concrete. Every fifty yards there were small watch-towers. They did not appear manned but powerful lights illuminated the immediate area. We cruised in ominous silence until finally the main gate appeared. It was like something from a Second World War movie: ponderous steel doors that would allow two trucks to enter side by side once opened. A guard house stood outside and two men lounged in front with what looked like Heckler & Koch MP5s slung around their shoulders. They stared at us with interest.

"Keep driving, keep calm," I instructed. Once again the bland wall stretched into the night. After five minutes it suddenly made a left turn and there were fields again. I let him carry on for a hundred yards then told him to stop. He turned to me with a quizzical expression on his face.

"I want you to wait here for one hour. I'll be back."

The driver looked at me as if I'd asked him to murder his own mother. "I cannot. It is too dangerous."

"What's dangerous?" I smiled reassuringly.

"This place. I cannot wait in the night. Someone might attack me."

"Who will attack you?"

"Some people." He nodded in the direction behind us. "From there. Those people."

"How old are you?" I said.

"Fifty-five, sir."

"Do you remember the Americans when they were here?"

"Yes, sure. I was young man. I can speak good English, right? I learnt from the Americans."

"And you are afraid of the dark now?"

"Not the dark. Those people." Once again he nodded into the darkness behind us as if the living dead would emerge from behind his red tail-lights.

"Why don't you come back in one hour and pick me up here?"

He stared at me for a while, wondering probably if I was sane. I took three twenties from my pocket and in the old Hollywood gesture tore each one in half. I handed him his mutilated pieces and kept the other three segments.

"You can tape them up later. Good as new," I said.

He hesitated, fingering the half-notes and finally slipping them into his shirt-pocket.

I looked at my Rolex and told him to be back at 0230 hours. Sharp. "Don't let me down." For a second I thought about it and then decided it was best to counter fear with fear. Greed wasn't always good enough as a persuader.

Suddenly the Beretta was in my left hand and my right gripped his shoulder. He stared wildly at the dark barrel, flinching when I moved it to stroke his cheek.

"Don't forget. Two thirty. You'll get the other half of the money." I paused. "If you don't come, you get this." I tapped the muzzle of the automatic on his shoulder then gave him a smile. I wanted to scare him, not have him paralysed with terror.

He swallowed a few times, hard, then said: "Okay, sir, okay. But you crazy."

A minute later I was stepping into the edge of the rice field and watching the limousine disappear back from where we'd come.

Now what was the plan?

I wanted to do a recce but it would be hard to see much without getting over the wall. There had to be one or more side-entrances. Perhaps they were not that well guarded, perhaps they'd be equally inaccessible. But it was worth a try. It felt good to be bringing the fight to the enemy. They'd had me on the hop for too long. The thought of the men coming to my hotel room, and the thought of Lavender Daai turning up at the lawyer's offices made the bile rise in my throat. The bitch. I was going to get her.

The weight of the nine millimetre felt excellent in my fist. I had a full magazine and a box of 50 in my jacket pocket.

It took me five minutes at a quick stride to get back to the outer wall of the factory. I veered off to the right, slowing down, wondering if they might have light sensors or trips. That seemed too sophisticated to me for this part of the world but one had to be careful. I stayed in the shadows, beyond the reach of the lights from the mini-watch-towers. I walked along the wall with cautious, deliberate steps. The earth felt soggy underfoot. The night smelt damp. I listened hard as my eyes ran along the wall for signs of any movement or a side-entrance.

There was nothing for a while. Just white wall and the dark watch-towers with their fixed search lights that lit up a three metre strip of ground in front of the wall. I kept on moving. Given the right tools and two healthy arms I could climb the wall and cut through the three strands of barbed wire. What were the chances that they were electronically rigged for motion or more simply hooked to a high voltage generator? It would be useful to know. I couldn't see any insulator posts so it was unlikely that the wire was electrified. I wondered how much security was needed out here. Wing Cam seemed to have put the fear of hell into the locals so a few goons with guns on the main entrance might be all he needed if he wanted to maintain his privacy.

I was here for reconnaissance so these were all useful thoughts but a bit limited on facts. At the back of my mind I was itching to get inside the place but it was the wrong time and if I fought my way in, I'd never make it out.

Pausing for breath, I crouched down and told myself I was being powered by anger. This was not the time for action. It was the time for deliberation and investigation. The glow on the hands of my chronometer told me it was already two in the morning. It was time to turn back. I'd found out some stuff. Not much, but it helped. I'd got a feeling for the place.

It was a sixth sense, more than hearing or seeing, that alerted me to danger. I turned, raising my gun, only to find what seemed like two shadows rising out from the ground. Then I felt the hard steel of a weapon pressed against my neck. Where the hell had they come from?

"Welcome, Mr. Jedburgh. We were expecting you," a familiar Geordie-Vietnamese voice said.

There was no percentage in fighting. The odds were against me. I gave up my Beretta reluctantly. So much for entering Danang quietly.

12

It was my old friend Mr. Ven who had relieved me of my gun and drained me of whatever confidence had driven me to come out alone into the treacherous night.

I cursed myself for the cockiness that now deprived us of the advantage we'd had by coming up to Danang and bringing the fight to the enemy. I'd delivered myself to them. They were smirking as they led me around the back of the wall and revealed to me the other entrance which I had assumed must exist somewhere.

It was just a standard iron door but there were electronics that controlled it. Ven punched some numbers into a touch pad and ran a swipe card through a reader and a loud click told us we could enter. One of his men shoved me forward. By now my wrists were strapped tight in front of me with plastic handcuffs. The ones you can cut off but not break off. The police in New York favour them and I could understand why. My wound began to ache from the awkward angle of my arms.

We came into a flood-lit courtyard. I saw several forty foot containers being loaded with cardboard boxes and two lorries stood at one end ready to haul them away. A man was driving a baby fork-lift moving palettes from one stack to another. All this in the middle of night.

"We make toys here," Ven said conversationally. We marched across the courtyard and entered a long, low building. Once inside I gasped with amazement. I had never seen a factory floor this large before. The room stretched into the distance, it could have been a mile or more. Rows and rows of what I knew to be injection moulding machines stood like inter-galactic fighters from a Star Wars movie.

"Eight thousand machines," Ven said with a hint of pride. "We have five buildings like this."

The function of an injection moulding machine is simple. One loads it with a steel mould and then pours plastic granules into the cylinder on top. The plastic is liquefied and squirted into the halves of the mould. Out pops a plastic form which is then usually assembled by hand in another part of the factory. The assembly is labour intensive which is why toys are made in countries where workers are cheap. At this time the machines were resting and so were the thousands of workers they probably had stashed away in dormitories somewhere else on the premises.

"Who do you make toys for?" I asked not expecting an answer but Ven replied: "McDonald's, Burger King, Wendy's, Kellogg's, many famous American companies."

I nodded. He was talking about premiums. The cheap give-aways that come with Happy Meals or are shaken out of cornflake packets. As we walked past the idle machines, I glanced around and saw boxes of discarded toys. It seemed they were Disney characters from the latest movie, just as Petersen had said.

"Where are we going?" I asked.

Ven didn't reply this time. He turned briefly to give me a knowing sneer.

We were only half way down the production hall when we turned left. I was still being prodded by a gun from one of the goons which kept me moving in the right direction. It hadn't taken them long to figure out that prodding me in my injured shoulder made me wince with pain. Every time that happened they chortled with pleasure. Ven unlocked another door, this time with a set of Yale keys. We walked down a corridor that was lined with more grey metal doors. He opened the second from last one and indicated for me to step in. A solitary light bulb lit the space.

It appeared to be a storage room for sacks of plastic granules. There were two wooden chairs against the wall and a small barred window high up. As good a prison as any I'd seen in my police days. One of the guards removed the handcuffs. They didn't think I would be squeezing through the bars of the window.

"Can I have some water?" I asked.

Ven just laughed and pulled the door shut. The swish of the key told me he'd turned it twice on the outside. I went to sit down on one of the chairs because the night, the medication and booze had caught up with me. I felt deadly tired and depressingly frustrated.

After a few minutes of rest I explored my prison. There were no tools in the room. Only the bags and in a corner some rat droppings. The room smelt musty and the floor was covered in a thin layer of cement dust. I rattled at the door and found no give. There was nothing more to be done for now.

My watch told me it was two thirty now but somehow I doubted that my taxi driver would be sitting waiting for me at the spot we'd agreed. And if he had come it was unlikely he'd be running to the authorities to report a missing foreigner. He'd been far too scared of this place to get himself involved. Wing Cam would have the police in his pocket and dancing to his tune. You could bet hard currency on that.

Dragging them along with my good left arm, I arranged a series of bags on the floor creating a bed of sorts. I used one bag as a pillow and made myself as comfortable as I could. It was hot in the room and it had been a while since I slept without an air-con or fan but fatigue has its way of overcoming discomfort.

I blanked my mind for the moment, expecting there would be further developments sooner or later. I'd need all my wits and my strength around me. A soldier sleeps anytime he gets the chance.

"Bill, wake up. Are you okay?" someone was saying. It was a woman's voice and I wondered what she was doing in my bedroom. I came up from a dreamless sleep to find that I was not in a comfortable five star hotel but lying with cramped limbs on a bed of nylon sacks filled with plastic pellets. My mouth was dry as a martini and I felt both shaken and stirred.

Kneeling next to me was Brigit Nguyen. Her face was anxious but the expression gave way to relief when I blinked back at her.

"You're a sight for sore eyes," I said. She was wearing a dark blouse and jeans.

"What happened to you?" she asked, laying a hand on my forehead. "You're hot. You don't look good."

I struggled to a sitting position and studied her for a few seconds then ran my palm across her face. I smiled and felt great pleasure seeing her again. She appeared unharmed although her clothes by now were covered in the same cement dust as mine.

"I'm okay and you? Did they mistreat you at all?" I said.

"No," she shook her head. "It's been fine. It was terrible at first but my brother is here and he made sure they did not hurt me."

"Your brother is here after all?"

"He's been working for them all this time. He's important to them so they have to give him respect."

I felt myself frown. "Why did they let you in here?"

"They told me they'd caught you trying to climb over the wall or something and I should bring you some food."

"Did you?"

By way of reply she sat back and revealed a plastic tray on which was a small bottle of locally distilled water and a bowl of white rice topped with scrawny chicken pieces. At this moment it seemed like a meal fit for a king. I reached over and grabbed the bowl and spoon.

"What time is it?" I asked.

"It's eight in the morning," she said and moved up to sit next to me on the sacks. She began stroking my thigh with a dreamy look on her face.

"Stop that, young lady. You might just get me excited and this is not a great venue for ripping your clothes off..."

She giggled and went to whisper in my ear but instead began nibbling it. I shrugged my shoulder and she stuck her tongue inside the ear-hole.

"Stop it," I said again, stifling a laugh. She seemed to be cheerful enough given the fact that we were both imprisoned by a notorious gangster who'd once made her family's life a misery and was starting all over again.

"What are you so relaxed about?" I had to ask her.

She grinned. "Now that you're here things will be alright. I know it."

I stared around the dire room and said, "How the hell do you expect me to make things alright stuck here?"

"You'll find a solution." Brigit looked me deep in the eyes, a flicker of concern showing in hers. "You will find a way out for us, won't you? You did come here to get me and my brother out of this mess, didn't you?"

"Well, sort of."

"You found out where they'd taken me, and then you came after me," she said as if repeating the mantra of my mission.

"I hoped that you'd be here when I figured out it was Wing Cam who was behind all this. But I haven't done a good job so far …getting caught like this."

"It doesn't matter. If they wanted to kill you, they would have done so last night."

I made a noise of disgust, "Now that's a sobering thought you've just put in my head." I chucked her under the chin and could see that behind the cheerfulness lurked a thunderstorm of desperate tears. "Tell me, sweetie. Have you seen or met a woman called Lavender around this compound? She's a Chinese-Filipina, speaks with an American accent?"

Brigit shook her head. I went on: "What exactly is going on here? Why is there so much security and what is your brother's role in this?"

It didn't take her very long to explain and it was pretty much as I'd suspected. Wing Cam was using this remote yet convenient location to manufacture MDMA and its variations. Her brother had specialised in similar synthesised products while at university, even written his thesis on the evolution of designer drugs. Wing Cam had somehow forced him to come and work here and apply his talents.

Once the drugs were complete they were placed inside some of the toys manufactured here and then either shipped out by conventional means or flown out on illegal flights from the enormous airport. It was a perfect location really. An hour and a half's flight East to Hong Kong and China. An hour in the opposite direction to Bangkok or the old US airbase of Korat. Two hours south-west to Phnom Phen, a bit further to Kuala Lumpur and Singapore. And there were many small, abandoned airports or landing strips that could be used in or around those cities and countries. Danang's port was the third largest in the country and could connect with Hong Kong where containers could be loaded onto ships bound for Rotterdam, Felixstowe and Los Angeles. You had to admire the man.

"But why is your brother doing all this? You always told me he's not a criminal. Have you been kidding yourself all along?"

Brigit shook her head and looked down. "It's our family responsibility to Wing Cam. We still owe a debt of honour from the time he helped our family leave Vietnam. It was not washed away by my parents. And

Wing Cam has come back to claim it from my brother. He told Stephen that he wanted five years of service from him and then he'd forget about us."

I stared at her. Asian ways were always strange for us Westerners. "How do you know he will keep his word? Do you trust a man who makes a living from the suffering of others?"

Brigit began to cry because I'd pricked the one bubble of hope she'd been floating on. Cursing myself for the insensitive words, I hugged her and whispered nothings into the top of her head. This was not a nice place to be. It made it worse being with a girl I suddenly cared for because she'd hamper whatever moves I could make. As a man once said, 'a woman hangs on your gun hand when you want to have a clean shot'. Well, these days women were always hanging around when the time came for shooting.

Ten minutes later the door opened and a Vietnamese guard yelled gruff words at the girl. She'd calmed down by now and dried her tears.

"He's telling me I have to go. I'll bring some more food later."

"Try and find out what they've got planned for me. And keep an eye out for that bitch Lavender. If you see her, be careful. She's more vicious than a rabid dog."

Brigit gave me a long look after I said this and then left with the tray and bowl. The door was locked again and I settled back on my makeshift bed. There was nothing else to do, so I began doing breathing exercises and started some basic meditation. My intention was to do this for an hour and if no one had bothered me by then I'd do some of my Wing Chun forms – as best as my injured right arm would allow me.

It was three hours later when they came for me. I'd done my exercises and was resting, running recent events around my mind and asking myself questions that presently were impossible to answer.

The door opened and Ven came in. He held a long black stick which looked very much like the riot baton I'd once found in the back of the armoury of Wong Tai Sin police station. It was the kind of tool you used to subdue recalcitrant prisoners and it had impressed the local population as I strolled down the high street in my pale green uniform with the navy blue peaked cap and the highly polished Sam Browne belt which was the police uniform of colonial Hong Kong.

"Planning to break up a riot, Ven?" I asked. "Or just happy to see me?"

"You talk too much," he replied, glancing around the room to ensure all was in order. I stood up in case he had it in his mind to whack me a few times just for fun.

"What's going on, Ven?" I said.

"You call me Mister Ven. Understand?"

He reminded me of some of the more sadistic prison officers I'd met in the past. They were always telling the prisoners how to address them and they enjoyed the beatings which it was their privilege to hand out.

"Mister Ven," I said and nodded. There was no need to antagonise him. He'd find a time and a place of his own choosing to get angry and work me over with the baton.

"You come and see my boss now." Two different goons were with him this time. They both carried MP5s and gave me hard stares with their black, oriental eyes. Their faces revealed no expression except a dedication to the task at hand. Plastic handcuffs were ratcheted around my wrists again, then I was marched along behind Ven and in front of the two gun-men. We exited the corridor at the opposite end, stepping into a smaller courtyard. From the big production hall we could hear the noise of the injection moulding machines pounding, as they flung out plastic pieces with each 'kerchunk' that sounded not unlike the breech loading of a semi-automatic rifle.

"McDonalds must be happy. Lots of plastic crap for Happy Meals."

Ven turned and half-raised the baton. I shrugged and gave a dry smile. We carried on through the courtyard, entered another building and walked through what appeared to be a canteen. A few men lounged around reading newspapers or smoking cigarettes. At one table a group were playing cards. When they saw Ven they paused respectfully for a short moment. Nobody seemed bothered at the sight of a white man being frog-marched by two armed guards. All in a day's work in the gangsters' paradise.

At the end of the canteen we stepped into another corridor. This time the floor was carpeted and there were pictures on the walls. Nothing fancy, just Vietnamese landscapes that gave the hallway a more homely atmosphere. It was also cooler, indicating air-conditioning coming from somewhere.

We arrived at a wide staircase and ascended three floors. I'd forgotten how hard it is to walk uphill when your hands are tied together. By now the general factory feeling had been replaced by an office environment. We came to a reception area and found two pretty girls answering phones. Ven said something to one of them and she indicated down the corridor. Probably something like 'he's ready to see you now'.

Ven led the way past offices where Vietnamese men and women worked at computers. In one room a group of technicians in lab coats were discussing what could have been a particularly knotty problem. Their senior was drawing a flowchart on the white board with a marker and everyone was staring at him intently. I wondered if there was a clear separation between the legitimate toy business and the illicit drug trade or if it all blended into the same commercial structure.

We came to another open area and found two more guards sitting alertly in armchairs cradling their MP5 submachine guns. It was a fine weapon. I'd fired it many times in training and in action. No well-dressed man in Danang seemed to be without one. The gun has a slightly curved, steel magazine with a 15-round capacity and if you flick the switch to the letter 'F' it fires in fully automatic mode. We always joked that the 'F' stood for 'fucking full-on'.

Over their heads – and accounting for their particularly vigilant demeanour – was a surveillance camera that swept the room languidly.

"Sit here," Ven instructed and pushed me down into an empty blue sofa. He exchanged words with one of the guards and then knocked deferentially on the big oak door. What sounded like a sharp bark came from the other side and Ven entered, closing the door behind him. I smiled at the four men who were left with me.

Somewhere there was a funny story here. How many Vietnamese thugs does it take to guard an Englishman? Three to point their guns at him and one to scowl fiercely?

A moment later Ven was back and snapped at the men to bring me forward. We entered the office and finally I got to meet the man everyone had been talking about.

Wing Cam stood in the centre of the room. A short man in a dark, well-tailored suit with an open-collared shirt. He looked much like his picture although in person there was an aura of violence about him which was oddly tangible. On the fingers of both his hands I noticed diamond rings, mostly large white diamonds but also red, green and turquoise. His hair was slicked back in a style from an earlier decade. He was an oriental Napoleon glaring at me with hard, charcoal eyes. I fancied there was some curiosity in those eyes. He was wondering who or what I was. And I wondered how much he knew about me.

In his hand was my passport, which they had taken from me when they relieved me of my wallet. He tossed the passport on to his desk.

"Welcome to Danang, Mr. Jedburgh. We have been expecting you," he said echoing the words and accent of his henchman Ven, where Northumbrian tones blended with Vietnamese inflections. The air was stale with cigarette smoke.

I cast an eye around the room and found we were not alone. Sitting on the arm of a comfortable chair was Lavender Daai and she was grinning at me. Grinning, as if we had just met at a tennis match. Old friends, not old adversaries. The woman was insane. Well, I knew that.

The short man said, "My name is Wing Cam. Which you will know by now, I'm sure.".

"I know who you are," I replied curtly.

"And this is a mutual friend of ours." He gestured at the girl. "Miss Lavender. I understand you've had business dealings in the past?"

I nodded. "Sort of."

Wing Cam's voice was even. Underneath the politeness I sensed a harsh, vicious personality. It most likely gave him pleasure to disguise it by using the common, polite phrases of daily intercourse. Some people would be lured into underestimating him and he would enjoy revealing his true proclivities. Lavender and Wing Cam were admirably suited, in my estimation, for working together.

"Hello, Bill," Lavender said, shifting slightly on her perch which drew my attention to the tight black clothes she was wearing and her fine, fit body.

It was a huge room dominated by three heavy sofas. Man-sized modern paintings hung on one wall and the other wall was a panoramic window which gazed out over endless rice fields. At the far end was a gargantuan antique desk, at least two metres long. I assumed it to be real. The owner could probably afford such trifles so why bother with copies? Three black telephones were lined up on the desk with two cell phones for good measure and what I recognised as an Macintosh Powerbook. Communication was vital for any business and the boss here didn't need an MBA to understand that.

"Sit down," Wing Cam ordered and he said something to Ven which resulted in my handcuffs being cut off. I massaged my wrists for a while and kept my mouth shut.

"I'm sure you are wondering why you are still alive?" Wing Cam began, after he'd sat down opposite me, hitched up his trousers in a gesture that reminded me of Grosvenor. He reached for a packet of Rothmans Kingsize Filter that lay on a side-table. "If Lavender had her way you'd be dead and buried over there by now," he waved in the general direction of the paddy fields while flicking fire from a gold Dunhill lighter. He blew out a plume of blue smoke from his mouth.

Lavender kept grinning at me. I stared coldly back but concentrated on Wing Cam.

"So you are wondering why are you are still alive, perhaps?" the man repeated rhetorically.

"Yes, I'm surprised," I said cautiously. "I'm sure there is a good reason. You seem to be a man who thinks about his actions carefully and plans wisely. I am impressed with your operation here."

He laughed loudly. "Hah. You are funny when you try to flatter me." He leaned forward and showed me teeth that were stained yellow like the inside of an old teapot. "I think you've been in Asia too long. Getting used to the art of empty compliments. It does not suit an English gentleman. You have to stick to your cultural arrogance."

"I don't consider myself a gentleman any more."

"Whatever, Jedburgh. My associate Lavender tells me you seem a gentleman on the outside but are a thug on the inside. A man after my own heart, I would say. Not that I ever had the benefits of a real education. Mine was on the streets of Newcastle. A harsh but fulfilling place."

"I'm sure it was," I said. Wing Cam gave me a sly, appraising look. I returned it and wondered what my chances were. Ven was standing by the door, silent and watchful. Lavender was quiet and wary, one booted foot touching the burgundy carpet. And then there was the window – an enormous pane of glass. If I leapt at it perhaps it might break, most likely I'd bounce back, only to be shredded by machine-gun fire from the guards outside the room. Another option would be to go for Ven's gun and turn it on Wing Cam. But the firepower opposing me made the odds very poor. Somewhere Lavender was probably hiding that compact Sig Sauer of hers. And my right arm was only half useful.

So I sat tight. Opportunities for escape were limited at this moment.

Wing Cam said: "Lavender here is very pleased that you finally got here. We heard you'd arrived in town and were sniffing around so it was just a matter of time. We have one very important question for you." He paused and took a long drag from the cigarette. "Where is the real package, the one with the real diamond I've been expecting?"

I slowly shook my head. "I have absolutely no idea. I brought a package of diamonds over to Saigon. As I was delivering it your tame bitch here came along, took the package and shot the hell out of an old man."

Lavender shifted on her perch and tut-tutted with her tongue. She was enjoying this. I knew that a solid backbone of sadism ran through her.

Wing Cam said: "I know you brought two packages to Vietnam. One was taken from the hotel safe by Mr. Ven here, the other was obtained by Lavender," Wing

Cam said. His voice dropped a few degrees in temperature. "Neither was worth anything. Where is the real diamond?"

"I don't know, Wing Cam. I guess the real package might be with Milford Grosvenor. But I've never seen it. It wouldn't surprise me if it didn't even exist."

"Of course it fucking well exists," yelled the little man, jumping to his feet and flicking the butt of his cigarette at my face. "We would not be here talking if the package did not exist. I want to know where is my fucking Red Teardrop?"

I shrugged and looked over at Lavender who was studying me with a pensive frown. "I've no idea what the Red Teardrop is or looks like. Grosvenor told me it's a special diamond. I've never seen it."

Wing Cam took a turn around the room and pulled another cigarette from his blue packet. Once he'd lit it he seemed to have calmed down again. He stepped up close and I was tempted for a second to head-butt him. I resisted the urge. The odds in firepower had not changed.

"Do you understand what I do here? This is an amazing place," Wing Cam said. He walked over to the window, his back now turned to me while he carried on: "I make drugs, excellent drugs, the best designer drugs you can imagine. I have outstanding chemists working for me and we experiment all the time." He turned and glared at me, his head half hidden in a cloud of smoke. "But we have not been so good at inventing things lately and so I'm always on the look-out for better ideas. Drugs to me are like any other product. You have to keep coming up with new ideas."

He strode back towards me and stood over me, his legs apart, one hand on his left hip as he sucked the life out of his Rothmans. I risked a glance at Lavender whose face revealed nothing. She'd heard the spiel before and wasn't going to react to it either way.

Wing Cam said: "I make a lot of money. I make millions every month. What do I do with this money? I spend it on beautiful things that increase in value. I invest, Jedburgh. Do you understand?"

I nodded.

"Where is the Red Teardrop diamond?" he demanded. Wing Cam stared at me silently, his eyes boring into mine, his malevolence hanging in the air like the tobacco smoke.

It was best to stick with our original game plan so I said: "I believe Milford Grosvenor has it."

"You don't have it?" Wing Cam asked again.

"I don't."

"Why did you come up here last night?"

"I wanted to check your place out."

"Did you really think," he said with a smirk, "that you could come to my factory and free the girl by yourself?"

I shrugged. "I was going to have a look at the situation."

"What do you think of the situation now?"

"Pretty ugly, Wing, to be honest."

"So, Grosvenor has my diamond."

"What's so special about this one diamond then?" I asked. The look on Lavender's face when I said this was pure disdain. It seemed obvious I was still missing some point here.

"You've convinced me that you don't have the diamond," the drug dealer said. "Ven, we will go and get this Grosvenor guy. Lavender, you take care of Jedburgh here. You can play with him a little bit if you want but don't kill him. He might know more than he's telling us."

The girl grinned and said. "You don't mind if he suffers a bit do you, Wing?"

"Suffer?" said Wing Cam. He turned and smiled at her. "Do what you want with him. Don't kill him until we've got Grosvenor and he's given us the Red Teardrop."

She nodded and got to her feet. Wing Cam swept out of the room.

From somewhere Lavender's Sig Sauer pistol appeared in her hand. I was closer this time and thought it might have been the German police version of the P225 which they called a P6. It's a perfect gun for the well-dressed lady killer. She came over and rested the muzzle on my nose. "I've been waiting to pay you back. Lermontov was my man and I know you killed him."

"Prove it," I said defiantly.

"I don't need to prove it. This isn't a court of law. I know what I know and I'll do what the hell I want." The girl chuckled spitefully.

Well, she had a point there.

13

Not so long ago I had been in a similar situation in the Philippines. That time Lavender had me gagged and bound to a chair with one of her friends drooling over her shoulder, ready to hack all my fingers off.

So I didn't have any delusions that what lay ahead for me was going to be either fast or painless. This was a bad situation and she had been left in charge.

Ven had put the cuffs back on and they marched me down the corridors along which we'd come. My mind was working hard to find solutions but I kept coming back to the obvious problem which was that Lavender wanted to enjoy her slice of revenge. There was nothing I knew now which was of interest to her or Wing Cam.

My only tiny hope was Brigit but I couldn't see how she could help when Lavender held the gun. Brigit probably had no idea what was happening to me now and was locked up as well.

Ven and Lavender took me to another room, this one was bare and empty except for what appeared to be a kitchen table in the centre. Each table leg was encircled with chains and the idea was obvious. The prisoner had to lie on the table and his arms and legs were restrained, spreadeagling him or her. It was an effective debilitating position. A position that allowed the captors to visit all manner of abuse on the captive.

I hesitated for an instant but could see no room for action. Ven, Lavender and the guards had me fully covered. Attacking them would be futile. I'd have to play the game as best as I could.

"Go lie on the table," the girl said. Her voice was cold and commanding.

"You sound like my doctor."

"I'll be your doctor, mother, father, uncle and priest by the time we've finished, honey," she said.

"You've got way too much anger bottled up inside you. That's not healthy."

"Get the hell on that table and stop screwing around," she ordered, her voice rising a tone. She grabbed my upper arm with her hand and the pain shot all the way down to my toes. I did as I was told, resting my buttocks first on the rough wooden surface, extending my arms, spreading my legs. It felt as if I was about to be crucified which, judging by the glint in her eyes, was pretty much what the hell-cat had in mind.

What chance of outside help was there, I wondered, as Ven shackled my wrists? You have to keep positive in these situations. He wrapped the chains around three times, then snapped them shut with bronze Yale padlocks.

"Comfortable?" Lavender asked. She was standing at the far end of the table. Raising my head I could see her between my feet. She'd stashed the pistol in the small of her back. A chilly smile played around her lips.

"How the hell did you get involved with Wing Cam? He seems a nasty piece of work," I said, trying to develop a dialogue. Anything to delay what was ahead.

"Nastier than me, do you think?" she asked playfully.

"Oh, you're nasty. You're like a gorgeous apple that has a worm eating through the core."

"That's a nice description," she said. "The last time, I didn't know you were a professional. This time we are going to do this properly."

I rolled my eyes. "Fuck you, Lavender."

"That's not going to happen. But, maybe," she paused and considered, "maybe I'll fuck you up with a long hard object. Would you like that? Something up your anus. I've been told that you English men like it up the arse because you were all sodomised at school when you were young."

"Ha-ha," I replied.

Ven had completed checking my shackles and now he retreated to a corner of the room. He said to Lavender, "What do you intend to do with him?" He seemed genuinely intrigued.

"Stay and watch, if you like," she said. Turning to back to me she asked, "Tell me what happened when you killed Lermontov?"

"I didn't kill him. I heard that the Reliable Man killed him."

"You killed him, I know it. My father put you up to it. That old bastard."

"Can we just get on with the main show?" I said.

"In a hurry to die, are you?"

"It's what you want to do, isn't it? Kill me. So get on with it." I wasn't sure of the wisdom of baiting her but it was all that was in my head at that moment.

She laughed, a low hoarse noise that came from the back of her throat. "Not so fast. I know that's what you want. You want me to get it over with quickly. But we're going to do this slowly." Her eyes glittered with a manic energy. She turned to Ven. "You don't have to be here. I can take care of this fucker by myself."

"It's up to you," he said nodding, a hint of disappointment in his voice. He really wanted to see what Lavender had in mind. That was partially professional curiosity, I guessed, and partially he knew that the girl was off her rocker and he wanted to make sure she didn't disobey his boss and kill me. Not until Wing Cam had given the green light.

"I'll leave you two then," he said, after a moment's hesitation.

Once the door had closed there was silence in the room. It was unbearably hot because the windows were not open and there was no fan. Lavender stalked around the table top, enjoying the sight of me strapped down.

I could feel my heart pounding like sub-woofers at a rock concert.

I didn't know how or when she wanted to start. I had no idea what she had in mind. She checked the chains again and found them to be secure. There was no way I could wriggle free.

"How does that feel?" she asked maliciously.

"It feels uncomfortable, to tell you the truth."

She stood over my face and our eyes locked. She ran a fingernail down my cheek. At any moment I was expecting her to dig them into my eyes. Blinding me was entirely within the scope of Wing Cam's instructions. But she simply stroked me, smiling coldly.

"You want to know what I'm going to do, don't you?" she said.

"Yes."

"We'll get to that part later. Don't worry. I'll make you feel pain you never knew existed. Lermontov showed me some of his KGB secrets."

I swallowed; my throat was dry while my entire body was soaked in perspiration from fear and from the humidity. Next I would lose control of my bladder and piss myself. And that would make me feel very stupid. It would please her, to see me lose control.

"Does Wing Cam really want to know where the Red Teardrop diamond is?" It was my best shot, hoping that the information might just be more important at this stage than her revenge.

"It's too late for that now." Slowly she began unbuttoning my shirt, starting with the top button. When she was done, she winked and yanked hard on my chest hairs. "You already told him you don't know where it is. You haven't even got a clue what it is. You think it's just some fancy diamond."

"Isn't it?"

Lavender laughed like the maniac she was. "It's a special diamond. It's worth a fortune."

"I know where Grosvenor hid it. We came up together and he is planning to sell it to Wing Cam."

"Where is it?" she asked.

"I'll tell Wing Cam."

"You're just bullshitting. You are terrified, aren't you?" Lavender stared hard into my eyes, some perspiration from her face falling on mine - the room was terribly hot - then said, "I'm going to leave you for a while and get my stuff. Then you can try telling me again where the diamond is." She chuckled hoarsely and stepped out of my view.

Nothing can prepare you for the kind of pain that comes when you are tortured by an expert. I knew this to be a fact from what I had been told by men over beers in dark pub corners.

I stared at the ceiling and tried to rein in my imagination. She could cut off my eyelids. She could punch holes in my throat. She could slice off parts of my skin. Pull out my fingernails. Cut off my testicles...

We'd done some interrogations in the police but the object had always been to leave no visible marks and the subject had to be able to walk away from the cell and appear unscathed in a court room.

If they complained, there could be no physical evidence to substantiate their words. Without some form of coercion few criminals admitted their crimes. That was not the case here. Wing Cam had given Lavender permission to play with me, to entertain herself, to indulge in her psychopathic urges. I was at the mercy of her sadistic creativity.

I considered how she had turned out so evil. Where had it all begun? Her father had been a gangster, but of the old school. He had a streak of decency in him, I recalled. He was tough yet fair. A thug with principles. Where had it all gone wrong for Lavender Daai, to turn her from convent girl into vicious torturer? Had her father's genes mutated into something more spiteful? Had her father ignored her, treated her badly, even abused her? It didn't seem likely, although Asians had a vast capacity for cruelty and much of it was practised on their immediate family members.

Concentrating, I tried to keep my breathing calm. What would come would come. I was not going to give her the benefit of seeing me beg and plead. At least it wasn't my intention to give in. There was no telling what would happen once she came at me with a scalpel or even hallucinogenic drugs. What brutality was trapped in that beastly brain of hers?

It could have been five minutes or twenty before I heard footsteps on the corridor and the she-devil was back.

"No Houdini then?" she said and checked that all my chains were still secure. I didn't reply. In her other hand was what looked like a black doctor's bag. She placed it on the floor and we made eye-contact. Her little evil grin was back.

"I was there when your father died," I heard myself saying although the thought had not formed itself before the words came out.

She paused. A glint of anger in her pupils this time. "Do you think I care about your relationship with my father?"

"He was a good guy. He loved you a lot."

"Bullshit." She spat the words at me, droplets of saliva hitting me on the cheek.

"He was a good guy," I repeated.

"He was an old bastard. You know that. He took what he could get and made others suffer."

"Like his daughter then." They were not the words I'd wanted. I wanted conciliation and reflection. But my guts were giving me anger and frustration.

She laughed. "You've got that right, Bill. Like father like daughter. Except as far as you're concerned I'm ten times the nightmare he could ever have been."

"So you're trying to outdo him? Is that what this is all about?"

Lavender walked around the top of the table. My eyes followed her, waiting for a reaction. Waiting for words or for a punch. I was annoying her and it felt satisfying. Given my situation it was madness to goad her. Was I hoping she'd lose her temper and finish me off quickly? She'd never do it. She was too smart for that. She wanted a slow, pleasurable progression of pain for me.

"My father had no time for me so I made my own way. And when I began to understand how the world worked I realised that he was just an old style Triad bully. There was nothing special about him."

"But he cared for you," I said.

"Maybe he did. In the end. It was too late by then. I'd lost any respect a girl could ever have for her father."

"And so this is what you've become? A harder, more vicious, less balanced version of him?"

She didn't like that. "Enough," she yelled and her hand struck my face so hard I could feel the blood immediately from the split lip. It trickled down my chin and along my neck.

There was silence in the room for a few seconds. She was breathing hard, staring down at my face. Ordinarily she could be an attractive young woman, now her features were infused with shadows that made her appear haggard and malevolent.

"Let's get on with it," she said matter-of-fact. A moment later she had the doctor's bag open and was brandishing a diminutive hammer with a rounded head. It looked harmless but I had an idea of its dangers.

"You are a shooter, aren't you? You were trained to fire guns? It's what you like to do?" she gloated. I said nothing.

Lavender took my right arm, holding it tight. She felt with her fingers, noticing the bandage covering the wound made by her bullet. "Is this where I shot you?" She prodded with a vicious index finger. She found the spot, found the stitches. "Here. Is this it?" My arm and head exploded in a world of pain. She dug and pushed and prodded and her smile grew bigger as I squirmed around on the table, gritting my teeth and when I couldn't hold the agony inside, letting it out by cursing her.

Hard Anglo-Saxon words poured from my mouth but she didn't relent. She kept on jabbing into the wound. Then when I was least expecting it, she let go. I inhaled a deep breath of humid air. A wave of relief swept over me, so intense that I missed the real purpose of what was happening. She'd grabbed my right wrist, forced it hard against the table top.

An instant before it happened I realised what she was about to do. All I could do was gnash my teeth, screw my eyes tight, in preparation for the pain. The little hammer fell swift and hard on my trigger finger shattering the bones. I opened my eyes and saw the hammer rise again, heard it strike again but without the pain, as if they were another man's fingers. Then when the nerves caught up and transmitted to my brain what I'd seen, I lost consciousness instantly.

"You disappoint me. You really do," the girl's voice said and I felt cold water splashing over my head forcing me back into the craven reality of my situation.

I remembered my finger, twisting my head sideways to see the damage. It was black and blue and bent but at least no bones were poking out through the skin. I groaned in despair. This was only the beginning. It was the most important finger. And she had destroyed it with a swift surgeon's movement. Tap, tap, tap. At least the pain was bearable. My body had shot adrenalin to all its extremities and for now it was like looking at someone else's limb. But that wouldn't last too long. It was a mangled mess and it would make itself felt later, sharply and surely.

"Did you think I'd use chemicals?" Lavender asked. She was perched on the right side of the table now. One hand resting on my thigh, an empty water bottle in her other hand. She had doused me with the water to wake me up.

"You... " I began but the words fizzled away. There was no point in wasting breath. I tried to lick the liquid from my face. I was thirsty as a mongrel dog in summer.

"Now, we're just getting started," she said conversationally and reached down to flourish the vile hammer again. "Lermontov told me that pure torture is all about pure pain. Truth drugs and serums are for the weak. It takes guts to beat the shit out of a man.... Or cut strips of flesh out of him. Chemicals are only there for later. To prolong the agony. To stop the victim from slipping away." I flinched as she tapped the hammer lightly on the table top next to my head, two inches from my ear. "We're going to have some fun, Bill."

She tapped the hammer again, harder this time.

"No. I'm going to have fun," she corrected herself, "and you're just going to lie there and scream... Does that sound fair to you? Pretty fair to me." The monster within her had taken control of her features again and she appeared as ugly as a shrivelled witch, keening on the heath.

She frowned suddenly, as an idea struck her, and stood up. She dropped the hammer into her bag and walked over to the window, opening it. "We need a fan in here. It's too damn stuffy," she said partially to herself.

She was gone for ten minutes while I lay on the kitchen-table doing breathing exercises waiting for the ache in my arm to subside and the agony from my finger to commence.

What was next? Which extremity of my body did she have in her sights for the second round? How long would this go on for? A day or two? Would Grosvenor come looking for me? Did Brigit know this was going on? What hope was there for survival? And of surviving with some form of decency. I could not let this bitch make me slobber in self-pity. I had to deal with the pain. I had to contain it. But how far could she push me? I'd never been pushed this far and, as she'd reminded me, this was just the beginning of the journey.

When she came back it was with a small standing fan that she placed on one of the tables. She plugged it into an outlet in the corner and a cool breeze began to waft around her work bench.

"That's better. I hate getting all sweaty and smelly," Lavender said. She came over to the table and reached for her hammer once more.

"The nose I think. A handsome hunk like you. A squashed nose is just what you need."

I braced myself for the blow but it never came.

"Leave him for now," Wing Cam's voice came from where I knew the door to be.

"I haven't even started yet," she replied, with a note of petulance.

"Ven says he heard him say he does know where the Red Teardrop is."

"Was Ven listening at the door?" she said. "Jedburgh's just bluffing. Let me work him over some more."

"You can have him later. Bring him back up to my office. I want to talk with him again." A billow of Rothmans smoke came at my nostrils. If I hadn't been tied down I would have gotten on my knees to kiss Wing Cam's feet.

There was silence for a while. I watched Lavender's face cloud over with fury. Then I heard Wing Cam say: "Now, girl."

That tone brooked no argument. But she wasn't happy.

This time it was only Wing Cam and Ven in the room. I had an ice pack on the broken index finger of my right hand and the cuffs were on again.

"She's a hell-cat that girl and she hates you pretty bad," Wing Cam said as he lit another cigarette. He smiled at me with his tea coloured teeth. The phone rang on his desk and he took the call barking Vietnamese commands down the line for a full five minutes.

"Your partner Milford Grosvenor. You came down with him right?"

I shrugged. There was no point in denying something every hotel employee could verify.

"He's gone, checked out of the hotel this morning. Was that part of your plan?"

"We didn't really have a plan. We came up here to sell you the Red Teardrop. And I wanted you to let Brigit go."

"So he has the diamond on him?"

"No, he doesn't. I was taking care of it. But maybe he has it now and that's why he's disappeared."

"We searched your room and his room already. There was nothing."

"I wasn't going to leave it in an obvious place." By now I had decided this was the best strategy to pursue. Lie as convincingly as I could about knowing where the diamond was.

"Where did you hide the diamond?" He stared at me coldly.

"If you let me go, I can bring you to my hotel room where I hid it."

He laughed. It was more like the bark of an Alsatian but it passed for humour with the man. "You think you still want to sell the Red Teardrop to me? Listen to this fool, Ven. The girl must have smashed his brains not his finger with that little hammer of hers." He took a deep puff from the latest Rothmans he'd lit. "I offer you a trade. Your life for the real diamond. If you really have it. If Grosvenor has it then you are out of luck. No deal. Back to the hell-cat and her toys."

This was my only chance and I had to make it sound convincing. I had to make Wing Cam believe that I really did have what he was after so he would let me go back to the hotel. Once there I had more opportunities to get out of this situation than here in this armed fortress. It was unlikely Brigit could help me and I was not counting on Grosvenor to storm the toy factory despite the weapons he had packed into the back of his vehicle.

"The Red Teardrop is hidden in a certain place in my hotel room. I'll show you where it is if you let me go back there. There is no way anyone can find it unless they know where to look."

Wing Cam weighed up my words. He picked up one of his phones and made a call, followed by a few more. Finally he said:

"You used to be a policeman in Hong Kong? I lived in Hong Kong for four years. In an internment camp for Vietnamese refugees. That's what they called us. We were locked up like animals. The men separated from the women. And you know what was my crime?"

"I don't."

"My crime was to want to be free to make money. To live like a normal person. So I had fled my country and the communists. We took a boat, a small fishing boat that was not intended to go so far and we were on the ocean for one week. We ran out of drinking water and food. Children died. My brother fell overboard and was eaten by sharks that had been trailing us. Then just before the boat started sinking we made it to Hong Kong waters. We thought we were free and had made it to a new life but instead we were locked up. Can you understand what that felt like?"

"I have an idea," I said.

"No, nobody like you, white and with your colonial attitude can understand what it was like to be a refugee and then, when we had lost everything, to be treated like scum and even lose our basic human respect."

I studied his bitter features. There was no knowing from which deep well of anger this lecture had come from. He'd obviously been through a hard time. I knew what he was talking about. Thousands and thousands of boat people landed on the shores of Hong Kong in the eighties and the only way of dealing with them was to pack them into internment camps. Many of the men were violent, with military backgrounds that made it easy for them to kill each other over a minor slight or a small advantage. Someone like Wing Cam would have been a hard, cruel man before he set sail from his impoverished home country. The tough experiences of a refugee would not have formed him but simply burnished the steel that was his personality.

"But in the end you were accepted to live in the UK. That was worth the wait wasn't it?"

He gave a resentful growl. "What do you think it was like as a young Vietnamese man in a country like England? Nobody wanted us and everyone hated us. Tell him, Ven. Tell this Englishman how we were hated by his people when all we wanted was to make a living."

Ven nodded grimly. He rolled up one of his sleeves and exposed what looked like a spider's web of scars.

"Chopper attack from the Chinese gangs." Then he raised his other hand and showed me something I had not noticed before. The tip of his ring finger was missing. "That was a local Geordie gang who tried to muscle in on our grocery shops."

I composed my face in a mask of empathy. It wasn't understanding that these men were seeking. I assumed they wanted respect for the hard times they had lived through. Respect for how far they'd come. From the mean streets of Newcastle to this multi-million dollar toy factory that serviced the needs of kids the world over – both the little ones that wanted to play and the older ones that wanted a high.

"I want you to let the girl Brigit go free."

"What do you care about her?" Wing Cam said.

"I don't care much about her but this has nothing to do with her. She is confused about her brother and his loyalty to you. If I get you the real package, let me and her go. I'll be gone from Vietnam within a day."

He considered me with a sly smile. Ven spoke a rapid sentence in Vietnamese which I assumed was something along the lines of 'let's get the diamond from him and then we'll kill them all afterwards.' If Wing Cam knew only part of my background he would never consider leaving me alive, but it was a chance I had to take, mainly to find opportunities for escape along the way. While I was strapped on the table with Lavender ready to poke my eyes out, my chance of survival was less than zero. Now things were decidedly looking up.

"You can have the girl, if you want. She is just distracting Stephen."

"Is Stephen important to you?"

The small tyrant nodded. "He is one of our best. The other's have learnt from experience but Stephen has the education that means he can analyse and deconstruct compounds like nobody else I have. Yes, he is important. But nobody is indispensable." He considered me for a while then reached for one of the Motorolas that was strapped to his belt. He gave some instructions over the phone and turned back to me. "You get me my Red Teardrop, I'll let you and the girl go. You will leave Vietnam within twenty-hours or Ven here will find you and hand you over to Lavender. Is that a good deal?"

I nodded. "The package is none of my business. I delivered it and that was enough. What you're up to here is none of my business." It was funny because I knew he was lying as much as I assumed he knew that I was lying. But if he actually believed my words then it gave me an edge. A part of me very much liked the idea of walking away from it all. But leaving Lavender and this man to carry on with what they were doing here turned my stomach. If I could get out of this one alive, I would have to come back and exterminate Lavender. She was far too dangerous and far too vicious a creature to have running around free.

"Ven has something else to do, so I will tell Lavender to bring you back to your hotel. Don't try anything. You know she is good." Wing Cam squinted at me as the smoke rose up from his latest Rothmans. A hard smile played around his lips.

14

Riding back into town in a Mercedes with dark windows I wondered if my taxi driver from the previous night was cursing me for the half dollar bills he'd been left with. I guessed that he'd tipped off Wing's organisation to my presence so it was unlikely he'd ever collect on that fare.

"What are you smiling at?" Lavender demanded. She was in the front seat and had turned to keep an eye on Brigit and myself who were trussed in the back with the usual plastic cuffs and the additional security of the seat belts.

"Private joke," I said. Brigit stared at me as if I'd just put my head in the jaws of a crocodile. She had spent enough time recently with Lavender to know that you did not make flippant remarks which might antagonise her. Try as I might, I could not control myself. Goading the bitch was the only way I could cope with my feelings of anger towards her.

The driver was one of the men who had been with Ven before. He'd hardly spoken but the scar across the side of his neck made it clear he was a man of violence. He guided the big German car through the streets, leaning briefly on the horn when a scooter or bicycle got too close. He rarely reduced speed. You could tell it would be of no consequence to him if anyone accidentally strayed into the path of the motor and bounced off the bonnet.

I thought of what we would find at the hotel. Grosvenor had obviously decamped. He must have got nervous when I disappeared and thought I was double-crossing him. We'd not known each other for long so it was a fair assumption to make. All he knew about me was that I was a malleable opportunist who didn't bat an eyelid at smuggling diamonds.

Most likely he was still in the area, hunkered down and waiting for the right time to get in touch with Wing Cam. If I had been in his position I would have pulled back and gone somewhere more low-profile, but that was hard in a one-horse town like Danang where a white man stood out like a red poppy in a wheat field.

Finally we pulled up at the Furama Hotel. Its comforting colonial style façade reminded me of how bad my day had been so far. I should have stayed here last night and worked things through with Grosvenor instead of trying to do a recce on the lion's den and then getting myself caught like an amateur. I should have known better than that. I must be losing both my mind and my touch.

I glanced over at Brigit whose face, normally such a pleasant light-brown hue, seemed nearly as pale as a shroud. I gave her a wink feigning a confidence that I had not yet found within myself. But I had to pretend. I stared blankly at Lavender who scowled at me over the top of her gun. They'd decided that turning up mob-handed would raise too many eyebrows. But if I arrived at the hotel with two pretty Asian ladies that would seem perfectly normal. The plan was for Brigit to stay in the car, guarded by the driver. Once I handed over the Red Teardrop to Lavender and she was satisfied it was the real deal she would call Wing Cam, then Brigit and I would be set free. It had sounded quite sensible when Wing Cam proposed it but of course it was a load of horse manure. The moment Wing Cam had what he wanted I'd get a bullet between the eyes. I knew that would make her angry, she wanted to torture me, not give me a quick, clean exit. But for now we were all pretending it made sense and sticking to our lines.

"You don't have the package. I know," she said. Her eyes got smaller. "Wing Cam should know better than to fall for that bullshit. We'll finish yet what we started." To emphasise her point she tapped the muzzle of her Sig Sauer on the back of her seat.

I simply nodded.

"The girl stays here with Owen. You walk in front of me. I'll have the gun in my coat pocket and I'll be a yard behind. Don't speed up or slow down. Any sudden movement I'll just shoot you in the back. We don't want to scare any of the tourists and give the hotel a problem but I really don't care. If I have to kill you there in the lobby it doesn't matter to me. I'll just get back in the car and drive off and Wing Cam will sort it out with the local police and the hotel management." She paused and raised her eyebrows. "Do you get it?"

"I get it."

"Everything clear with you, Owen?" she asked the driver. He grunted in confirmation. With a western name it was likely he'd been one of Wing Cam's gang in England but he wasn't much of a talker.

"Right, get out," she said pointing a red-varnished fingernail at me. I hesitated a second, looking into her large brown eyes. What a shame that a woman who was so attractive was so evil. I'd come across a few like her before, but she was the worst. Even the Indonesian bitch had had some redeeming features. Or perhaps - on second thoughts - they were cut from the same cloth that was woven in some dark recess of the Seventh Circle of Hell.

I stood at the bottom of the steps waiting for her to come around the front of the car. She nodded for me to proceed. The bell-boys glanced at me with little curiosity, they looked more carefully at Lavender, admiring the form. She must be an expensive one, would have been going through their heads.

I stood in the middle of the lobby, waiting.

"Get your key."

The receptionist passed me a note that was in my pigeon hole along with the heavy key ring. I pocketed it quickly, unsure if Lavender had noticed. The receptionist smiled at both of us and then turned away to answer a phone.

We walked over to the lifts, where Lavender stood close enough for me to smell the perfume she was wearing. She must have sprayed it on before we got in the car. I had an idea it was Dolce & Gabbana. All the airline girls had been wearing it when it was launched. I watched her eyes carefully but she was so wary that making any move would have been fatal. This would be difficult, far more difficult than I had imagined.

A short, chubby Japanese man emerged from the lift bowing as they always do and allowing us to take his place. He'd be a manager in one of their local electronic factories.

I said nothing while she watched me carefully, tapping her right booted foot to an unheard melody. The lift stopped at my floor.

"You first," Lavender ordered.

I went down the corridor to my room and opened the door.

"Go stand by the bed."

I did as I was told.

"Where is the package?"

"It's in my laptop."

"Get it out."

"It's under the bed."

She regarded me suspiciously. "How can it be in your laptop?"

"It's in one of the two battery compartments. There is a false back. I've configured it to hide stuff."

"Stand back from the bed."

She'd pulled the Sig out from her pocket by now and was waving it at me. I stepped backwards towards the connecting door. Once she was sure I was far enough from her, she bent down and pulled aside the counterpane to check if the laptop case was there. She found it and pulled it out with her left hand.

I smiled at her caution and admired her backside. If you had to die violently, it might as well be at the hands of an attractive woman. But better to die an old man's death, in bed, surrounded by all your ex-wives and grand-children.

She nudged the laptop case with her foot and said, "Get it out."

I stepped forward and pulled it towards me then slowly placed it on the small table by the window.

"Be very careful. Any funny moves and you are dead."

"I'm well aware of that," I replied dryly, gently unzipping the black nylon case. All I was doing was playing for time. I had no idea if the package was still there. The Compaq Contura laptop did not look as if it had been touched. I took it out from the carry case and turned it over, slipping the catches that held one of the battery compartments in place. This was a model that had been designed for additional battery power and it had not taken much work to reconfigure the space for concealment.

I fiddled with the catches while keeping her in sight. It was good news, the dummy battery came out and behind it, tucked away, was the package. Neither Grosvenor nor Ven had known where to look. The problem of course was that this still wasn't the Red Teardrop. They were my diamonds which I was planning to sell in the Philippines. But they were wrapped up in the same way and they were not worthless.

"It's here," I said.

"Toss it over," she said sharply. The muzzle of the Sig was dark and lethal. The theory was that people telegraph in their eyes when they are ready to pull the trigger. In my limited experience that was simply nonsense.

"This is bullshit, isn't it?" Lavender said. She was hefting the duct taped package in her hand. "This isn't the real Red Teardrop either, is it? It's been a fake all along."

I shrugged. "Frankly, I have no fucking idea. All this diamond shit has had me confused since the beginning. I can't tell a ruby from a cherry lozenge."

She smiled grimly. "I don't care if this is the real one or not. I'll tell Wing Cam you didn't have it."

I squared off against her. "Okay. Do it then."

She shook her head. "Too easy. I need you to suffer more."

I was straining to watch her eyes. I wanted to see that twitch in case there was one. It was usually me at the other end of the gun pulling the trigger and so I hadn't done much research standing on this side of the muzzle.

"Do it," I taunted her.

"On your knees," she ordered me.

That part wasn't in my escape plan.

"On your knees," she barked. I swayed forward a bit, not sure what my next move was going to be. Then a gun popped twice and for an instant I was waiting for the pain to set in.

But it wasn't her gun. It was someone else's. And a gun with a suppressor on it. Not a lot of noise.

Standing in the partition door that separated my room from the next one was Hank Petersen, the bum from Christie's. But this time he was sober and there was a very sharp edge to his words as he shouted at the girl: "Drop your weapon now. Drop it or I will shoot to kill."

I looked from the girl to the American and back again. Lavender's face was a mask of fury. But she hadn't been hit.

Kill her, Hank. Kill her. But my mouth was silent. I was watching her gun hand. Her muzzle was still pointing at me and she could swing at him or just blast at me. Behind her head I could see the two bullet holes in the wall. I wouldn't have fired any warning shots. I would have taken her out, first chance I got.

I dived sideways, behind the useless cover of the rattan arm chair. That was enough distraction to make her flinch and hesitate some more. Hank advanced on her and finally she saw reason and dropped the Sig on the carpet. It bounced once and I grabbed it with my left hand before anyone else could.

"I'm a Federal Agent. Hank Petersen, Drug Enforcement Administration," he said to the girl. "Do not move or I will shoot to kill. Bill, don't do anything funny with that gun. I'm trying to help you here."

"Sure, that's cool with me. Watch her. She can be unpredictable."

"Here's a pair of cuffs. Put them on her, Bill." He tossed them over and I got her to kneel down now and snapped the metal tight around her wrists.

"This isn't over," Lavender said, spitting saliva with her words as they came out of her mouth.

For me, this bit - the one where I was in her custody - was over. That was good enough for now.

I could have bought Hank Petersen a bottle of Scotland's finest but he wasn't interested in any liquor this time round.

He explained rapidly that the DEA had been observing drug manufacturing activity in Danang and he had a small team in town. However they were unofficial and effectively illegal. The Vietnamese would never allow an American law enforcement agency to run freely around their country.

Part of being undercover had been his identity as the local expat drunk. He'd been good at it, I congratulated him. He'd fooled me and I'd a lot of experience with drunkards.

"We're after a guy called Wing Cam, as you probably realise," Petersen was saying. "The trouble is, he's too damn influential here. We just don't have enough on him yet and in Vietnam we can't bring him down. We need to arrest him when he's in a country that cooperates with the United States, like Thailand or Hong Kong."

Lavender sat cross-legged on the floor, glaring at us, like a black Panther finally trapped in a cage after a long hunt.

"What's the next step then?" I asked.

"We've got a safe house. We'll get her there and ask her some questions."

"There's a driver in a Merc downstairs guarding a girl who is a friend of mine. She's a hostage," I said.

He nodded. "Let's handle that carefully. If we can jump him without any fuss that would be good."

There was a second man with Petersen who looked Thai but spoke with an American accent. Petersen called him Chuckee. He produced a handkerchief and a roll of duct tape. He jabbed Lavender in the stomach with a Glock he was carrying. When she opened her mouth to breathe he rammed the handkerchief in and then wrapped it tight with two turns of the duct tape.

"Can you mask her eyes. I hate her staring at us like that," I said rubbing the various parts of my body that were fused with pain. From the bathroom I took my box of medicines and swallowed a few tablets with tap water. The second man ignored my request. Lavender was sitting cross-legged on the floor and he had his gun to her head for good measure. I liked the look of things.

"What is this shit?" Petersen was saying indicating the wrapped package and the open laptop.

"Who knows," I said, shaking my head. "I thought it was a diamond but then it wasn't the right diamond and now it could be baking powder for all I know." I picked up the duct-taped package and slipped it casually into my front pocket.

"How did you get mixed up in this?" he asked.

I looked at him for a while, then replied, "Doing favours for people who don't appreciate me."

He studied me for a while. There was something he knew but was not ready to talk about. He was treating me like one of the good guys but how did he know I wasn't one of Wing Cam's business associates who had fallen out with Lavender? I had an idea about that and it annoyed me. But you can't complain about being rescued by the U.S. Cavalry.

He gave me a knowing smile. "Let's get to the safe house."

"Okay, how the hell are we going to handle this?"

"Chuckee, you stay here and keep an eye on this bitch. Bill, I'll trust you with a gun. Don't get any ideas of cutting loose. We're your best bet of getting out of here alive."

"I'm not going anywhere. I have unfinished business to attend to." I cocked my head at the girl on the floor.

"We'll go down and check out the Merc and then decide how to approach it."

I took Lavender's Sig, removed the magazine, worked the action and replaced the round. It felt well-maintained and clean to the touch.

We descended in the lift and walked back through the lobby. Nobody paid us any attention. When we got to the last column Petersen peered cautiously around it. The Merc had moved forward ten metres and parked under some trees that partially hid it from the front entrance. With the windows tinted it was impossible to tell if they were still inside.

"You see that tree?" Petersen said. "Move around the side and go and stand there. They can't see you from the front but you can give me cover if I need it."

I told him that was clear. The Sig felt good tucked into the waist-band of my trousers under my shirt. He waited until I'd taken up position behind the tree. I pretended to be lighting a cigarette. The door-man was nowhere to be seen.

Petersen came out and staggered, doing his drunk routine to perfection as usual. He appeared to be heading for the car third in line next to the Merc. It was a battered Toyota Crown. It looked like he dropped his keys for a moment. He bent down to pick something up, then turned, which brought him closer to the Mercedes.

He staggered some more and I reached for the butt of the Sig. He'd have to move fast unless the guy in the car was asleep.

Petersen jumped like a cat. He ducked behind the second car, reappeared and tore open the driver's door of the Merc. Then there seemed to be a struggle.

Petersen's body half disappeared, then reappeared with a crooked smile. He beckoned me over, a black cosh in his hand. The driver was unconscious. Brigit huddled in the back, a look of confusion on her face. I winked at her.

I helped Petersen drag the driver out of the car and we slung him into the bushes.

"We'll leave him here. He can't tell Wing Cam much," Petersen said. He pulled out his mobile phone and called Chuckee, telling him to come down the service staircase with the girl and meet us by their pickup truck. I managed to free Brigit and we walked away from the Mercedes without anyone from the hotel having seen what had happened.

The base for the DEA's undercover operation in Danang was a commonplace Chinese style shophouse. We drove into a downstairs area that served as a garage and parked behind three Honda Dream bikes.

Chuckee pulled the folding gates shut, padlocking them from the inside, while we walked up the stairs to the first floor.

Brigit was in shock, shivering white-faced and not saying a word. Petersen dragged Lavender along by the arm. She was being awkward but not really resisting. He told her to sit in one of the PVC arm chairs that were clustered around the centre of the long wide room. At one end was a dining table on which stood four computers and monitors.

"You should have killed her when you had the chance," I said to Petersen nodding at Lavender.

"It's not standard procedure for us to kill people," he said with a sardonic smile and went to a small fridge from which he extracted several bottles of the local mineral water, tossing Brigit and me one and dropping another into Lavender's lap.

Petersen offered me a cigarette from his pack of Red Marlboro and we both lit up. He then got a monster-sized first aid kit and taped up my broken finger tightly.

"Call me old fashioned," he went on, "I think everyone should be given a fair chance."

"This woman is about as dangerous as they come."

"I believe you but where I come from we have some pretty mean bitches and I've dealt with some of them."

"Hmm," was my reply to that.

"Tell me your story then," he said. "You seem to know how to handle a weapon."

I shook my head cautiously and accepted a glass he was offering me into which he'd poured two fingers of Johnny Walker whisky. "Take the edge off," he suggested.

"I was in the Royal Hong Kong Police for many years," I said. "We got to see dead bodies but we didn't have to do much shooting. I was in VIP protection for a while and their equivalent of your SWAT teams."

He nodded and smiled. It seemed to me that he already knew this. He wouldn't be treating me this nicely if I was just the stranger he'd met at Christie's. We'd walked to the other end of the room where the girls couldn't hear our conversation. He pulled out two chairs at the dining table and invited me to sit down.

"We've been working this for three months here, trying to get enough evidence on Wing Cam to put an international arrest warrant together. But the man is slippery." He emptied his glass of whisky in one quick shot and pursed his lips making a hissing sound. "Sometimes we'd all just like to do it the easy way. Walk up to the man in a restaurant and take him out. Save the tax payer a whole bunch of money."

I shrugged. "No comment."

He laughed. "Never going to happen. Forget I said that."

"You care about your job," I said.

"Just getting rid of nasty drug dealers."

"Someone has to do it. How long have you been with the DEA?"

"I've been with the Agency ten years. I was with the CIA for nearly fifteen years before that. I've seen drugs doing bad things to our youth and I've seen politics and terrorism use the drug trade for their own purposes."

"You're a man of conviction."

"My niece died from a heroin overdose."

"That's close to home."

"And my grandson lost half his mind to ecstasy and now spends his time painting pictures that make Edvard Munch's Scream look like a man having a bad hair day."

"Shit."

"It all starts with people like Wing Cam and his hangers-on. Like Lavender Daai. We've got a big file on her as well."

"So how come you turned up in my hotel room just at the right time?"

He laughed and poured me another glass from the bottle he'd brought along with him. "It's about time you got around to asking me that question." He put his glass to his lips and looked at me slyly over the rim.

"So?"

"We've been keeping a close eye on the factory and we knew you were coming down to the hotel."

"How did you know?"

"Classified, Bill."

I got it. "You've got an undercover asset at the factory."

"Don't go jumping to conclusions," he said but I could tell from the twinkle in his eye that I was right and it wasn't a lowly factory worker.

"Thank you for turning up," I said. "She was just about to put a bullet between my eyes."

Two other men entered the room and I recognised them as the pool players from Christie's. They nodded to us and sat down at two of the computers. I couldn't see the monitors and what they were doing.

"We've been keeping a close eye on the guy you came into town with, Milford Grosvenor," Hank said. "What's the deal with him?"

"He's a big shot lawyer and a dodgy diamond trader. This was all about him selling a diamond to Wing Cam. Do you know where Grosvenor is?"

Hank shook his head. "No, he bugged out of the hotel early this morning. We don't know when. But his room has been cleared out." He gave a light chuckle and explained: "We've got some of the front desk staff on Uncle Sam's payroll."

"Grosvenor must have known they'd caught me last night," I mused. "Where the hell is he?" And did he have the real Red Teardrop diamond with him? That was the half a million dollar question. By now I had a strong suspicion that Grosvenor had the real diamond from Rosenstein all along but was too careful to admit it to me. He played his cards close to his chest.

That reminded me of the note from the front desk that I'd pocketed. It was crumpled up. When I opened it up it simply said: 'We're out getting things organised. Catch up with you later. MG'

I excused myself and went to check up on Brigit. She was feeling much better. They'd locked Lavender in a bedroom upstairs and Chuckee was keeping an eye on the door.

"We have to go back to the factory and get my brother," Brigit said, pulling me down so I sat on the arm of her chair.

"Are you mad?" I replied. "We've only just escaped from there and you want to go back?" This would be a real opportune moment to get out of Dodge and leave all this mess behind me. The DEA could deal with Wing Cam and Lavender and, frankly, I didn't care what happened to Grosvenor. I'd played my little part and had a hole in my shoulder and a broken trigger finger to show for it. However I'd got Brigit back and that should be the end of the road. Wing Cam still had my passport so getting out of the country would require a visit to the embassy in Saigon.

Except of course there was that open contract from the mysterious Thanatos which I hadn't got around to accepting yet. Thanatos wanted Wing Cam dead and was willing to pay 88,000 US dollars for the Reliable Man to do his work.

15

My sense of optimism did not last very long.

Brigit had gone into one of the other rooms on the third floor to have a rest and I was thinking it was time to turn the tables and interrogate Lavender. I wasn't planning to use any of the tools she'd been lining up for me and so was wondering how I would be able get her to talk.

I had returned to the main living room. Hank was leaning over one of his men and they were studying some documents when there was loud banging on the door downstairs.

Hank poked his head out of the window and we all heard the words that someone shouted: 'Police, you must open up now or we will break the door down." It was a Vietnamese voice. I went to stand next to Hank. Sure enough there were three police cars standing in front of our shophouse.

They were old Toyotas with the local police livery and about ten police officers in uniform stood around. Some of them were holding Armalite rifles which must have been left over from some American weapons pile. Leaning against one of the police cruisers, picking his teeth with a toothpick and grinning up at Hank and myself was Ven. Beside him was the driver we'd coshed and left unconscious in the bushes.

"That was quick," I said, feeling deflated. Now I knew what the British POWs must have felt like who escaped from Stalag-Luft III only to be recaptured five hundred yards from the camp.

Hank swore fluently in his Southern drawl. The ancient Anglo-Saxon words sounded somehow less offensive in his accent. One of the policemen started banging on the folding steel garage doors with a hammer.

"Wait, wait, we are coming down," Hank said.

Chuckee was standing in the middle of the room and the other men were on their feet. They all knew what was going down and they had a protocol for it.

"Pull the plug. Trash it all," Hank ordered and waved at his team. There was no time to burn any of the paperwork lying around but everything that was on the computers could be deleted through some instant re-formatting of the hard drive. I watched as Chuckee turned to the computer nearest to him and typed in a rapid sequence of letters and numbers which resulted in a big dialogue box appearing on the monitor. 'You are about to delete all data on the hard drive. Yes/ No?' was the message.

Chuckee hit Yes and Enter.

The computer was obviously still a bit nervous about this drastic action and asked one more time: 'Are you sure? Yes/ No?'

Chuckee hit Yes and Enter and a little image of a campfire appeared on the monitor with a message. 'The hard drive is now being reformatted. If you wish to use this computer again you must upload a new OS.'

The other men had been doing the same, after which they grabbed all loose pieces of paper and file folders and threw them into a big empty oil drum that had been standing in the corner. I'd wondered earlier what it was used for and had assumed it was just a Vietnamese-style trash can. In a way it was.

One of the men was already dousing the contents with a small can of petrol he'd taken down from the shelf above. He then stood back and waited for the others to complete the clear-up. In his hand was a matchbox, the kind with a logo you pick up in a bar.

Hank had already made his way down the stairs to open the door. The clock was ticking, the police were still banging but it had taken no more than three minutes to execute the emergency protocol. They must have practised this on boring Saturday nights.

The man with the matchbox looked at the others. They all had an ear out for the garage doors being opened. That would be the final signal. As Hank started pushing the doors back to let the policemen enter, the man with the matchbox struck a few and dropped them into the oil drum. The contents went up with a loud swoosh and I could feel the searing heat of the petrol igniting the paper from ten metres away.

"That was slick," I said to Chuckee. "I hope you have back-ups."

He shucked his shoulders and put his hands on top of his head to make sure that nobody thought he might be interested in resisting arrest. All the guns we'd used earlier had been replaced in a cupboard by the door. With a bit of luck nobody would be hurt or shot.

A minute later the first police officer came into the room. He was sighting down the barrel of his heavy revolver and wore a bullet proof vest. There was an obvious look of relief on his face when he found everyone standing quietly in the living room with their hands on their heads.

"There are eleven different words in the Vietnamese language for corruption," Chuckee said under his breath. "Everybody has his hand out in this country."

Within five minutes we were all handcuffed and lined up against the wall. One of the policemen with particularly large shoulder boards was obviously the commander and he gave instructions for the fire to be doused and the place to be searched.

Ven came to stand behind me. "Did you think we were that stupid? Where are the two girls?"

I told him because they would find them as soon as they went up to the bedrooms.

"So it's true," I said. "Wing Cam has got the police in his pocket."

Ven gave a short, mirthless laugh. "How else do you think we can operate in this town and run the biggest factory outside of Saigon?"

"Makes sense."

"We've had these Americans under observation for weeks. What are they CIA, DEA or what?"

"You'll have to ask them yourself."

He laughed again. "Commander Vuong will be doing the asking. You and the girls are coming back to the factory with me."

"Is that really necessary?" I tried at some levity.

"Where is the red diamond?" he asked.

"In my front pocket," I said. He reached around and dug into the pocket. It was a singularly unpleasant feeling. Being groped by an Asian man had never been one of my vices. He pulled the package wrapped in duct tape out from my pocket and said into my ear. "Is this the real one?"

I said, "I've no fucking idea. It could be. You'll have to take it to an expert."

"Mr. Wing Cam is an expert. He knows everything there is to know about diamonds." Ven then gave me a light slap over the back of my head and said something to the police commander. I assumed he was telling him that he was satisfied with the way things had gone.

The police weren't that happy about the computers all showing green screens and the smell of petrol and burnt papers in the air. They yelled for a while at Hank and his guys, got excited when they found the gun cupboard. I wondered if possession of a weapon without a license was a capital offence in this country.

"What's going to happen now?" I asked Hank, who was standing next to me. We were still all facing the wall with our hands cuffed behind us. I could hear Lavender's voice now. She was giggling with delight and telling Ven what a useful fellow he was. Brigit was crying.

We stood like that for about twenty minutes while the police tried to salvage what they could and searched everywhere in the house. I had a feeling they would not find much to incriminate the operation Hank had been running.

"Was it our fault that we were compromised?" I asked Hank.

"No, I think they've been on to us for a while."

"Will you be alright?"

"I guess they'll take us down to the police station and they will crank it up into a full blown diplomatic incident. My boss will tear my balls off."

All I could do was give him a painful look. But I was starting to worry about what part of my anatomy Lavender might be tearing off once we got back to the factory. This was not good.

Ven grabbed hold of my arm and began marching me towards the stairs. The driver was pushing Brigit along who stared at her feet. Lavender gave me a wink as I passed her.

There was another exchange between the police commander and Ven. Something along the lines of 'nice doing business with you. See you at the policeman's ball later in the month.'

I hoped Hank and his team would be okay. I hadn't known him for long but he'd impressed me with his professionalism. But having your undercover operation blown would not look good in his annual assessment. That was, if he didn't get thrown into jail for ten years. Surely Uncle Sam would take care of his own?

16

The factory hadn't changed since we'd left a few hours ago. I had hoped never to see it again. Wing Cam's office hadn't changed either except this time, Milford Grosvenor was there, sitting on one of the big guest sofas.

Ven prodded me in the back. They'd taken Brigit off somewhere and Lavender was ahead of me.

"Mr. Jedburgh, so nice to see you again," Wing Cam said giving me a supercilious grin. "I think you know your associate Mr. Grosvenor here?"

Grosvenor turned and gave me a warm smile. He wasn't handcuffed and he appeared rather pleased with himself so I assumed he hadn't been abducted and had come here of his own volition.

"Bill," he greeted me.

"Sorry, I seemed to have screwed up our plan when I went off on my own," I pre-empted any accusations.

"Not at all. All worked out really well," he said, his face still covered by a Cheshire Cat grin. "You've just arrived for the best bit."

Ven pointed for me to sit in the armchair opposite Grosvenor. I sank down into the cushions and said to the lawyer. "So where have you been hiding?"

"Here and there."

"And why are you here?"

Wing Cam, who had been standing by the window, strode back over to us and sat down in the largest of the armchairs. Lavender was on the same sofa as Grosvenor, eyeing him up with the curious interest of a piranha seeing a foot. Ven went to stand by the door, a quiet, efficient sentinel if there ever was one. I didn't like the man but so far he had impressed me with his competence.

"Mr. Grosvenor here has come to sell me a diamond," Wing Cam explained. I stared at the diamond-encrusted rings that were on eight of his fingers. Didn't the man have enough diamonds? You couldn't go down to the Seven Eleven and pay for a six-pack of beer with a diamond so what was the point, apart from looking like a rich prat?

Yes, I concluded, that was probably the point in owning lots of diamonds.

Lavender handed over my duct-taped package to Wing Cam who accepted it with interest. She said, "That's all he had hidden in his hotel room. I don't think it's the Red Teardrop." She turned her head and smiled malevolently at me.

Wing Cam snapped his fingers and Ven brought him a pair of scissors from the desk. Wing Cam then cut open the tape and the bubble wrap to reveal a black jewellery box a cubic inch in size. He snapped it open and my collection of one and two carat white diamonds lay there in the box.

I looked at Grosvenor who winked at me. I hoped he had the real diamond or some other trick up his sleeve. He appeared confident enough.

"Not the Red Teardrop," Wing Cam said, "but let's see the quality."

Wing Cam took a jewellers loupe from his pocket and screwed it into his eye. He held each gemstone up to the light from the window and studied them one by one for a minute, turning each one as he held it carefully between thumb and forefinger.

"These are not bad. Good enough for bribing officials," he concluded. "I will keep them, Jedburgh. Now where is the real diamond that I'm interested in?" His jolly mask dropped and he glared coldly at the lawyer.

"The real Red Teardrop is in a safe hiding place known only to me," Grosvenor said.

"Hmm," was Wing Cam's reply. It's what he'd expected. Lavender stared some more at Grosvenor. Her eyes narrowed like a cat that was about to pounce.

"So what's so bloody special about this Red Teardrop?" I spoke up. Grosvenor had told me in Saigon he thought it was worth about half a million. That is a decent chunk of pocket change but I still felt there was some part of the story missing.

Wing Cam gave a low chuckle. He frowned and stared at me. "You have no idea what this is all really about, Jedburgh, do you?"

"It's about a fancy diamond. You like diamonds."

"Not just any diamond," the drug dealer said. "Potentially one of the most unique and famous diamonds in the world." Wing Cam pointed at Grosvenor. "Why don't you tell him."

Grosvenor gave a disparaging shrug and said, "The Red Teardrop was discovered a few years ago in Brazil by a farmer near the Abaetezinho River. It was originally 13.9 carats but after being cut in New York in a triangular brilliant shape it became 5.11 carats. It also increased substantially in value. Our dear departed friend Jeremiah Rosenstein managed to acquire it and we thought Mr. Wing Cam here would be a perfect buyer."

"So what's it worth now?" I asked the obvious question.

"As much as Mr. Wing Cam is willing to pay for it," was Grosvenor's sensible answer.

"Okay," I said. That still didn't tell me what sort of numbers we were talking about. But I suspected we were in the middle of the negotiations.

"So you do have the real one hidden out there? And I've been the decoy bird all along?"

Grosvenor shrugged his shoulders.

The drug dealer placed my box of regular diamonds on his desk and said: "Mr. Grosvenor here wants me to pay 8 million US dollars for the Red Teardrop. That's too much for my taste."

"The real one is a brilliant cranberry colour and no red diamond this size has ever been found before," Grosvenor rolled into his sales pitch. "Only thirty true red diamonds have ever been discovered. Most of them weigh less than half a carat."

Now that I had heard the asking price, I had to admit that I was impressed. You could understand people getting excited for that sort of cash. I looked over Wing Cam's shoulder at one of the paintings on the wall. I knew nothing about art but I thought it might be a Kandinsky and they weren't cheap. To me it was all lines, colours and squiggles. But to a man like Wing Cam it could also represent a way of investing the huge amounts of cash a global drug operation generated.

Rare and beautiful diamonds were another way of investing money and of course so much more portable.

"I am willing to pay 5 million US dollars," Wing Cam proposed. "In cash, here and now. You can walk away with it."

Grosvenor smiled and said 'no'.

"How about I throw in your friend Mr. Jedburgh here? Lavender would like to keep him and cut out his eyes and tongue but if his freedom helps our negotiations..."

Lavender glared at Wing Cam. I glared at Grosvenor when his answer was: "Jedburgh isn't my friend. I'd never met him before until he turned up in my office."

"Shame," said Wing Cam. "Anyway, 6 million US dollars and you take Mr. Jedburgh away with you." Lavender didn't say anything, she knew her place in their business relationship but she wasn't happy at all.

I cleared my throat loudly to remind Grosvenor that he should do the decent thing.

"7 million and I'll take Jedburgh and his girlfriend Brigit along with me," was his counter-offer. I suddenly liked the man a whole bunch more.

"No, no, no, Grosvenor," said Wing Cam and barked a long sentence at Ven who nodded and left the room. "We still haven't seen the real Red Teardrop so maybe we should wait until you have produced it."

"I have it and I will produce it once we agree on a decent price."

"Decent?" Wing Cam challenged him.

"There are collectors out there," said Grosvenor, "who would cut off their right arm to possess the Red Teardrop."

There was something that flickered in Wing Cam's eyes which made me realise he was one of those collectors. He'd cut off his own right arm and as many arms belonging to other people as was required.

"6.5 million and you take the two of them. I want to see it first before we discuss any further."

Here I jumped into the conversation and did a risky thing. "Brigit won't leave here without her brother Stephen. He has to come with us if we are to be part of the deal."

Grosvenor frowned at me and I thought for a second he might abandon us after all. I didn't know much about his moral compass but I knew it didn't point to True North. I was gambling that there was a sense of decency and loyalty in the man's heart. A long time ago he'd started off as an English gentleman, whatever that meant these days.

Ven returned to the room accompanied by a wizened Vietnamese man in his sixties. He was clutching another old-style battered, leather doctor's bag. They stood quietly by the door.

Grosvenor rolled his eyes, then waved his hand casually and said: "Fine, we leave with Jedburgh, Brigit and her brother and I will settle for 6.8 million US dollars."

I could sense that Wing Cam was on the hook. It was all just monopoly money to him. The drugs being made in this factory were probably earning him 10 million US dollars a month, according to what Hank had told me. And even though he lorded it over the town and the local population there wasn't much you could spend your ill-gotten gains on in Danang. Spending it on my freedom and a fancy red bauble seemed like a great investment to me. I wanted to yell at him to take the deal but that would have been bad form.

Wing Cam stared at Grosvenor for a very long time without twitching a muscle on his face. Then finally he allowed a big smile to appear.

"Okay, Milford. You have yourself a deal. "I'll agree to 6.8 million and the three of them as part of the deal. But I have one final demand. Just a tiny, cosmetic one."

He looked sideways at Lavender who was glowering, not pleased at all with what her business associate had decided.

17

Wing Cam waved over the old man with his doctor's bag, talking to him in Vietnamese. The man approached diffidently.

"This is Mr. Duong. He is a very important member of my team," Wing Cam explained, as he raised his arm in the air and the cuffs of his shirt and his diamond-encrusted Rolex fell back to reveal his left wrist. I hadn't seen it before but there, like with Bridget and Ven, was the Buaya tattoo. The small crocodile on Wing Cam's wrist was faded and blurred. The tattoo had been done a long time ago.

"Mr. Jedburgh must have something to remember us by. To remind him every day that he owes me his life and he owes me a debt," Wing Cam said grinning at me. It was now pretty obvious what this was all about.

I wanted to shake my head but to be fair Grosvenor had made a sacrifice on the deal and it was now my turn to contribute.

Pointing at me, Wing Cam made it cuttingly clear: "You will have a Buaya tattoo." He tapped his left wrist. "Then I will allow you to be released to Grosvenor if the diamond is the real one."

I looked at Grosvenor and gave a mild shrug. It was my turn to take one for the home team as an American had once said when he left me with the ugliest girl at a party.

"Very well then," I agreed.

"Mr. Duong is an expert," Wing Cam said. "He has been a tattoo master for fifty years. You see I adopted the Buaya as the symbol of our organisation when I took over leadership. It has a long history for Triads but had died out. Even our ecstasy tablets are all stamped with the brand of the Buaya."

"Will it hurt?" I said peevishly. Wing Cam translated my words into Vietnamese and they all had a good laugh.

Strangely I had never had a tattoo. It had always seemed a senseless thing to do, mostly by drunk men after too many beers in dirty Wanchai parlours. The worst thing about a tattoo was that it identified you. It put a mark on your body. It was harder to claim you were someone else in a picture or when arrested if the tattoo clearly marked you.

Whatever, I decided, I could just have it lasered off when I was back in a civilised city.

"It will be a fine memory of your time in Danang, Jedburgh," Wing Cam said with a smirk and then instructed the tattoo master to lay out his tools on the big desk.

Ven advanced and grabbed me by the arm and, not ungently, dragged me up towards the table. There were still plenty of pain killers coursing through my body, I reminded myself. And it was just a tiny needle with blue ink in it.

As I passed her, Lavender hissed: "I should have cut your eyes out. Count yourself lucky." I smiled at her because I knew that would wind her up.

Grosvenor sat impassively and watched the proceedings. I still wasn't convinced that he was completely on my side, but at the moment things were looking positively bright so there was no point in complaining.

They had dragged the two guest chairs together and I was made to sit in one while Mr. Duong sat opposite me, our knees touching. My left arm lay on the desk on a small cushion that the tattooist had produced. Gazing at the instruments he produced, I felt I was in the hands of a professional.

"Make it a nice one," I said to him. He smiled without appearing to understand but he heard from my voice that I was not making a fuss. Perhaps many of his clients had struggled and screamed in the past as Wing Cam had his mark branded on them.

Duong wiped my wrist down assiduously with alcohol then produced an instrument that had the shape of a Flash Gordon space blaster. At the end was a needle which began to whirr.

"Still, no move," Duong instructed me as he had probably done thousands of times. He held my arm down with a firmness that betrayed his frail appearance. He shifted to get the angle right and I caught the smell of his lunch from his mouth. I watched with interest as he applied the needle to my skin. The device whirred some more and there was a pricking sensation on my wrist. It wasn't painful but it was irritating.

It took Duong about ten minutes to draw the Buaya. It was the exact shape that I had first noticed on Brigit's wrist in London. Duong was obviously an artist and he prided himself on consistency. The tail of the crocodile stuck up and bent backwards slightly. It was only just over an inch long but you could see the fine detail of the sharp teeth in the reptile's mouth.

When he was done, Duong cleaned up the area and applied a dressing that went all the way around my left wrist. I was starting to look like an Egyptian mummy with all the bandages on my body. He said something to Ven who translated: "He says keep on the bandage for two days and then it should be healed. Don't scratch."

"Let's have a look at yours then," I said chirpily.

"Fuck off," he told me in his Geordie accent and walked off.

While I was being branded, Grosvenor and Wing Cam had been continuing with their conversation. The handover of the Red Teardrop had now been worked out and agreed.

Wing Cam explained, "Jedburgh, the girl and her brother will remain here for the next few hours. Grosvenor will get the diamond and meet us at 6 p.m. at the airport. He has a private plane there, waiting to take off. We will meet by the plane and I will examine the diamond. If I am satisfied that it is the real one and as beautiful as they say it is, then I will hand over the 6.8 million US dollars and you can fly into the sunset."

Grosvenor added, "Only three other people with you, Wing. I will be armed and so will my plane crew. No funny business."

The drug dealer laughed cheerfully. "No funny business. Maybe we will do more deals like this one in future. You seem to be good at selling diamonds. You are wasted as a lawyer."

"Let's see about that." Grosvenor turned to me and nodded at my wrist. "I'm sorry about the tattoo but let's get this deal done and get out of town. I will see you in an hour or so."

"Don't screw me over, Milford," I reminded him.

He appeared genuinely upset at my words. He leant closer and whispered: "Don't worry. This will all work out well. The diamond is truly unique and he desperately wants it." He gave me a wave and turned to follow Ven out of the door.

Then Lavender spoke up: "Wing Cam, I am disappointed."

"In business sometimes we make compromises," the drug dealer said as the door closed on Grosvenor. Mr. Duong was packing up his tools and there were two new guards now in the room, probably to take me off somewhere.

"I can't accept that," Lavender said with a nasty edge to her voice. "You promised me Jedburgh. You said I could torture him."

Wing Cam frowned and glanced at his Rolex. "I need to go and get the money from my safe and prepare for this evening. We need to tell the police at the airport so that they won't interfere with us."

"If you won't let me have Jedburgh then I will terminate our business relationship. I will leave right now," the girl said with determination. If she had a gun on her I would have been worried if I'd been Wing Cam, but I guessed Ven hadn't returned her Sig. The girl was too unpredictable.

Her face was contorted in an angry scowl. I didn't put it past her that she would launch herself at Wing Cam. He glared at her, willing her submission. He was the boss here and he called the shots.

"Maybe you can have a little time with Jedburgh," he said.

I didn't like that at all.

Then he added: "Maybe not. I don't trust you, Lavender. You will mutilate him and kill him. I have my deal with the lawyer. That is the most important."

"If you don't give me Jedburgh, our business arrangement is over and I will not finalise the distribution network in America for you," she threatened.

Wing Cam didn't like her attitude at all. "Is that so?"

The office door opened and Ven re-appeared. He said something in Vietnamese. Wing Cam told him: "Miss Daai here wants to terminate our business association. She wishes to leave Danang. Will you escort her out of the factory and drop her off in town."

"You bastard," Lavender snapped at him.

"When you are the boss of a big organisation, sometimes you have to be a bastard. Lavender, you are fired."

"I am not your employee. You can't fire me."

"Ven, please take her away." Wing Cam stepped closer to the girl who stood in the middle of the room, looking for all the world like an Asian Adrestia, the Greek goddess of vengeance.

The drug dealer said, "Do not challenge me. You will now leave. It has mostly been a pleasure to work with you. Maybe we can work with each other again when you understand that I make the decisions."

Lavender snorted with disdain, turned on her heel and marched past Ven. She would have banged the door except that it was heavy and was controlled by an automatic door closer.

"Women, Jedburgh," Wing Cam said, shaking his head and moving back to his desk. "You can't live with them or without them." He studied me quizzically for a moment then added with a smile: "Welcome to the Honourable Buaya Society, you are now one of us for the rest of your life."

Somehow I got the feeling he actually meant it and that was why he had kept me from the clutches of that Chinese-Filipina hell-cat.

18

They brought me back to the same store room where I'd been locked up before. They hadn't swept up the rat droppings since the last time. Brigit was already there. She looked frightened and had been crying. I took her in my arms and made comforting noises. That seemed to calm her down. I kissed her gently on her forehead. It was clammy from fear and the oppressive humidity.

"I'm so sorry for getting you involved in this," she said. We sat down on three large sacks that contained something called acrylonitrile butadiene styrene. I guessed the contents were probably used to make toys rather than drugs. The sacks were firm and scrunched as we moved around.

"Trouble is my middle name," I said because it seemed like an amusing thing to say to make her stop sniffling.

"What is your middle name?" she asked, looking up at me. "Really?"

"I don't have a middle name."

"Oh," she said, then added after a pause: "Do you think Wing Cam will have us all killed?"

I gave her shoulder another firm hug. "I don't think so. What was the point of going through the whole palaver of having me tattooed then to go and have me killed."

"But you don't know him. He is crazy. One minute he is nice and the next he is like a raving demon."

"Let's hope he stays nice and doesn't change his mind. It all depends on Grosvenor coming through with the real goods and," this was the bit that still made me nervous, "not letting us down."

"Could he let us down?" she asked nervously.

"Yes, I just don't know him well enough. It could all have been an act. He agrees to us being part of the deal but when it comes down to it he doesn't even have the real diamond, he grabs the money and does a runner." I stared up at the barred window and reminded myself that escape from here was impossible. We were in Grosvenor's hands as much as Wing Cam's. "He's got a plane waiting at the airport with an experienced bush pilot who came up from Saigon with us. Grosvenor could jump in the plane and be half way down the runway before Wing Cam could call up his mates in the police and deploy some heavy artillery."

"Does Grosvenor have the real Red Teardrop?" Brigit said.

I shook my head. "That's the 6.8 million dollar question I have no bloody answer to. He might have. But it could have just as well been a fake deal all along cooked up by Rosenstein, the diamond merchant and Grosvenor who knew that Wing Cam is besotted with diamonds and has more money than Donald Trump."

Brigit asked, "Who is Donald Trump?"

"Some American property billionaire. Owns a lot of skyscrapers named after him."

We were silent for a while, then she said, "We will get out of this won't we, Bill?"

I patted her arm and gave her a smile filled with much more confidence than I was feeling.

The lock turned and the door opened. A short, young Vietnamese man was pushed into the room. His face expressed delight when he saw Brigit and she leapt up and gave him a hug. This was obviously her brother, Stephen.

She introduced us and he pulled up three more bags to sit with us. Stephen was in his late twenties and had a receding hairline. He wore round, horn-rimmed spectacles and there was a dark brown birth mark on his forehead above his left eye, the size of a fifty pence piece but more oval shaped. On his left wrist I found the same Buaya tattoo that we now all shared. His was mildly smudged at the edges, like his sister's, indicating that they had been branded when they were teenagers or even younger.

Brigit addressed him rapidly in Vietnamese explaining the latest developments while he listened with a frown. They had obviously seen each other over the last few days and had had some conversations.

"Was Wing Cam holding you against your will?" I asked him.

"Not really. At first they kidnapped me in Saigon and tried to remind me of my family debt to the Buaya Society and to him personally." His accent was the same as his sister's: mostly London but with the tones of someone who had come to the country as an older child. "They showed me pictures of Brigit and where she worked and said they would harm her if I didn't cooperate. I was to work here for two years."

"I assume you will be happy to get out of here?" I said.

"If I can be sure my sister will be safe, of course."

"Wing Cam's buying a fancy diamond from an associate of mine and we are part of the deal as your sister will have told you. With a bit of luck we might all be on a plane out of here in a few hours."

He stared at me and nodded dourly. "You can never trust Wing Cam. He is an evil man."

"What sort of work were you doing for him?"

"I have a degree in chemistry. I specialised in the synthesising of pharmaceuticals. I wrote my thesis on ring-substituted amphetamines." He gave me a quizzical look. "Do you know what ecstasy is?"

"Sure, little pink pills that make people dance all night long."

"Yes, and have seizures, amnesia, heart-attacks, paranoia, you name it. Classically it's methylene-dioxymethamphetamine but Wing Cam has had me experimenting with a whole variety of additives to reduce costs, increase effectiveness, create greater dependence." He shook his head and stopped talking. It was a burden that he carried.

"And have you been successful with these experiments?"

"Sure, it's not rocket science. The thing about synthetic drugs is that it's relatively easy to assemble the components. Ordinary chemicals can act as precursors to producing a variety of amphetamines. Take Sassafras oil, Camphor oil or Ocotea oil. They can be used to produce Safrole, which is a direct precursor to MDMA. There's plenty of all that in this part of Asia."

"You must be very good at your job. Strange that Wing Cam is willing to let you leave."

"Any competent chemist with a specialisation in the field can do what I do," he said. "There are four other guys that I work with. Two of them are from China and two Vietnamese."

I stood up and walked to the door and put my ear to it. There would be one or two guards outside but the door appeared to be made of steel and no sound could be heard coming through it. I beckoned Stephen Nguyen to the far corner and put my finger up to my lips to indicate that we should whisper. It was unlikely that there were any listening devices in the room. It was a storeroom most of the time and the walls were bare concrete with cheap whitewash.

I whispered: "Earlier we were with a man called Hank Petersen who works for the American Drug Enforcement Administration. He told me he had an informant here in the factory. You are his informant, aren't you?"

A terrified expression took hold of his face and even if he denied everything, I knew my guess was correct. He sniffed and brushed his nose, looked over at his sister who had been observing us with curiosity from her seat on the sacks of plastic granules.

Stephen nodded and simply said, "Yes."

19

Stephen explained in hushed tones that he had been approached by the DEA while he was working in Saigon. Wing Cam and Ven had been trying to persuade him to come to Danang but he'd been resisting and it was just a matter of time before they started applying more emotional pressure.

Hank and his team had been aware of this because they were watching Ven. They came to see Stephen as he sat in a coffee shop one afternoon and made it clear to him that he would never escape the fangs of the Buaya Society if he didn't help in taking them down.

When Ven came the next time - this time with a gun and two of his usual heavies - bundling him into the back of a Toyota Landcruiser SUV, Stephen didn't put up too much of a fight. He had been given a small transmitter device that allowed him to send out morse code messages that were sent out in an encrypted format as a flash transmission. The transmitter was hidden in his belt buckle. He'd been sending out regular reports over the last weeks but today he'd sent a desperate plea for help.

"You know they won't be coming in like the cavalry to rescue us, don't you?" I said.

"Brigit said they'd been arrested by the Danang police."

"Yes, and if they're lucky the US government will pay a big penalty fee and they might be quietly sent back home." I turned and looked across the room to give Brigit a smile that she returned. "If they're unlucky they might be locked up for 10 years in a dirty prison for spying."

"I know," Stephen said. For all the doi-moi new economic openness of the country it was still a tightly controlled communist totalitarian state and they didn't like foreign federal agents running operations under their noses. The fate of Hank, Chuckee and the rest of their team concerned me. But they had known the risks and Uncle Sam could be pretty persuasive when he wanted to be.

Stephen whispered to me: "If I leave here now with you and Brigit, I will have failed in my mission. Wing Cam is still there and will come after us." He looked miserable. His time here would have been wasted and the work he had been doing would be used to improve drugs that would make Wing Cam even wealthier and more powerful.

"You have to leave Vietnam," I said, "and go as far away as you can."

"He can find us in any country of the world. He will come after us again. You don't understand the family debt bondage that we were placed in when we were just children."

"I have some idea." I patted him on the shoulder. "Let's take this one step at a time. Let's get out of here on Grosvenor's plane first." I wanted to tell him that this game wasn't over yet and that just because I had a neat little crocodile carved into my skin didn't mean I was part of Wing Cam's fan club now.

I would be coming back for the man if we got out this evening. Not only for revenge but for the money that Thanatos had offered to have him killed.

We went to join Brigit again and spent the next hour talking about unimportant things. They told me about their childhood. I told them some stories from my early years in Hong Kong. There was a palpable tension among us as we waited for the next move in Grosvenor's game.

Finally they came for us. Ven stood back from the open door. "Time to go to airport," he said. There were two other guards with him carrying their usual MP5s. My shoulder was starting to ache as the drugs in my system were starting to wear off. I was also feeling an irritation on my left wrist under the bandage.

We walked along a different corridor and came out through a side door that led us to the courtyard where all the vehicles were parked. Five containers were being loaded up at the far end of the courtyard with boxes. I could just about recognise the name of the world's largest toy company on the cardboard boxes and the description of the product: 'Pocahontas, set of 8' was stencilled in big letters. It was an animated film that had recently been released. I wondered if these were just regular toys or if they contained little packets of pink, blue, yellow and red pills with the Buaya logo. Because that was the brand they used on the ecstasy tablets, as Wing Cam had mentioned. You can be assured of excellent quality, sir, if you buy under the trademark of the crocodile.

I wondered which advertising agency did brand development for Wing Cam? I had once dated a girl at

Grey's who was a dab hand at product placement and she had tried to baffle me with the science of it all.

We were squashed into the back bench of the Toyota Landcruiser and the driver took off in a cloud of dust. Ven sat in the front holding one of the MP5s. Grosvenor had limited the number of guards who could be at the airport.

The workers loading the containers paused to watch us go. There seemed no inquisitiveness in their eyes. Just another regular day at the largest factory in Danang. Stephen had mentioned they presently had 8,000 workers and Wing Cam was planning to grow to 20,000 workers if sales in America went well.

The airport was a single storey, newly built cement structure with no grace or style. Simply another ugly provincial airport which happened to have two 10,000 feet long runways that the Yanks had built during the war. Two Russian-made Tupolev TU-134s in Vietnam Airlines livery were parked on the runway. One had just arrived while the other one was getting ready to fly back to Hanoi or Saigon.

The Landcruiser pulled up in front of a locked side gate which was opened after some exchange with the military guards. The site also served as a major base for the Vietnamese Air Force and in the distance we could see bomb-proof hangars and fast jets lined up.

Our destination was a collection of private propeller planes that huddled next to a maintenance hangar. I wondered who was permitted to keep their own plane in this country? A good guess would be men like Wing Cam who had power, influence and the money to buy it.

He was already there, his black Mercedes lurking next to a twin-engined propeller plane that I recognised as a Beechcraft Super King Air. Milford Grosvenor, dressed now in a khaki safari suit, was standing at the top of the staircase watching us approach and I hoped he had the Red Teardrop in his breast pocket.

One thing was niggling at the back of my mind. Would Wing Cam be crazy enough to risk a shootout in public if he decided not to honour his part of the bargain?

I craned my head backwards towards the commercial terminal building. It was about half a mile from the Beechcraft so you would have to be watching us carefully to notice any funny business going on.

The second question that troubled me was whether the drug dealer owned any surface-to-air missiles. There were plenty of RPG-7s floating around on the illegal arms market since the Soviet Union had disintegrated. Although designed to take out tanks, an RPG-7 could be very effective, at a pinch, in stopping a plane accelerating down a runway.

But would Wing Cam be so brazen to risk such a public display of fireworks?

Then I remembered Jake, the dour Aussie bush pilot and comforted myself with the notion that he'd be a dab hand at risky take-offs and landings. You have to believe in something when your own scope for action is limited by a man holding a 9 mm parabellum submachine gun.

Our Landcruiser pulled up alongside the Mercedes and the three of us were shepherded out and lined up in the open space between the Beechcraft and the cars.

We were not tied up or handcuffed because there was nowhere to run for cover.

It felt uncomfortably as if we were being lined up for a firing squad. I really hoped that Grosvenor wasn't going to pull a fast one on this sultry Danang evening.

20

Jake, the bush pilot, ignored us all as he walked around the plane going about his business of pre-flight checks. He kicked the tyres and examined the propellers and hummed some Australian pop song to himself. I could have been mistaken but it sounded like 'I should be so lucky…'.

There was an Asian face visible in the cockpit sitting in the co-pilot's seat. A grizzled Western man in combat trousers and a faded 'Grateful Dead' T-shirt appeared in the doorway at the top of the steps and he held one of our AK-47s in a casual but assertive manner while the grip of the other Beretta peeked out of his waistband, against the swell of his belly.

Grosvenor had come down the steps and walked over to meet Wing Cam. There was a wary smile on the lawyer's face. The drug dealer watched him approach.

"Where is the money?" Grosvenor asked.

"Where is my diamond?" Wing Cam replied. He clicked his fingers and the driver from his Mercedes jumped out with an over-sized aluminium Zero Halliburton briefcase. Holding it to his chest, he flicked open the catches, popped the top so that all of us could see rows and rows of American dollars lined up like so many pretty green sardines.

Grosvenor reached into his trouser pocket and took out a small, black velvet pouch. He held it up for Wing Cam to see.

"You give me the briefcase, I give you the Red Teardrop. You check it over while I count the money."

Wing Cam nodded in curt agreement. He told his driver to hand over the briefcase. He reached inside his jacket and took out a piece of paper that he unfolded. From where I was standing with my hands interlocked on the top of my head it looked like a large and detailed picture of the diamond, probably showing every cut.

Grosvenor placed the small packet into the drug dealer's hand and stepped back to grab the silver-coloured briefcase from the driver. The first of the two engines on the Beechcraft came to life and the propellers started spinning. What price freedom, I thought? It was ten metres to the bottom of the plane's steps and three large bounds up into the safety of the cabin.

I gave the guard closest to me, with his MP5, a wink and he stared at me stonily. He'd seen all the movies so he knew you didn't simply smile back.

"If I say run," I instructed in a low voice to Brigit and her brother, "make a dash for the Landcruiser and hide behind it." I glanced sideways and caught her startled eye. "If I say plane, we go for the steps."

Neither of them said anything. They stood frozen, like ancient obelisks in a jungle clearing.

Wing Cam had screwed his jewellers' loupe into an eye socket and was giving the small red stone in his hand a detailed examination. He kept comparing it with the picture he held in his other hand. Grosvenor was riffling through the stacks of US dollar notes.

"There's only a million here," Grosvenor said glancing up.

Wing Cam laughed. "I was hoping you wouldn't notice." He snapped at the driver who had been standing by the boot of the Mercedes and now popped it open. There were six more identical over-sized Zero Halliburton briefcases lined up and the driver began taking them out, lining them up at Grosvenor's feet.

"Hewie, get down here and bring this case into the cabin," Grosvenor called to the man with the AK-47. There was a gleam in his eyes that you only see when a man has become possessed by Mammon and the fever is upon him. The Chinese call the god of wealth Bi Gan. When they are gambling and they are winning, their eyes take on the same gleam.

He riffled through the second case while Wing Cam continued his deliberate inspection of the tiny red item in his hand. It didn't appear cranberry colour from where I was standing but the drug dealer was treating it with some reference so I was hoping it was the real deal this time.

Wing Cam said without looking up: "One million US dollars in $100 notes weighs about 8 kilograms, Mr. Grosvenor. We don't count money in my business. We weigh it."

Grosvenor shot him a distracted look and kept on going through the cases. He was on the fifth one by now and Hewie of the AK-47 was going up and down the steps, bringing each checked briefcase into the plane.

Finally Wing Cam said: "I am satisfied. This is the real Red Teardrop. I am delighted. It is perfect. It is a vision." There was a huge grin on his face which not even Lawrence Olivier could have faked.

I was starting to feel marginally optimistic. What mattered was what came out of Wing Cam's mouth in the next minute. I fixed Ven with a firm stare. He took the toothpick he'd been gnawing on out of his mouth, shifted the MP5 he had tucked under the crook of his arm, and shrugged. Was that a good sign?

He said: "You must take care of the Buaya sign. It is an honour to have that tattoo."

"I am honoured," I said, trying to keep the words free of any sarcasm.

By now both propellers on the plane were spinning and the fuselage was shuddering mildly, as if in anticipation of getting away. I knew what that felt like.

Wing Cam said, "I need a green diamond for my collection. I heard that Fawaz Gruosi might be willing to sell one of his."

"Only Rosenstein would know the answer to that and your Chinese girlfriend killed him," Grosvenor said, stretching his back after being hunched over for the last ten minutes. The last Zero Halliburton was now on the plane.

"Oh, she's a crazy bitch that one," Wing Cam said and turned to me. "Isn't that right, Jedburgh? I saved your arse this time and you owe me. That tattoo will be a lifelong reminder. You have a debt to me."

I nodded. I didn't trust myself not to say anything which might upset the delicate situation.

Wing Cam informed us: "You may go. All of you." He waved at us theatrically and I fixed Ven's eye to make sure there were no alternative instructions. He stepped forward and handed me my wallet, and our three passports, which was a positive sign.

"Plane, quickly," I snapped at the girl and her brother, and as if by magic they came alive and bolted for the steps. I followed at a more leisurely pace keeping a careful watch on the muzzles of the two MP5s to make sure they were all still pointing at the asphalt. Hewie stood at the top of the steps and his AK-47 was now in both of his hands. I hoped Grosvenor wasn't thinking of doing anything stupid. Take the money and run, I willed him. Or fly, in our case.

I was the last one up the steps into the plane. Now there only remained that final niggle of mine. Would Ven produce an RPG-7 from the back of the Landcruiser? Reason told me that didn't make any sense. Wing Cam wouldn't want to incinerate 6.8 million dollars. If he wanted his money and the Red Teardrop he'd have done the dirty earlier.

I turned at the top of the steps and nodded at Wing Cam. I wanted to give him respect but also check what emotions his face might betray.

All I could see was contentment. That gave me some comfort.

21

The Beechcraft Super King Air was configured to seat 8 people on slim seats with an aisle down the middle and storage space at the rear. The aluminium cases were stowed and tied down and we all buckled up. The interior appeared functional, relatively new but not luxurious. I sat in the front right seat with Grosvenor on the other side of the aisle.

"This baby only needs 3000 feet for take off," he said and gave Jake the thumbs up. The cockpit door was open and we could see Jake and his Vietnamese co-pilot prodding and poking their instruments. The plane began to shudder more. Jake advanced the throttle lever, released the brakes and we shot off.

"Why didn't we fly up in this thing?" I yelled at Grosvenor over the engine noise.

"We only bought it yesterday from an oil company executive whose company couldn't afford it any more," he yelled back.

"How long will it take to Saigon?" I yelled, remembering the 17 hour journey we had driving up.

He grinned. "We're not going to Saigon."

I heard Jake in the cockpit say to his co-pilot "And... V1, V2.... Rotate." Then I saw him pull back on the yoke and the wheels left the ground. I craned my head to look out of the window but couldn't see what we had left behind. I held my breath. This would be the moment that the plane would disintegrate if Wing Cam wanted to be vindictive.

Nothing happened for five minutes. Jake took us up at a steep rate of climb. I sat and listened to the engines, held on to my seatbelt and thought calming thoughts.

After a while, I remembered the last thing Grosvenor had said.

"We're not going back to Saigon?" I said.

"That's right," he said. By now the howling from the two turbo-prop engines was becoming less intense.

"Where are we going?"

"Across the water," he said cryptically. I looked out of the window and noticed we were over the sea. I thought about the map and what it looked like. What was North East of Danang? First there was Hainan Island and then came Hong Kong. Further east there was Manila.

"This plane has a range of 3100 kilometres," he said.

Jake was still taking us up, although the rate of climb was less steep now. The plane was being buffeted mildly by the winds but he avoided the fluffy white clouds and kept heading into the blue yonder.

I said: "We're going to Hong Kong, aren't we?"

"Correct in one," he said. "It's only about 900 kilometres. We should be there in less than two hours." He gave me an amused look. "I wasn't going to land at Saigon airport with seven cases filled with American currency. You may have forgotten that Vietnam is still a communist totalitarian state."

I laughed.

"I've got several banks lined up in Hong Kong who can't wait to get their hands on this lot." He jerked his thumb at the back of the plane.

"Really?" I said. "I hope it's not the Hong Kong and Shanghai Banking Corporation. They'll charge you for counting each bank note."

He thought that was funny. "No, proper professional private banks. Ever heard of Lombard Odier, Julius Baer, LGT?"

I nodded. All three of them would serve him well with the discretion he would require for such a hefty cash deposit. In Hong Kong money was worshipped and a smart banker rarely asked questions regarding provenance. Thank heavens for capitalism, freedom of speech and the rule of law. All of which were going to go out of the window in less than two years' time when Britain handed the territory back to China.

For the moment Hong Kong was still a free port so nobody was going to check his bags for illicit cigarettes or booze. I nodded at him. It was a smart move to fly out of Danang and straight up to the big bustling metropolis of Mammon.

The Beechcraft levelled out and Jake came down from the cockpit and stood between our two seats.

"We're at 25,000 feet. That's what they've given us. Got to keep away from the big boys higher up on this lane." He pointed at the roof meaning the wide-bodied jets that ploughed this route on their way to Saigon, Bangkok and Singapore. "Weather's looking fine."

"You did a good job getting us out there fast," Grosvenor said.

"I didn't like the look of those fuckers," the Australian said in his casual drawl and returned to his seat.

I glanced around and caught Brigit's eye. She still looked nervous and her brother, on the other side of the aisle, was holding her hand. I gave her a thumbs up sign and she smiled weakly and returned it. Hewie sat on the last row, his AK-47 laid on the floor. It looked as if he was dozing.

"Where did you find him?" I asked Grosvenor.

"Old Vietnam vet. Been back in country for a few years after living in Thailand. I helped him get through a messy divorce." He unbuckled his seat belt and walked down the aisle. The plane wasn't steady like a jet aircraft and it wobbled mildly, so he had to hold on to each seat as he made his way to the rear of the plane. Hewie opened one eye like a languid alligator and watched.

Grosvenor unclipped one of the bungee cords and extracted the top briefcase, then tied the rest down again. He balanced the case on the empty seat beside Hewie and snapped open the hasps. He reached into the case and extracted two bundles of greenbacks. I guessed one bundle, secured with mustard and white currency bands that wrapped around the middle, was 100 x $100 notes. The lawyer handed them to Hewie who by now had both eyes and his hands open.

"20,000 dollars, as agreed."

"Easy money," said the American.

"Could have gone either way," Grosvenor said gravely.

"That's what my lieutenant always said when he welcomed us back into KSCB after a good patrol."

"What was a good patrol? No casualties?" Grosvenor asked.

Hewie gave him the sort of look and shake of the head you give someone who doesn't have a clue. "If half the patrol came back home, that was a good day." He looked out of the window at the sky and into the past. "That was during the retreat from Khe Sanh. Operation Pegasus, what a fuck up."

He caught my eye as he'd noticed me, craning back in my seat, listening. He shrugged and banished the bad memories to the place where he kept them locked up. That had been 26 or 27 years ago. He would have been a teenager, probably, not legally permitted to drink beer in America but killing Commies in the Orient had been perfectly acceptable.

Hewie stuffed his bundles into one of his shirt pockets. That should keep him in beer and totty for a while. Grosvenor took out two more bundles, then closed the case and came back to his seat. He placed the Zero Halliburton on the floor next to the other AK-47 and handed me the bundles of Benjamin Franklins he was holding.

"That's for your troubles, Bill."

I took the stack of dollars and flicked them as if I wanted to fan my face. "I didn't add much value. Sorry about that."

"You did great. You provided vital diversion and confusion so we could get organised."

"That was the reason you wanted me along?" I asked.

"All along you've been a decoy. Right from the start when Jeremiah asked you to carry the fake diamond package."

"Yeah, funny that," I said, trying to hold down a feeling of bitterness that had risen in my throat.

"We had to be smart about this," Grosvenor explained, "Wing Cam has eyes and ears everywhere. So we let it be known that you were the one carrying the Red Teardrop. It made sense. Former Hong Kong

Policeman. Hard bloke like you. It all fitted the profile."

"You could have told me," I complained.

"You wouldn't have been so convincing." He shook his head gravely. "You did just as expected. You set up a triple decoy so that Ven took your wrong diamond. Then Lavender turned up and that confused the issue even more." He clapped himself on the leg in delight. "Perfect, my son, it just worked out perfectly."

"Except for Jeremiah getting shot."

He suddenly appeared contrite. It seemed he'd already forgotten that bit. "Yes, that was bad luck. He shouldn't have gone for the girl. There was no need. I still don't understand what was going through his head."

"Maybe he was confused as well, which was the real diamond after all."

"No, no, Bill. He had the real diamond on him all the time."

"Where was it then?" I noticed that I'd sat up in my chair with sudden interest.

Grosvenor laughed. "He had it sewn into the lining of his old jacket. It's so small you had to know where to feel for it."

"And you knew where it was in the lining?"

He nodded. "I cut it out before the police arrived in my office. Palmed it and then the rest you know."

"You bastard." I smiled though when I said this because, after all, he could have left us at the mercy of Wing Cam.

"I like you, Bill. You're a good bloke and with Jake and Hewie here we could make a good team. We should do a few more jobs together."

"Just what I need, another geezer who wants to tell me what to do," I said sarcastically, mainly to myself.

"You obviously have problems with authority," Grosvenor said jokingly. "You need to be part of a team. The Rat Pack, you know."

"Spare me, Frank. Call me when you need help and I'll consider it but I'm used to bumbling along on my own."

Jake leant through the open cockpit door and yelled down to us: "We're coming into Hong Kong airspace now."

Grosvenor said with a smirk, "I hope you've got your passport. Or Hong Kong immigration might send you back where you came from."

I patted my breast pocket. "He kept my bloody diamonds but at least Wing Cam was kind enough to return all our passports. I've still got a Hong Kong ID card so I can come and go as I please."

"Not for much longer," he said.

"What are your plans after this? Are you going back to Vietnam now that you've won the lottery selling the Red Teardrop?"

"I'm going back to England. I'm going to buy a house in Dorset I've had my eye on for some time, and become a boring provincial lawyer."

"Really?" I said with a note of incredulity.

"It's an old manor house that needs doing up a bit and has 50 acres of land with it and a little river with trout."

"What's that going to cost?"

"I won't get change from a million pounds. But I have a few million tucked away already apart from this lot. This was the big one."

"I thought we were all going to be part of this great new Rat Pack?" I said.

"Dorset isn't the middle of nowhere. Get up to London within two hours on the train. Plenty of commercial action in London. I've got a nice apartment in Mayfair. I'll come up with a new wheeze within a few months."

"Sounds like you've got it all worked out," I said and then Jake started taking the Beechcraft down towards Kai Tak Airport.

22

There was a ding-dong sound that wouldn't stop and I began finning up from a great depth. Finally I woke up, confused and disorientated, still very tired, realising that it was the doorbell of my hotel room.

"What?" I yelled. There was a muffled sound from the other side. I turned the light on. The room was in complete darkness although a sliver of light told me it might be day time outside.

I went to open the door and found a Chinese girl standing in the corridor. She had homely breasts, wore tight jeans, a yellow blouse, red lipstick and her hair was tied up in a bun. There was an expression of impatience on her face. She rolled her eyes and said, "Finally," then pushed past me into the room.

"What time is it?" I asked.

"It's two in the afternoon."

"Can't a man a sleep?"

The girl was Jane Tan. Officially employed as a stewardess by Singapore Airlines she also worked for Brigadier Wee in whatever capacity he saw fit. She was qualified to carry a gun and had proven to me that she could handle it effectively. About three weeks ago she'd been shot in the shoulder by a man in Manila.

"How's your shoulder?" I asked, then looked down quickly to check that nothing was hanging out from my shorts that could be considered rude.

"Fine," she said and busied herself with opening the curtains that let the blinding sunlight into the room.

"Ouch, I feel like a vampire," I said.

"You look like Frankenstein's monster," the girl said and gave me a slow appraisal, up and down, once she'd flung herself into the corner of the sofa by the window. "You should get those bandages changed. They look a bit dirty to me."

"I will. I was planning to go and see a doctor once I'd had as much sleep as my body needed."

"You arrived at Kai Tak at ten last night. You came straight here and went to bed. I make that about 14 hours sleep."

"I feel like someone drove a Chieftain tank over me and then reversed just to be sure."

"What's that bandage on your wrist for?" she asked and pointed. Her fingernails were a colour that someone had once described to me as being 'Rouge Puissant'. It's the sort of colour you want a girl raking down your back while her ankles are around your ears.

I smiled crookedly at Jane Tan. That was a nice image to have pop into your head out of nowhere.

"I've got a tattoo," I explained.

"What sort of a tattoo?"

"It's a Buaya."

She nodded knowingly. "And you think you're a bit of a Buaya so that's why you've had yourself tattooed?"

"Am I not a Buaya?" I said, slightly offended by her dismissive tone.

"Yes, you are a Buaya. Dirty, sleazy, but occassionally quite charming."

"That's not the reason I have a Buaya tattoo."

"You joined Wing Cam's gang. That's the reason."

"How did you know?" I said, surprised but really not at all. I was just slow and tired and muggy headed. There was only one reason Jane Tan had turned up at my hotel and it wasn't to take me out for lunch.

"Let's go out for lunch," she said.

I snorted. I found my watch and put it onto my right wrist. It really was early afternoon and I was feeling peckish. It had been a long time since I'd last eaten anything of substance. There had been a Mars Bar when I arrived in the hotel room.

When we landed at Kai Tak, Aussie Jake took us to the part of the airport reserved for private aviation. There were about forty planes there, some bigger, some smaller than ours. There were several Gulfsteams IVs, probably all belonging to wealthy Chinese property magnates.

An immigration official had come along and politely checked all of our passports. A Mercedes limousine turned up, sent by one of the banks Grosvenor had mentioned and whisked him and Hewie off. They also took the briefcases. Another limo arrived to take the rest of us wherever we wanted to go.

Brigit, Stephen and I had had a quick conversation and they'd already decided that they wanted to get back to England as soon as possible. I gave them 5000 US dollars and told them to get on one of the Cathay, BA or Virgin Atlantic flights that left around midnight.

The girl cried a bit and thanked me for everything. Stephen told me to be careful. I told them to be careful. I didn't tell them that I wasn't quite finished yet with Wing Cam.

Then I'd asked the limousine driver to drop me off at the Grand Hyatt Hotel in Wanchai. I had walked into the lobby, demanded a room and paid cash in US dollars which they thought was perfectly acceptable. The Hong Kong dollar is pegged at 7.8 to the US dollar but somehow they didn't give me the same exchange rate.

Jane Tan said: "Get in the shower, have a shave, put some clean clothes on, then we'll go for lunch."

"I don't think I have any clean underpants left."

"Too much information. Get on with it," she commanded.

Half an hour later we were downstairs in the coffee shop. I'd asked the hotel if they could book me an appointment with the closest doctor so I could get some clean dressings and more medication. There was a clinic in the building next door, they told me, and sorted me out for an hour later.

I ordered the biggest pot of coffee they had and Eggs Benedict with three eggs. Jane ordered a salad.

"What does he want?" I asked once the waitress had left.

"Who?"

"The Brigadier."

She gave me a fake smile and kept me in suspense for half a minute while she poured herself some jasmine tea.

"Do you know who Thanatos is?" she finally said.

"No idea, but you're going to tell me."

"Apparently he's the Greek god of death."

"Very funny. That's not what I meant."

"Now, I had to look this up," she continued in all seriousness. "He was the son of Nyx, the goddess of night, and Erebos, the god of darkness and brother to Hypnos, the god of sleep."

"You are an erudite little flight attendant."

"Don't patronise me, you jaded old chauvinist."

"I'm not that old."

"You look terribly old and haggard from where I'm sitting."

I rolled my eyes and tapped the table top with my fingers. "Tell me who Thanatos is, really."

"He's a person who commissioned you to kill Wing Cam, who is a drug dealer in Danang."

"Okay," I said neutrally.

"Is Wing Cam still alive?"

"Last time I saw him, as I was waving out of the aircraft window at him, yes."

"Should he still be alive?"

"The bloody Brigadier is Thanatos. I should have known it all along," I said and of course I had suspected it. It had just been his new sneaky way of engaging my services.

Jane stared left and right dramatically at the other tables around us which were mostly empty because it was nearly 3 p.m. "I did not say the Brigadier was Thanatos."

"Yes, I get it." I poured myself another cup of coffee and dumped two sugars into it. My brain needed all the fast energy it could get.

"So, let me get this straight," I said. "Brigadier Wee is pissed off with Wing Cam and Lavender Daai because they're making MDMA and getting it into the hands of what's left of your Triads in Singapore. Poor little party boys and girls getting addicted. Right?"

Jane shrugged and made a face indicating 'no comment'.

I continued: "Larry made all that clear. So, knowing that I was on a little commercial mission to Vietnam he engaged the Reliable Man to take out Wing Cam."

Jane said sarcastically, "But Wing Cam is still alive and you've got a Buaya tattooed on your wrist." She hummed to herself for a few seconds, enjoying every minute of this. "Spectacular failure on your part I would say."

"It's not too late," I said with a 'humph' at the end of the sentence. My Eggs Benedict arrived, and I ignored the girl for the next five minutes as I shovelled protein into my mouth. She nibbled at her Salade Nicoise.

A thought occurred to me. "Did Wee tell Hank Petersen from the DEA about me possibly turning up in Danang?"

"Probably," she said, then popped a baby tomato into her mouth. I could tell from the way she said it that her answer was more like 'Definitely'.

"Any news about the DEA guys?" I asked.

"Being kicked out of Vietnam as we speak," she said. "Cost the Yanks a big bribe."

"How much?"

"Enough to buy five of the new T-90 Main Battle Tanks that the Russians have just put on the market."

"Ouch."

"Better than being locked up for ten years in a Vietnamese prison."

"Uncle Sam takes care of its own," I agreed, wiped my plate clean and then added, "So, why exactly are you here again?"

"I'm on my way to San Francisco on SQ1."

"That explains everything."

"I'm a familiar face, the Brigadier feels, that you respect and will listen to."

"You're right. I love your face and all the other bits that belong to the rest of your body."

"Thanatos has a job that needs doing," Jane reminded me. "And apparently there is even payment for it."

"I recall. Actually the going industry rate, from what people have told me. Not that I would know about such things."

"Well?"

"I'm going back to Vietnam as soon as I am feeling a bit better. In a day or two."

"There is no need to go to Vietnam," the girl said with a knowing smile.

"Explain."

"The Hong Kong Jewellery and Gem Fair starts tomorrow. We've just found out that Wing Cam is booked on a flight from Saigon this afternoon. He's taken a booth and plans to exhibit a new acquisition of his."

"The Red Teardrop."

She nodded.

"Which hotel is he staying at?" I asked.

"The Peninsula in Tsim Sha Tsui."

"So he'll be in town for a few days and I've got time to prepare."

"I guess so," the girl said.

"What are we doing now?" I was feeling much more energetic after my late brunch and the prospect of revenge arriving in town.

Jane said, "I'm going back to my hotel to get some shut-eye before flying out this evening and you're going to the doctor to get your tattoo checked out."

"That's it? You haven't even got an hour for some sweaty sex?"

"Let's keep things on a professional level from now on, Bill." She smiled warmly to show me that no insult was intended. "Once with you was quite enough."

I love Singapore girls. They give it to you straight.

23

The doctor said my index finger wasn't as bad as it looked. He put a proper splint on it and wrapped it up, binding it to the middle finger. I certainly wasn't going to shoot any gun with my right hand for a while.

He gave me a painkiller called Ponstan, an antibiotic called Augmentin, a tetanus jab and charged me 700 Hong Kong dollars. I tottered off and ran a few more errands. Like depositing the remainder of my cash into a US dollar account that I had with Standard Chartered Bank.

Before Jane left I'd asked her to find out where Lavender Daai had gone. There had to be a record of her flying out of Vietnam to somewhere. I had to know where she was. She might not be working with Wing Cam any more but she could pick up crooked partners like a dog picks up fleas. She would turn up again somewhere, coming after me for unfinished business, and I had to be looking over my shoulder all the time unless I knew that there was an ocean and at least a thousand miles separating us.

I also did a recce of the Hong Kong Convention & Exhibition Centre which conveniently was located in the building next to the Grand Hyatt Hotel. They had started building an extension last year which was going to stretch into the harbour on reclaimed land and was planned to be completed in time for the glorious handover ceremonies in June 1997.

The HKCEC was run by the Hong Kong Trade Development Council and they ran exhibitions there nearly every week. It started in January with the Toy Fair and went on with textiles and electronics and this week it was all about diamonds and pretty baubles. Traders came from all over the world to buy, sell and show off. They spent a lot of money in the hotels, restaurants and nightclubs and that's how the city maintained its buzz and kept on getting richer.

With a population of 6.5 million souls and a Gross Domestic Product of 129 billion US dollars, Hong Kong - measured as a separate entity from the United Kingdom - was the 28th richest country in the world. China's GDP was only 850 billion US dollars but they were working hard at getting richer too. Adding Hong Kong to their pot would give them a big boost on the global league table.

The Exhibition Centre had a large foyer entrance where visitors would register and receive their badges, then they could stroll around several halls which were filled with booths of varying sizes and splendour. Since this was the jewellery fair there was a much higher level of security visible than would normally be the case for consumer products. Men and women in uniform, showing the logo of Securicor, were stationed at every entrance even though the fair was not officially open yet. The company would have won the contract to manage this event which involved storing all of the precious stones overnight for the duration of the fair. I wouldn't like to be in charge of this project, I thought, as I ducked behind a pillar to avoid an old sergeant of mine who had obviously retired and moved on to being a security guard.

First thoughts were that I didn't want to be taking out Wing Cam in the trade fair. I didn't want to have to sign in and then make a quick exit. It would be much easier to set up with a nice sniper rifle and a good scope and target him as he arrived or departed. The Shui On Centre across the road had a decent roof, I remembered.

But of course I couldn't hold a rifle steadily or pull a trigger properly. I'd have to do a walk-up and use a handgun with my left hand. With that in mind I took the MTR from Wanchai under the harbour and popped up in Tsim Sha Tsui. I knew the Peninsula Hotel pretty well, and had just stayed there a few weeks ago with McAlistair, so it didn't need much reconnaissance. I just wanted to remind myself of all the exit routes. They were as good as anyone would want. Tsim Sha Tsui was one of the busiest square miles in the world.

I chuckled quietly. You could cross Nathan Road and disappear into Chungking Mansions, and in that rabbit warren of a building nobody would find you for months. It had fifteen entrances and exits as I recalled from some long distant briefing when we did a raid on one of the illegal curry houses to arrest a Sindhi people trafficker.

By 7 p.m. I was back in my hotel, sweaty and ready for a shower. By 8 p.m. I had decided that a quiet evening and a Wiener Schnitzel might be in order. In Thailand they always used pork and most people couldn't tell the difference. But a proper Austrian Schnitzel was made with the thinnest slice of veal covered in breadcrumbs and the best place in town for one of those was the German bar Schnurrbart in Lan Kwai Fong.

It wasn't that busy when I arrived so Inge, the Manager, gave me one of the booths at the back and I read the South China Morning Post while my Wartsteiner beer was being poured.

"We haven't seen you for a long time, Bill," the German woman said.

"I spend most of my time in Thailand or Singapore now," I said.

"You are not a police any more, I remember?"

I nodded. "I left a few years ago. I'm a consultant now."

"We had a big group from the Police Tactical Unit here last night," Inge said, rolling her eyes. "I had to ask Schnurrbart in TST to send over five more bottles of Schnapps." She held out the menu card but I shook my head.

"The usual," I informed her.

"We have some nice white Spargel. It is just in season. I can add some to the Schnitzel. And you like the Bratkartoffel, don't you?"

"Perfect," I said.

The usual Yuppie crowd of bankers and lawyers came and went. There was always a regular group of young trendy Chinese who enjoyed the German atmosphere; the decoration was straight from a Bavarian beer-hall. In the corner, on the big long Stammtisch sat a group of jovial middle-aged, stout-bellied Germans playing the popular card game Skat. It was a three player trick-taking game and it was usually played for money. There was much howling coming from the men as they thumped down their cards, abused each other in their harsh language and tossed shot-glasses of white liquor down their throats in between sips of beer. Just a regular weeknight in Lan Kwai Fong.

I'd just cleaned my plate, popping the last fork of fried potatoes into my mouth, when Bob Kenworthy and Theo Scrimple appeared at my table.

"There's that wanker, Jedburgh," Kenworthy said, sliding onto the bench opposite me. I made room for Scrimple who was a large man, with a big gut.

"Where've you been since the funeral?" Kenworthy, who looked a bit like George Michael if you squinted, said.

"I've been here and there."

"You're like a fucking travel agent. Never longer than a day or two in any one place."

"You're not entirely wrong about that," I laughed. "This week I've been in Amsterdam, Singapore, Saigon and Danang."

Scrimple who'd been studying the menu said, "Bloody hell. Don't you get sick of all that traveling?"

"Some weeks are busier than others," I replied and waved at Inge to get the lads some beers.

"What are you up to in Hong Kong then?" Kenworthy asked.

I tried to look nonchalant. "There's a jewellery fair starting tomorrow so I've been advising a client on personal security and all that guff."

"Do they listen to you?" Scrimple wanted to know.

"Mostly they do. Sometimes they don't. As long as they pay me, that's fine by me."

"Do they pay well?" Kenworthy asked.

"Enough to keep me in cold beer and hot women. Are you still ADVC Ops Yuen Long?"

"They're going to move me to Traffic New Territories when I get back from long leave.

"Is that good?"

"Only if they let me ride on the big bikes."

"You know, you have to be sober when you ride a 1000 cc motorbike, don't you?"

"Fuck off. Would I be that stupid?" Kenworthy said and received the tall glass of Wartsteiner beer from the Filipina waitress. He gave her a lascivious smile and she scuttled off.

"Where are you at, Scrimple?" I asked.

"Back in CID, Tze Wan Shan," the fat man said.

"They must have been desperately short of local inspectors," Kenworthy said with a wink. "They're all jumping ship and leaving for Canada and Australia. So old Scrimple here is back running a Reserve Team."

"Can't be much happening in Tze Wan Shan," I commented.

"We get the occasional TCWA," he said, then took a deep, thirsty draft of his beer which emptied half the glass. He had always been a man who liked his ale.

"Half the time it's not really 'Taking A Conveyance Without Authority'," Kenworthy said. "It's more like, I crashed my car and I can't afford to pay the insurance, so I'll report it as stolen."

"We had seven burglaries last week," Scrimple said, trying to impress.

"What did they nick?" Kenworthy asked.

"Mostly women's underwear," Scrimple said with a shrug.

"Have you solved the crime yet?" Kenworthy asked.

"D-Sergeant will solve it. He says he's meeting an informant next week who has some facts pertinent to the case."

"Thank heavens for D-Sergeants," said Kenworthy with a chuckle.

"Where are you going for your long leave?" I asked him.

"I have this new Eurasian bird and her Daddy's a banker and he's going to let us borrow his yacht for a month."

"Are you sure you will be able to spend a whole month in the company of the same woman?" I gave him a look of fake concern. "Have you thought this through carefully?"

"Fuck off, Jedburgh. You got any regular woman in your bed then?"

"Nah, they can't put up with my travel schedule. What's Simon Foxcroft up to these days?"

"He's heading up a Regional Crime Unit now," Scrimple said, placing down his empty glass and waving at the waitress to get us all another round. "He just got another CP's Commendation. He's like a one man crime solving machine. It's a bit embarrassing for us regular blokes."

Kenworthy laughed. "I wouldn't lose any sleep over it, Scrimple, mate."

"I'm not. All I want to do is get my salary every month, have a decent shag once or twice a week and come home to a clean flat."

"Sounds like you need a nice Filipina maid," I said.

Scrimple frowned. "My last one went and got married to a German engineer so I'm on the look-out for a new one."

"Taking him down to Wanchai later," Kenworthy explained. "Let's have some of those nice apple-flavoured shooters. Don't have to be in the office until afternoon tomorrow."

24

I left the two coppers in the German bar shortly after 10 p.m. telling them that I needed an early night. Kenworthy waved me off with good natured abuse that involved comparisons to fairies and other lightweight folk. Scrimple grinned vacantly because he was already on the other side of five tall glasses of Wartsteiner and I'd lost count of how many Apple-Schnapps. I hadn't matched their consumption, reminding them that I was on drugs. I'd told them that I'd broken my finger while training with my Kung Fu sifu.

As I walked down the steep, cobbled stones of Lan Kwai Fong, passing trendy bars like California on either side, my mobile rang.

It was Jane Tan. "I'm off to the airport," she yelled. "I've got some information about Lavender Daai from the Brigadier."

"Where is she?"

"She flew from Saigon to Hong Kong then onwards to Los Angeles yesterday."

"LA," I said by way of confirmation.

"That's right."

"And you're absolutely sure about this?" I said.

"She checked in on the flight and immigration has her on all the border checks."

"Isn't it great to be able to hack into everyone's computers," I laughed with relief. LA was a long way from D'Aguilar Street where I was standing.

"Anyway, we're going to keep a close eye on her and keep you informed. That's what Brigadier Wee says to tell you."

"That nice of him."

"Don't forget you've got a job to do."

"Yes, Miss Thanatos," I said.

"Don't screw it up," she said cheerfully and then hung up.

No pressure there, I thought grimly and walked on until I reached Queen's Road. I was just about to cross over to go down into the MTR station when a man's voice called my name. I looked around and saw Milford Grosvenor coming up behind me.

"We've got to stop meeting like this," he said cheerfully. His face was florid and spoke of more than one bottle of wine.

"Where have you come from?" I said politely.

"Just had dinner at Jimmy's Kitchen," he jerked his thumb over his shoulder, "with my bankers."

"Couldn't they have taken you anywhere more fancy? What about the Mandarin Grill?"

"I love Jimmy's Kitchen. They've got the best Dover Sole in the whole of Asia. I always eat there when I'm in Honkers." He clapped me on the shoulder and I could smell half of a vineyard on his breath. "I got them to buy me the best claret on the wine list. Can't get decent wine in Vietnam."

He paused and looked me up and down. "Where are you off to anyway?"

"Bed, early night." I held up my bandaged fingers. "I need some rest after the excitement of the last few days."

"Ridiculous. Come and have a night cap with me in the Captain's Bar. I'm staying at the Mandarin." He pointed across the road and in the general direction of the hotel.

I only hesitated for a few seconds. I did crave an early night but having an unguarded conversation with a drunk Grosvenor might be interesting. He appeared to have consumed a lot more alcohol than I had.

"Alright," I said. "Where are the rest of the Rat Pack, Jake, Hewie and the Vietnamese pilot?"

"They've all gone back to Saigon already."

"What about the plane?"

"I've already sold it to some bloke called Leung. My Swiss banker fixed it up. Three phone calls and the deal was done. Apparently the Super Air King is highly sought after in China." He pushed me across the road as the pedestrian lights turned green.

As we walked along and he explained to me why the apple crumble in Jimmy's Kitchen was the crowning glory of British colonial cuisine, I mulled over whether I should tell him that Wing Cam and entourage were coming to Hong Kong, perhaps had already arrived.

"When are you going on to London?" I asked.

"Oh, in a day or two. Got a few people to catch up with. Need to sell an apartment I have on Conduit Road. I used to work for Lovell's here in Hong Kong in the 1980s, snapped up a cheap property with a sea view. Can you imagine how low the property prices were after Maggie Thatcher signed the Joint Declaration? They were giving them away in Corn

Flake packets." He stopped and put a hand on my arm, turning me around to face him. He had a serious expression on his face although his eyes were slightly unfocused. "Let me give you a piece of advice from a cunning old lawyer who's been around the block a few times. If you've got any property in Hong Kong now, sell within the next year. The market is as high as it's going to get and after 1997 it will tank. It will come screaming down like a bloody Stuka on a London bombing raid. Hong Kong is going to crash and burn. Mark my words."

"How much is your place worth in Conduit Road?" I asked, trying to lighten his mood with a question he had to concentrate on.

"I bought it for half a million Hong Kong dollars. The property agent has five interested buyers who are all offering over ten million." He poked me in the chest with a hard index finger to make his point. "Rule Number One: 'Always take the money and run'. Got that, Jedburgh? Take the money and run."

"It's good advice," I said and nudged him so that we would start walking again. Having a night cap with Grosvenor might be a lot harder going than I had anticipated. Although at this rate he'd be nodding off in his Madeira as soon as we sat down in the Mandarin Hotel's bar.

We crossed Ice House Street and it was then I should have noticed the shadow leaning in the dark doorway of Prince's Building. But I was listening to Grosvenor's hackneyed aphorisms and making sure we weren't run over by the passing red taxis.

I suddenly became aware of swiftly running feet behind me and my instincts began twitching. I turned to check and was rammed hard by a solid shoulder which sent me flying onto the pavement. I screamed in pain as I landed on my hands and injured finger. A shock jolted through my shoulder as it took the entire weight of my body. But I rolled sideways and scrambled to my feet. The fight was half lost if you were on the ground.

There was only one assailant and he'd grabbed Grosvenor's swaying form, steadied the lawyer for an instant, and then shoved a long thin blade between the fifth and sixth rib, just above the arch of the diaphragm. I didn't need to count the ribs because I knew where the heart was and how I usually did it.

I was back on my feet and in a fighting stance when I recognised the assailant as Ven. He was wearing a black, roll-neck sweater and he grinned wolfishly at me as he released Grosvenor and kicked him hard in the groin so that the stiletto could slip free.

"You next," he said and held up the slim blade. It looked like a V-42 Commando knife and I realised Grosvenor was not much longer for this world because Ven had handled it like an expert.

The Vietnamese man leapt at me like a panther but I got my leg up and kicked him in the chest. He staggered, found his feet and came at me again.

There was no cutting edge on the blade. It was all about the thrust. The close quarter Wing Chun style that I'd trained in for many years used trapping techniques and something called 'Sticky Hands, Chi Sau. But with a hole in one shoulder and two fingers strapped together I was barely functional.

On a perfect day Wing Chun was ideal for close contact combat, using quick punches and kicks with a tight defence, coordinated through agile stances and footwork. But I was feeling less than hunky dory. Ven kept on coming at me, probing for an opening with the flickering blade. Trying to get through and hit my liver, the carotid or popliteal arteries at my neck and on the leg.

He was panting, his face was covered with a sweaty sheen, and his nostrils flared with fury. He was intent on killing me but time was running out. There was the sound of police sirens in the distance.

Finally I trapped his arm between both of mine and my elbow caught him hard on the jaw. The stiletto went spinning off into the night. Ven hissed at me and kicked at my groin but I got my knee up in time and our shins connected in a shock of searing pain.

Then Ven turned, picked up the stiletto, and ran in the direction of the MTR entrance. A taxi skidded to a halt as he slid across its bonnet. I fell to my knees gasping for breath. It had been a long time since I'd had a full on fight like that one.

I crawled to Grosvenor and went to staunch the blood flow from his chest but there was no point. His throat rasped as he tried to say something. I leant closer and thought he murmured: "I just need a bit more time for some fun."

25

There had been no point in hanging around for the police to arrive. I didn't need my name in the papers or on a crime report again. I had fled in the other direction. Ven was too far ahead for me to chase him down into the underground so I'd bolted past the Cenotaph lawn and snared a taxi outside the Hong Kong Club building.

Fifteen minutes later I was in my hotel room examining the scrapes and bruises on my arms and legs. At least I had all the painkillers a man could wish for. I had a long shower, took some pills and went to bed, waking up about 9 a.m. feeling fragile but better.

I thought about Grosvenor and the attack for a while as I lay in bed, then I called room service for some breakfast.

It would not have been difficult for Ven to find the hotel that Grosvenor was using. Ven and his boss would be able to find me as well so I'd have to tread cautiously today and it was time to switch hotels and identity.

An hour later I was in Hok Yuen Street East in Hung Hom where a company called Guardforce provided state-of-the-art safe deposit boxes. Most banks in Hong Kong offered this service but Guardforce were open from 7 a.m. until 11 p.m. which, for the time-pressed assassin, was more convenient than banking hours.

They also had discrete private rooms for accessing your valuables.

I had several boxes there. The one I was opening this morning was about half a metre long and a quarter of a metre high and wide. I kept some spare passports here and parts of my armoury. What I wanted today was a particular piece of kit for a special occasion.

Mossad, the Israeli intelligence agency, has always denied that it runs a team of sanctioned assassins. But they do exist and the Kidon Unit commissioned the manufacture of a lovely handgun called the Meraglim Mark III which was made in the same factory as the Galil assault rifle. The Meraglim is a four-shot throwaway pistol made from hardened epoxy resin. It can be disassembled to avoid detection and its grip is covered with a sticky coating that destroys fingerprint traces. The last two inches of the barrel are a built-in suppressor that reduces the sound of any shot to a small burp. The four rounds that come with it have a very low velocity and self-impacting heads that cause maximum tissue damage. It is a highly engineered, disposable semi-automatic, perfect for the close up, walk-up kill.

I'd picked up five from a Lebanese dealer who'd acquired them from a rogue Mossad quartermaster with a gambling habit. They'd cost me 10,000 US dollars each so the decision to use one was not taken lightly. A brand-new Glock 26 would set me back just under 300 US dollars.

I had used the Meraglim in London, one on a job in Dubai, and the remainder were in this safe deposit box in Hung Hom. I had been sniffing around for months to buy some more but it wasn't the sort of kit you bought at a gun-show in West Virginia.

Apparently there was a Mark IV which had come out recently because a friend of mine had heard that the Duvdevan, the counter-terrorism unit of the Israeli Defence Force, had recently been issued with a batch for their work in Arab-held territories. Just thinking about it made my mouth salivate with desire.

I retrieved what I wanted from the safe deposit box, locked it and called the young attendant to take it back. Then I took a taxi to Reclamation Street in Mong Kok to visit a shop that sold party costumes, sexy lingerie and cos-play outfits for kinky Japanese men or anyone else so inclined. What I bought here was basically a fat-man suit and several wigs that would disguise my appearance.

One of the things I'd learnt during my time in the police was that when you asked five witnesses for a description of the same suspect they would rarely come up with the same answer. People's memories worked in different ways and focused on different elements of an image. The witnesses would only be consistent when there was something glaringly obvious to remember: he was old, he wore glasses, he had red hair, he was fat. Like with many things in life keeping things simple was usually the most effective.

I'd checked out from the Grand Hyatt already and now found a room in the Kowloon Hotel which was located directly behind the Peninsula Hotel where Wing Cam was supposedly staying. The Kowloon had been built in 1986 and its rooms were tiny but that meant there were many of them and it sat conveniently on top of the MTR station. This time I used a Belgian passport. My photo was matched with the name of Jean Vandenborre.

The mobile rang just as I was getting in between the sheets for a brief power nap.

It was Larry Lim. "Did you get all the messages from Jane?" he asked.

"Yes."

"Have you seen the papers? They are full of the stabbing of some English lawyer. What do you know about that?"

"I was there," I said and waited for his reaction. He swore briefly and asked me to tell him what I could over the open line.

"It was Ven. He and Wing Cam must have arrived in Hong Kong during the afternoon and worked out that Grosvenor was still in town, then tracked him down. Ven was waiting for us outside the hotel."

"And you're okay?" Larry asked. There was real concern in his voice. I knew he was a good friend and he cared.

"Close run thing, to quote old Nosey. He was trying really hard to prick me with his stiletto."

There was a long moment of silence from the other end and then he said: "Would it be helpful if we gave the police an anonymous tip? They are never going to connect Ven to Grosvenor. The papers are saying it was a robbery gone wrong and that's about it."

I thought about that one for a while. It was true. Unless someone pointed them in the right direction, how were my old buddies from the RHKP ever going to know where to look for the vicious knifeman? But it couldn't be me who passed on any information. I had to keep as low a profile as possible, given the plans I had for later that evening.

"You guys talk to Special Branch all the time, don't you?" I said, examining the logic of the idea. "You could slip it into the conversation and they could then pass it along the line and muddy the waters so that CID has no clue where the information really came from?"

"We could."

"Who is the Director of Special Branch now?" I asked.

"You haven't heard then? It's in the process of being dismantled," he explained.

"Why would anyone tell me?" I laughed caustically.

"They're transferring bits of it to Security Wing, Department B. There's a bloke called Prendergast we talk with now."

"So, why don't you point him in the right direction and see if they can pin anything on Ven. But he'll have got rid of his Commando knife by tossing it in the Harbour by now."

"I'll get right on to it. What are you up to now?"

I chuckled. "I'm working on this little project for a geezer called Thanatos."

He laughed down the line. "Wasn't my idea. Honestly," he apologised.

"It's fine. You'll know when it's done." We cut the connection and I mulled it all over some more. Then the drugs knocked me out and I woke to the low beep of my alarm.

The fair would be closing by 6 p.m. and I wanted to be waiting for Wing Cam by the time he got back to his hotel. I'd made a call earlier to confirm that he did have a suite at the hotel but of course they wouldn't tell me which one.

It took me half an hour to get into costume. I strapped on the padded belt which would make me look like a man forty pounds heavier in the gut. I placed two rubber balls in my cheeks to puff them up. I rubbed a cream into my face and hands which made my skin colour darker. I applied a goatee beard and moustache with theatrical glue. I donned a grey wig, horn-rimmed glasses and grabbed a wooden walking stick. Checking myself in the mirror on the back of the bathroom door, I now looked like an Italian professor on a lecture tour of the Far East.

The final and most important item was snapping the Meraglim onto my belt. It fit snugly into a nylon holster designed for a full-sized automatic like the Glock 17.

Nobody gave me a second glance as I limped across the marbled lobby. I crossed the road and entered the Peninsula Hotel through its shopping gallery, passing the Louis Vuitton shop.

The lobby of the Pen was something entirely different. It was a huge vaulted chamber, not quite as opulent as Grand Central Station in New York, but equally impressive. There was a whiff of elegance and tradition in the air and most of the guests looked well-heeled and pretty impressed with themselves. The hotel kept a fleet of Rolls Royce Silver Spurs to pick them up from the airport. The Japanese made the hotel their headquarters during the Second World War and then signed their surrender documents in a ballroom on the third floor.

Last year the Kadoorie family, who owned the place, had added another thirty floors to the back of the building so it appeared that they at least were confident about the future of Hong Kong under Chinese rule.

I took a little tour of the lobby and then approached the receptionist to ask if Mr. Wing Cam had returned yet as I had a package for him. She smiled pleasantly at the old Italian gentleman whom she saw in front of her and confirmed that the guest had not returned to his room yet. I said I would come back later.

I found a good table in the lobby with a view in all directions and ordered a pot of Earl Grey tea. This was how a civilised man did a stake-out.

It was about 6.30 p.m. when I was on my second pot of tea and had languidly smoked two cigarettes that a young lady came to sit at a table on the other side of the room from me. She gave me a cursory glance, then turned to face the entrance.

Lavender Daai looked good in a tight black jump suit, a pearl necklace around her throat and red leather cowboy boots. My heart rate went up a few notches but I resisted the urge to walk over and shoot her with my Meraglim. Why wasn't she in Los Angeles?

26

There was no other option but to sit tight and wait for Wing Cam to return. Was Lavender waiting to meet him or kill him? With that woman you could never tell.

I had a little chuckle into my fake beard at that one. If Lavender had decided she was going to get her own back on Wing Cam it would save me using up my precious Meraglim and I might still be able to collect on the money Thanatos was paying. But of course if Lavender were to attack Wing Cam out of spite, or for whatever crazy reason was coursing around her head, I'd still have to put her down like the rabid bitch she was.

So there we were, sitting in the lobby of the Peninsula waiting for the next act. I asked for the bill because it would soon be time.

A little while later Wing Cam arrived, having been deposited at the front entrance by one of the hotel's Silver Spurs. He was laughing at something Ven had said to him and following close on their heels were two of the guards I recognised from Danang. They were wearing black suits and stared sullenly around the lobby as they would have learnt from all the gangster films they had watched.

Wing Cam's eyes flitted over me and spotted Lavender who had raised a languid hand and lowered the sunglasses she'd been wearing.

"There you are, my lovely," Wing Cam said in his curious Geordie-Asian accent. He seemed very pleased with himself. He must have had a good day showing off his new acquisition, and perhaps a few other ones from his collection. I couldn't hear the rest of their conversation but Lavender seemed to smile and allowed the drug dealer to give her a hug.

Ven, as he had walked past me at a few metres distance, had not given me more than a casual glance either. He now turned and examined the vast room again.

Nobody paid Wing Cam and his entourage any attention as there were two other groups of wealthy Asian men surrounded by acolytes and bodyguards in the hotel lobby. Wing Cam looked exactly like what he was, a rich factory owner in town for some shopping and entertainment.

It seemed as if Lavender and Wing Cam had kissed and made up and she wasn't here to put a bullet in him. That was a shame. I'd have to carry on with my plan then.

The four men moved over to the lift area and went upstairs. Lavender remained in her seat, flicking through a fashion magazine she'd produced from her cow-hide Birkin bag. She looked surprisingly relaxed for a psychopath. But I knew there was a geyser of violence that bubbled below the surface.

I assumed that Wing Cam would freshen up and then they'd go out for dinner. I didn't want to do the shooting in the lobby because there would be security cameras dotted around. I wanted to do it in the busy street, out on Nathan Road. I was hoping they would go for dinner close by. If they took a limousine to the other side I would wait until they came back. This was simply a stalk now. My back-up plan was to follow them up to the rooms. I was confident in my disguise, but my preference was to follow them on the street and take advantage of the hustle and bustle that was Tsim Sha Tsui on any given night.

As expected they came downstairs twenty minutes later. Ven was a few steps ahead of his boss and the two goons were bringing up the rear again. Lavender stood up and joined them. They had a brief conversation. Lavender laughed at Wing Cam's words. She seemed a cheerful sprite this evening. I wondered what that was all about.

I did have one serious problem: the Meraglim only held four rounds. One man would be left standing. I had to get the order of preference right. Ordinarily I would shoot the bodyguards first because they would be carrying guns, but in Hong Kong bodyguards were not permitted to carry firearms. I was going to assume they were not armed with anything more than the sort of knife that Ven had used to kill Grosvenor.

So my order was going to be: Ven, Lavender, Wing Cam and then hold one round back in case there was any fight left in the bodyguards. If they were sensible, both of them might even survive the carnage.

There were a thousand excellent restaurants in Tsim Sha Tsui but the one they choose was simply above us. Felix had opened the previous year. It was on the 28th floor with spectacular views of the harbour. It had been designed by Philippe Starck and had received rave reviews for balancing glamour and sophistication with the conservative nature of the hotel's history.

Ven led the way to the lift that ascended directly to the restaurant. I watched and thought it through. I'd been in the bar in Felix only a few weeks ago with Jane Tan so the layout was familiar. If I could get into the fast lift back down to the lobby it would be a very efficient escape route. It felt workable.

I waited another five minutes and then took the same lift upstairs. A giggly American couple who behaved as if they were on honeymoon shared the swift ride with me. The lights changed colour dramatically, the doors opened and we emerged into a dimly lit lobby followed by the main restaurant area with its soaring double height ceiling and top-to-bottom glass walls on both sides. The city sparkled all around us. Energy flowed from one glass wall to the other.

At the far end of the restaurant was a long table, similar to what one might see in an old university college but without the timber mustiness. Felix was all chrome and glitz.

I turned right and went up a spiral staircase to the American Bar. It was not too busy around the circular marble counter. Two Filipino waiters mixed drinks and when I leant backwards slightly, I could look down, as if I were in a minstrels' gallery, and see Wing Cam and his gang at one of the round tables in the centre of the restaurant.

I ordered a glass of champagne and enjoyed the view of Hong Kong Island that was stretched in front of me.

What a city!

When a man becomes bored of Hong Kong he becomes bored of life. And what would it all be like in a few years' time? Nobody knew, except the old men in Beijing. And perhaps even they had no idea how they were going to handle this wild, bastard daughter of theirs that had eloped and followed the siren call of capitalism in 1842.

My watch, still on my right wrist, told me it was coming up to 8 p.m and the waiters were flitting around Wing Cam's party with the menus. He and Lavender were deep in conversation. Perhaps they were re-negotiating their deal and as part of that deal, she was demanding that I be found, and my head brought to her on a platter.

I was going to finish my glass of Cuvée Peninsula Brut and then I would amble downstairs to wreak some carnage with my excellent Israeli death-bringer.

But it was not to be.

As I was on my final sip, a group of men appeared from the lift lobby and marched intently towards Wing Cam's table. I couldn't help roll my eyes in irony as Detective Chief Inspector Simon Foxcroft addressed Ven, and one of the other tough-looking Chinese detectives proceeded to handcuff him.

The restaurant had fallen completely silent. You could have heard a rat run through the kitchen.

The police officers led the hand-cuffed Ven away, leaving Wing Cam to glare at their backs. He was touching his chest as if he were clutching a sacred amulet that hung around his neck. Lavender, I noticed, had a mordacious smile on her lips.

27

Wing Cam's dinner had been spoilt by all the unwanted attention he was now getting from the other diners. He had a quick conversation with Lavender and then they both got up and left their table accompanied by his guards.

I had to follow them. Grabbing my walking stick I leapt down the spiral stairs and got to the lift just as the doors were closing. There was only one lift and it had to go to the ground floor first before it could come back up to the 28th floor. I uttered the short Anglo-Saxon expletive that was always a panacea in such situations.

I walked back to the reception lectern that was manned by an attractive Chinese girl in hotel uniform.

"Mr. Wing Cam, he left something on the table and I just missed him getting into the lift. Can you tell me his room number? I can bring it to him."

It was worth a try and I looked like such a harmless old professor with my horn-rimmed glasses and grey goatee beard that she fell for it. Everybody was still shocked and titillated by the sudden appearance of the constabulary and the public arrest of a man in one of the trendiest venues in town. The receptionist was dazed and assumed we had been dining together. She had been attending to another guest as Wing Cam walked past. Automatically she glanced down at her list where his reservation would be showing his room number. I smiled at her with my most disarming manner. Come on, my love, I heard a voice say in my head.

"Oh, I'm so sorry, sir," she replied. "Yes. He's in Room 2503."

I thanked her and hobbled off, emphasising my imaginary limp. She'd remember me when the time came. That nice cuddly grandfather with an Italian accent.

It took another three minutes before the lift was back and a group of three exited before I could get in. When I walked out into the lobby there was no sign of them. Had they left the hotel or taken the regular lift up to his suite?

I walked around the corner and got into the next lift that was free and took it up to the 25th floor. The corridor was quiet. I walked cautiously along the ochre-coloured pile carpet, listening for voices and identifying the two security cameras at either end of the hallway.

The suite was at the far end and the door, curiously, was behind the security camera so only the one at the far end would be recording me.

I banged on the solid black door and said, "Police, open up Mr. Wing Cam." I'd done this for real a few times in my younger years so sounding convincing was not difficult. "Police, open up," I yelled again and stabbed the doorbell repeatedly.

The room door opened and one of the goons peered out at me. I pushed him hard in the chest and as he stumbled backwards I shot him in the same place to put him down permanently.

It was a large comfortable lounge that led off into two bedrooms on either side, separated by folding doors that had been pulled back. Wing Cam was standing by the window looking over the harbour with a glass of amber fluid in his hand. There was no sign of Lavender. The other goon was on his way to his boss with the room service menu in his hand. I took off the side of his head with my second shot from the Meraglim. Once again it just gave a nasty little plop and then the man disappeared behind one of the sofas.

"Who are you?" Wing Cam demanded, remarkably calm as he turned and faced me. He placed the whisky glass down with some care. I advanced on him, the muzzle of my gun pointed at the centre mass of his body.

"I am the Reliable Man," I said. "I have come to kill you."

"Who sent you?" he said quietly, as if we were discussing the stock market. "Whatever they are paying you, I will double it."

"Where is the girl that was with you?" I asked.

"She's gone. The police spooked her." He took one step closer to me. Whatever else he was - drug dealer, sex trafficker, and all round vicious bastard - he was a brave man. You don't get to reach the top of your own crime syndicate without having nerves of steel and iron balls.

"You don't have to do this," he said. "I will pay you half a million US dollars."

The clock was ticking so I wasn't going to have any long conversations with the man. In any successful assassination you had to be in and out as fast as you could, then disappear into the crowd. Only fools got caught.

"Look," Wing Cam said, a tiny hint of desperation had crept into his voice after all. He knew who the Reliable Man was. He knew my reputation. When you placed an order with the Reliable Man it was executed. No ifs, no buts. Reputation, as the bard said, was everything. Wing Cam had ripped open his shirt and pointed at the velvet pouch that had been hanging around his neck, resting just over his sternum.

"This is a very expensive diamond. It is worth millions," he said quickly and pointed at the pouch. "You can have this diamond if you don't kill me. Just walk away. Take this diamond."

"Sorry, it's a bit more complicated than that," I said and using my right hand pulled back the cuff of my shirt, so he could see my left wrist with the Buaya tattoo that he had given me. I was still holding the Meraglim steadily with the same hand.

"I don't understand," he said and there was confusion on his face.

I said: "It doesn't really matter," and shot him just below his Adam's Apple. His jaw and half his nose disintegrated. He fell backwards on to the carpet.

I stepped up to him, surveyed the carnage and grabbed the silk pouch, tugging hard so the string snapped. It felt the right size. It must be the Red Teardrop. He would not have trusted Securicor to take care of his most prized new possession. It made sense that he would carry it on his person, surrounding by his bodyguards.

Five minutes later I was back in the lobby. I still had the Meraglim. I didn't know where Lavender had disappeared to, so I was saving that final round for a clean getaway.

I crossed Nathan Road by the Sheraton Hotel, walked along Middle Road, turned by the Mariner's Club, all along checking if anyone was following me.

Nathan Road had been packed with people but it was less busy once I got to Minden Row which ran along the back of Chungking Mansion. I turned into the steep path that led to Signal Hill Park, a strange little oasis of green. It was dark and the occasional couple sat in the shadows, paying attention only to each other. At the top was Signal Hill Tower and in the early days it held a drop ball contraption that signalled time for mariners. These days it served as a lover's park and next to the tower was a public toilet.

In the toilet I took off my disguise and stuffed it into a trash can. When I came back down the hill and turned into Minden Row again, I tossed the Meraglim into the rubbish container opposite Star Mansion. The chemicals on the grip ensured there were no fingerprints on the weapon.

Hart Avenue was two streets along. Grant, the English manager, was at the door glowering at punters as always.

"You again," he said and gave me a nod.

"What's the crowd like?" I asked.

"Not drunk enough," he said.

"It's still early."

"What's the DJ like?"

"He's fucking useless. Like all of them."

"Good job you're here," I said with a laugh and clapped him on the shoulder then descended the steep stairs into the belly of the club. The stench of sweat and spilled beer hit my nostrils. I found a corner at the end of the bar where I could watch the totty on the dance floor. An Aussie girl took my order. I touched the velvet pouch that was in my pocket and felt the tiny hard item that was inside it. I'd had a quick look at it earlier in the Signal Hill toilet. It was the real deal. I wondered what I would do with it? Leave it for twenty years in a safe deposit box was the obvious answer. Only take it out when everyone had forgotten about it.

An hour and three San Miguels later I had spoken to enough people to be sure I had a decent alibi. I was thinking of going and hitting the sack when a man pushed up to the bar next to me.

"Jedburgh, how are you?" he said.

"Foxcroft," I acknowledged him. "Get you a beer?"

"Yeah, I'll have a Carlsberg."

"Been working late?" I asked.

"Just arrested the bloke who stabbed that English lawyer in Central last night," he said. "We had to bring him to TST nick to do all the paperwork."

"So what's the story?" I said. The DJ had just slowed the music down to let the blokes grab hold of some girls, and it became easier to talk.

Foxcroft shook his head. "He's not saying anything. We found him on the Interpol database as a hard-nut Vietnamese who lived in Newcastle for a long time. Must be some sort of grudge between his boss and the English guy he killed. They all flew in from Vietnam within a day of each other."

"How did you identify the killer so quickly?" I said.

He laughed and put down his beer on the bar counter. "You know how the phrase goes: 'acting on information received'…"

"Anonymous tip off?"

"Yeah. Once we knew where to look we found video of him crossing the concourse of Central MTR station at the time of the stabbing and that was good enough for us."

"Murder weapon?" I asked.

"No, long gone. This bloke's a professional. Unless something else turns up a good barrister will have him back on the streets in no time."

He looked down at his belt where he had a pager which was blinking red and vibrating. "Hang on, make a call."

Foxcroft was back in two minutes. "No rest for the wicked. They want me back at TST now. Seems the shit hit the fan at the Peninsula Hotel. After we arrested that guy someone else came along and topped his boss in his hotel room." He grinned and nodded at me. "Couldn't have happened to a nicer fellow from what I've been reading on the database."

He gave me a farewell wave and went back to work.

I thought about it all and had another San Miguel. It was time to go back to my house on the beach in Thailand and have a few months off. Time to chill out and spend time with my girl Nuhm who might be in urgent need of some horizontal bed gymnastics by now. McAlistair should be back in a few days and we could hang out at the gym and bullshit and I'd tell him some of my story and he'd call me a useless wanker.

I reminded myself that Lavender Daai was still out there and sooner or later I'd have to go looking for her or she'd be coming after me. And then there was Ven who might be back on the streets if the evidence wasn't solid enough for a judge.

There are always loose ends in life. I touched the diamond in my pocket and smiled sadly, then had a final beer, raising it in silent salute in memory of Rosenstein and Grosvenor.

END

Printed in Great Britain
by Amazon